Seas
and
Greetings

By Julie Murphy and Sierra Simone

A Merry Little Meet Cute
Snow Place Like LA
A Holly Jolly Ever After
Seas and Greetings
A Jingle Bell Mingle

Seas and Greetings

A Christmas Notch Novella

JULIE MURPHY
and SIERRA SIMONE

AVON

An Imprint of HarperCollinsPublishers

Excerpt from *A Merry Little Meet Cute* copyright © 2022 by Bittersweet Media LLC and Sierra Simone.

Excerpt from *A Holly Jolly Ever After* copyright © 2023 by Bittersweet Media LLC and Sierra Simone.

Excerpt from *A Jingle Bell Mingle* copyright © 2024 by Bittersweet Media LLC and Sierra Simone.

SNOW PLACE LIKE LA. Copyright © 2023 by Bittersweet Media LLC and Sierra Simone.

SEAS AND GREETINGS. Copyright © 2024 by Bittersweet Media LLC and Sierra Simone.

HarperCollins books may be purchased for educational, business, or sales promotional use. For information, please email the Special Markets Department at SPsales@harpercollins.com.

Avon, Avon & logo, and Avon Books & logo are registered trademarks of HarperCollins Publishers in the United States of America and other countries.

Originally published separately in ebook format as *Snow Place Like LA* and *Seas and Greetings* in the United States by Avon Impulse in 2023 and 2024.

Designed by Diahann Sturge-Campbell

Christmas palm trees © Radiocat/Stock.Adobe.com

Library of Congress Cataloging-in-Publication Data has been applied for.

ISBN 978-0-06-344312-9

25 26 27 28 29 LBC 5 4 3 2 1

To Lizzie McReynolds, who once had a
Twilight poster in her room

Seas and Greetings

Chapter One

*I*n a world of bouclé armchairs, I was a velvet settee, and nothing proved it more than the room I was standing in right now.

"Make a note that I want the welcome basket to be set on the table by the balcony doors on future sailings," I said to my cousin, and last-minute assistant, Bailey. My mother had insisted I bring her when my aggressively capable assistant, Michael, had come down with a case of cat scratch fever and wasn't able to work on the cruise because his armpits hurt so badly.

And I loved my twenty-three-year-old cousin to bits, *truly*, but she was no Michael—and also I was pretty sure she only agreed to come because it was a free cruise on a ship with eleven different bars.

"And going forward, the bouquets near the accent walls need to have more eucalyptus, I think. I want more pop against the yellow." I squinted at the bouquet again, wondering if eucalyptus was the right vibe for July. Maybe I should save it for the winter sailings. "Or possibly bay leaves. Write down 'bay leaves.' Bailey?"

I turned to see my cousin patently *not* writing anything down, as she was staring at the door—and fuck me in my nonswollen armpit. This was important! Details mattered! It was why I'd insisted on doing a walk-through when I'd embarked: because I wanted to make sure that every single element of a guest suite—the gold sconces, the artisanal toiletries, the vegan chocolates handmade by radical nuns—was ready for that crucial snap or reel or post. It wasn't good enough for things to look good in real life. They had to look good online too. And actually it still wasn't enough for things to look good online; the posts from our cruises needed to look good enough to convert the curious into the *believing*. Into guests who then became tripod-carrying missionaries and evangelized the good news of aesthetic ocean travel to the world.

I needed these believers because I needed Lemon Tree Cruises to work. If the cruise line didn't work, that set me behind on expanding into hotels, and if I was behind on hotels, then I was behind on the Rest of the Plan.

Cruises! Hotels! Rest of Plan!

In that order!

Plans were what made the world turn; plans were how money was made. Plans were how you took uncertainty and loneliness (and the gnawing suspicion that maybe your life was a cold and empty crater) and shoved those feelings into little boxes so that they couldn't bother you anymore. In the words of the Bible: Consider the lilies of the field, and look at how they always have kanban boards and planners with highlighters in muted pastels.

"Bailey," I said patiently. "Are you—"

"Tall," Bailey whispered, her brown eyes awestruck. "Hot."

I saw symmetrically faced people all the time, so I wasn't bracing myself when I followed my cousin's gaze to the woman standing in the doorway. And then I wished I *had* braced myself, because holy Dyson Airwrap, Krysta Morton was a cold, cold mommy straight from my dirtiest daydreams.

The low ponytail she'd sported for her entire tenure guarding Isaac Kelly was gone and had been replaced by a sharp undercut, the white-blond hair on top just long enough to pull into a neat bun. Her skin was fair, her mouth was a full but stern line, and her eyebrows were so light that they were almost hard to see from across the room, although I could guess that they were pulled together in irritation.

Blue eyes, a black suit with a white button-down shirt, and sunglasses on top of her head completed the vibe. A vibe that was fully *don't fuck with me*, with just a dash of *but if you behave, I might deign to sit on your face later.*

God only knew why that was so hot to me. Probably trauma.

But she was here to do a job, and so was I, and I was already four minutes behind the schedule I'd made for myself this morning on the way to the Long Beach cruise terminal.

"Krysta," I said, stepping forward and offering my hand and my biggest smile. "Thank you so much for taking this job. I know it was a little spontaneous, but I appreciate it."

She strode into the suite to meet me and shook my hand with a very firm clasp. Once. And then she pulled her hand back like she'd reached her quota of human touch for the day.

"Your manager was very persistent, Ms. Hayes," Krysta said. She was looking behind me—not at Bailey, but at the balcony doors and the steps leading to the second story of the suite. "I assume she sent over my rules."

"Yes!" Which was the truth.

"And you read them?"

"Of course!"

Okay, that part was not . . . as truthy. I generally tried to be diligent about reviewing everything sent my way, because *details mattered*, et cetera, et cetera, but just between you and me, these were the kinds of details that didn't interest me as much as the TikTok-ability of a cruise ship's outdoor pool. So as Krysta strode deeper into the suite and then took the stairs two at a time, I discreetly pulled out my phone and summoned up the email with her bodyguard-engagement agreement.

Ah, okay, here were the rules:

The Rules:
- No sneaking off alone.
- No secrets.
- No bodyguard-client fraternization.
- No olives.

I could see why Krysta didn't want any bodyguard-client fraternization, given that shaking my hand had seemed like a chore (which, excuse her, but did she even know that she had touched some of the most exfoliated and moisturized hand skin in the business???).

But olives? What the fuck.

"We need to talk about your sleeping arrangements," announced Krysta, coming back down the stairs with the staccato tread of a military general.

Bailey blinked up at her with big horny eyes. I really just needed to put this baby bird in a bikini and send her out to the pool, because she was clearly already in cruise hookup mode.

Krysta continued, "You've got me sleeping across the hall, but there are multiple entries to your suite, and I think it's safer if I sleep in the second bedroom, so I can be closer in case of a breach."

That was not the plan. The plan that I had planned on. This wasn't it!

"Bailey's sleeping there," I said. "She's my assistant, and I need *her* close. Plus, she's excellent at handling breaches—she's basically a breach legend. So."

Krysta stared at me.

"I promise I'm not being high-maintenance," I said. I had a lot of experience explaining why what I wanted was perfectly normal and reasonable. "It's just that I need someone nearby to record my thoughts, observations, and notes for improvement. It's the maiden voyage, you know," I added.

Krysta's blond eyebrow lifted, but she still didn't speak.

"And across the hall isn't so far away. And that room is such a fun room! It's next to a slide that leads down to the speakeasy—"

Bailey stepped forward with her hands clasped together, all noble voluntarism. "Addison, I think Krysta has a very important point about staying in the suite with you. As your cousin, who cares deeply for your unbreached security, I think we should switch rooms, and we should do it right away, and you know what, I'll go get my things right now. For your safety. And stuff."

I saw through her game. She wanted to be close to that slide, and the speakeasy, and the potentially sexy people therein. But before I could call her on it, Krysta said, "Good," in a voice that clearly signaled the decision was final.

My watch buzzed on my wrist, and I glanced down. I was now nine minutes behind schedule. Shitnuggets!

"*Fine*," I said, "but, Bailey, this doesn't mean you're getting out of assistant duties. Let's go."

I started walking to my next destination, a reluctant cousin trailing behind me, and when I made to shut the suite door, Krysta was there too.

"Where are you going?" she asked. "The rules clearly say *no sneaking off alone.*"

"A of all," I said as we started walking down the hall, "I'm not alone. I have my cousin-assistant. B of all, my manager agreed to those rules, not me!"

"You *will* follow them, Ms. Hayes," growled Krysta. Ooh, I did like that growl. Then she stepped in front of me. "Tell me where you want to go."

"To the theater!" I sang, delighted in having gotten my way somehow, although we'd need to be brisk if we wanted to make up for the lost nine minutes.

A muscle in Krysta's jaw flickered, like I'd just told her we were going to a self-catheterization workshop, but then her detached expression returned. It looked unfairly hot on her, with the high cheekbones and high forehead, the deep blue eyes.

Yes, stare coldly at me, Mommy. And then tell me what a bad girl I am!

Alas that hooking up with my bodyguard wasn't part of the plan, and also that I was sure Krysta had a healthy, if mild, dislike of me.

It could have been a fun cruise.

Chapter Two

Krysta had done her cruise ship homework and led us straight to the theater via service doors and back hallways to avoid the still-embarking passengers. We emerged into the backstage hallway-cum-dressing-room, which was filled with open pots of glittery makeup and what could only be described as panic.

God, I hated stage entertainment. Had since I was a kid and my mom strapped Dansoft shoes to my feet and made me go twirl on a stage. Something about having an audience right there, able to see the edge of your wig or the sweaty creases in your makeup, was just unbearable. But ships needed sure-to-be-beloved shows, and there was only one sure-to-be-beloved story I loved enough to imagine commissioning a cruise ship musical for.

"Where is my brother-doctor-dad?" the makeup artist called over the fray. "I need brother-doctor-dad in the chair right now. And tell flannel-dad not to touch that mustache until the adhesive dries!"

I skirted around some extras slurping iced coffee while they waited in line for costumes, and stepped onto the stage, looking for the director and the scriptwriter. I heard Bailey ask one of the extras where they got their drinks and resigned myself to losing my assistant to the siren song of caffeine.

But I didn't have time to argue with her about it. I needed to be done in the theater in ten minutes so I could go check on the kitchens, the spa, the margarita bar, and then make it through the mandatory muster drill before I went to my suite and had exactly forty-five minutes to change, refresh my hair, and practice my welcome speech.

As I spotted the person I'd hand selected to pen my musical tribute to *Twilight* at the far end of the theater, my watch buzzed. I looked down to see a text from my manager and caught the words *August* and *sit-down interview* floating on the tiny screen.

My stomach sank to my slouchy boots and then slithered across the stage floor. No, I couldn't think about this now—

I'd deal with it later.

Decision made, I scampered over to my scriptwriter, Pearl Purkiss. She was even paler than Krysta, with skin the color of cold milk, and silky hair now dyed a light pink. She was currently holding hands with her girlfriend, Gretchen Young, who was in an oversize racerback onesie, with long twists hanging to her waist and her nose piercing winking in the low light of the theater. She had warm medium-brown skin, a heart-shaped face with high cheekbones, and a tropical cocktail in one hand that she was currently most of the way through.

I was relieved to see Gretchen, because Pearl—while very budget-friendly and surprisingly a *Twilight* fan—was famously a migratory bird when it came to work. Gretchen, however, was an industry veteran like me, and even though we'd taken very different paths, the paths had been paved with getting shit done.

"I am here entirely in the capacity of supporting my girlfriend and lying flat on my back with no one talking to me, so I can't help you—ask Pearl," Gretchen said all in one breath, holding up her drink to demonstrate that she was indeed in vacation mode.

"I'm just checking in, seeing how things are going, making sure that we have everything we need," I reassured her. "Do you both like your room?"

"Love the minibar," Gretchen said at the same time as Pearl said, "The waves are already speaking their language to me, Addison. Shhhhh, boooom. *Shhhhh, boooom.*"

That presumably was the language of the waves.

"So about the show," I chirped, since I was short on time, and also didn't speak ocean, "last time we spoke, you and the director were reworking the music for the final scene. Is it ready, you think, or is the mind battle still better with a ballad rather than an up-tempo song?"

From my position next to her, I saw the faintest quiver of Krysta's mouth.

I wanted that quiver to be a GIF so I could watch it over and over again, so I could figure out what it *meant*. So I could figure out how she could make the smallest movements of that shell-pink mouth seem earthshaking.

Gretchen, who'd met Krysta once or twice back in Krysta's guarding-Isaac days, seemed to interpret the quiver as a question. "It's a *Twilight*-themed musical," she explained. "But for legal reasons, it's not *Twilight*, and instead a love story between two characters named Isabel and Edmund."

"Don't forget Jason," said Pearl, with an artist's affront.

"Right, and Jason. Anyway, it's called *The Lion and the Lamb*, and Pearl did an amazing job, and . . . I need to go."

Gretchen kissed Pearl on the cheek and then practically bolted away without looking behind her once. I realized why once the show's director appeared next to me.

Mack Anderson was a steal. On paper, he was a Broadway director with a résumé so stacked, Stephen Sondheim would probably come back from the grave just to create a new show for him to direct. That was until three years ago when Mack was found to have been living in the attic of his theater after gambling away a rent-controlled apartment when he bet wrong in Atlantic City on the Tonys. That part wasn't ideal, but the story went from bad to worse when rumors began to swirl about him solving the theater's rat problem with a newly found DIY taxidermy hobby.

I heard there were dollhouses. Dollhouses full of dead rats.

But he was a genius. A desperate genius. Mack was more than ready to take a West Coast job with a living stipend and housing, albeit temporary and at sea. I only hoped he hadn't brought the rats.

Mack *tsk*ed as he flung his silk scarf over his shoulder. "Gretchen!" he called. "I'd love to talk to you about a musical you might be interested in adapting with me." But Gretchen was already long gone, so he turned to Pearl and me. "The property I have in mind would be such a box office gimme. It was a book first, then a movie, then a Broadway musical, and now I'd like to adapt the musical back into a movie. Genius, isn't it? Adapting adaptations is the future. There are no new stories. Truly."

Pearl sighed a thoughtful sigh.

"Give the people what they want," I said. My watch buzzed, and again, my stomach threatened to drop right into the sea, but I realized it was just my alarm and not my manager pushing me to confirm his plans for August.

Whew. Time for the kitchen walk-through.

"Thank you, my beautiful chickens of the sea," I told Mack and Pearl. "I can't wait to see what opening night brings."

I gave them my jazziest jazz hands, a signature Addison Hayes smile, and made to leave—just as Bailey reappeared on the stage, double-fisting iced drinks, one of which was violently pink.

"Addy!" she called. "I got that hibiscus shit for you!"

Hibiscus shit! Ah, forgiveness, ah, *agape*.

I was about to go get it myself when Krysta said, "Stay put," and left. Which was unnecessary, but perhaps would take less time with her long legs, and time was money, baby! I needed to get moving!

But *wow wow*, also I could definitely watch Krysta walk all day. Her suit was cut so that the power in her shoulders was evident, and as she moved, I could see the muscles of her thighs press against her trousers.

"Addison," Pearl intoned in that hazy, slightly wondrous voice, like she'd just woken up from a dream.

I grudgingly pulled my gaze away from Krysta's thighs.

"I meant to tell you earlier," Pearl went on. "I have something for you."

Chapter Three

*P*earl handed me a red scalloped envelope that I distinctly recognized as stationery from the Wishes by Addison Galentine's Day stationery line. "Isn't red such a powerful color?" she asked before floating away.

I tore open the envelope. There was no Galentine to be found. Instead, there was a piece of paper torn from the Lemon Tree notepad that I'd curated for the guest welcome basket.

11 PM. Infinity hot tub. Stern of the ship. You've got skin in the game.

Well, wasn't that cryptic? I didn't have time for cryptic. Cryptic was not on the schedule.

So I folded the note to revisit during my fifteen minutes of free time after dinner and announced to Krysta like a *West Wing* character, "I'm walking."

I should tell her about the note. There were those rules about secrets and whatnot, and Bodyguard Mommy liked her rules. But as I went to open the note again, Krysta caught up to me in three strides and handed me my iced tea with a look that rivaled revulsion. Like actual disgust.

Maybe a hibiscus drink killed her father?

And maybe now wasn't the time for cryptic notes. Besides, Krysta would probably just do something silly like slow down my ETA and lock me in my room when this was nothing more than an overzealous fan in search of a moment of connection. Because what the fans expected from the entire Addison Hayes experience was connection. Via thoughtfully curated goods, services, shows, and parties. Every single one of my followers had the opportunity to have a little piece of me for a price . . . but sometimes a piece wasn't good enough, which explained the issue of the cryptic note and why it was without a doubt harmless.

After I checked on the kitchen and the spa, and previewed the sail-away sip-and-paint party for VIPs that would be held in the margarita bar, the captain announced that it was time for muster.

Krysta, the most serious human being of all time, led the way to our muster station, where she drilled the poor cruise employee on exactly which lifeboats we would use to evacuate and how many life jackets were available and what the plan was if a lifeboat failed to properly deploy.

Halfway through the safety drill, she turned to me. "Are you even paying attention?"

I looked up from the color-coded to-do list on my phone. "If the big boat goes down, we get on the tiny boats. That's basically the gist of it. Besides, you seem to be very good at your job, so I'm sure if things go sideways, you'll just drag the whole ship to shore with those muscly arms of yours."

For a millisecond, her lip twitched into something that almost resembled a smile before she looked away again and raised her hand to ask another question.

After muster, Krysta parted the sea of cruisers so I could go back to my room and change for the official send-off.

Fans waved and reached in front of me for selfies and autographs, which was actually really overwhelming considering the narrow hallways. Krysta stepped in front of me, shielding me from the eager guests before herding me into a crew-member-only corridor.

"Doing okay, Ms. Hayes?" she asked as the door shut behind us, searching my expression for any sign that I wasn't all right.

I nodded, enjoying her concern for me a little too much.

But then her shoulders straightened and she was all brusque and businesslike again.

"AND I HOPE you'll all raise a glass with me and toast the first-ever Lemon Tree voyage!"

I lifted my flute of sparkling grape juice to the crowd below me. I was on a balcony in the atrium, having finished my speech, knowing my glittering jumpsuit was set to its most content-ready effect with the wall of windows behind me framing the sunset. The better part of four thousand passengers was assembled below me and on the many balconies and staircases, and all of them had a phone in one hand, a custom cocktail or mocktail in the other, and all of them looked happy. My speech had gone perfectly, the music started just as we all tipped our glasses back, and when I took a discreet glance at my watch, we were perfectly on time. The guests would have thirty more minutes of libations and conversation before dinner and then the rest of the evening to explore. Exactly what I had on my planner, and my Miro, and my Notion.

So why did I feel like I was made of piano wire?

Oh, right, the note. The note for me. The note meant especially for me. My note.

I reminded myself that it was harmless and that the worst thing it represented was a blip in the schedule. And usually I would ignore it, but as I'd gotten ready for the welcoming ceremony, one word jumped out at me.

Skin.

You've got skin in the game.

This person couldn't know about—no. They couldn't know about my single greatest disaster! The most mortifying thing ever to have happened to Addison Hayes!

But if they did . . .

I had enough PR battles to fight. From comments calling me out about the carbon emissions of a cruise ship to the fact that the megachurch I'd gone to until I was twenty-three was currently in the throes of an FBI-level fraud investigation.

And then there was *August*. With the *sit-down*.

My stomach bounced and then burst like a water balloon.

No, I had to find out what this person knew. I couldn't handle professional ignominy on top of everything else this year. Ignominy was not in the plan, and ignominy definitely wasn't on the kanban board.

I made it through dinner, an exclusive tour with a group of hand-chosen influencers, and managed to give Bailey stern instructions to meet me for the morning yoga class at seven. And then I feigned exhaustion to Krysta.

"I really better get to bed," I said, setting down the sparkling grape juice I'd been nursing.

Krysta nodded and gestured for me to lead the way back to my room. Somehow, despite her full day of walking, glaring, and bodyguarding, Krysta's suit was still perfectly uncreased and her hair above her undercut was still neatly in its bun, as if even her hair was afraid to disobey her.

She didn't speak as we walked back to the room, and every time I glanced back at her, she had an expression that could charitably be called *frosty* and realistically called *I hate this place and everything that brought me here*, but it looked good on her, I had to say. I kind of wondered what it would feel like to let my face show emotions beyond the Addison Hayes Approved Range of Feelings, but then immediately dismissed the thought. It didn't matter what it would feel like. I'd never be able to do it, to be that person. It wasn't what the brand was built on . . . and also, I generally didn't feel too negatively about anything. Tomorrow was always another day, a fresh page in the planner with a new sheet of stickers. All you had to do was make it to the morning alarm and a brand-new start was yours for the taking.

It was strange having Krysta in the suite as I took a quick shower and pretended to get ready for bed. Of course, I'd shared a bathroom with people before, had planned on sharing it with Bailey for the duration of this trip, but I realized with some disorientation that I'd never had to navigate sharing a bathroom with someone who wasn't family or who wasn't already a friend. And when it came to hookups, well. I didn't even stay for conversation afterward, much less stay *the night*.

As I watched Krysta emerge from the bathroom in a sports bra and low-hanging athletic shorts, arms and shoulders flexing as she toweled off her hair, I decided it was a good thing that I'd made a point to compartmentalize my sex life. Because walking past her— her skin still glistening with lingering damp from her shower, her breasts firm, and her nipples taut under her white sports bra—to do something as mundane as brush my teeth felt . . .

I didn't even know how it felt. Exposing? Terrifying?

Illicitly thrilling?

And there was a moment when she slid behind me in the bathroom to hang her towel on the hook and her hip brushed mine that I became immediately *un*compartmentalized. My skin hummed. My belly went liquid. I could smell the sharp, clean scent of her bodywash and something almost woody underneath it, like cedar. I wanted to press my face into her neck and smell; I wanted her to slide her hand in my hair and hold me against her throat until I kissed it to her liking.

But when our eyes met in the mirror, I saw only that same cold, flat expression from before, the one that almost looked like disgust. And there was no iced tea here, no crowds, no ambient cruise ship goings-on. It was just me.

She was wearing that expression because of me.

Chapter Four

*M*y skin stopped humming and started burning instead. A hot flush scalded my cheeks—a flush that I couldn't even hide behind a red-blocking foundation because I'd already washed my face.

Okay, I had to get out of here. It was one thing to need to move Vibrator Night to tonight, but it was another to know that a hot mommy of a bodyguard literally found me repellant. It was a real boner-shrinker, and you know what? It shrank the boner of my self-esteem too.

Before I could finish brushing my teeth, she was gone, having put those long, muscled legs to good use to stalk off to her bedroom. I spat out my organic toothpaste, remembered to call my manager about that meeting with a toothpaste start-up—I'm coming for you, Tom's of Maine—and swished my mouth with water. And then I surreptitiously sniffed my hair to make sure I'd rinsed out my conditioner and didn't smell like an air freshener.

Nope. Fine. It must be my bubbly personality she was opposed to . . . or the fact that the faith-based media apparatus that birthed my career was patently homophobic and she probably thought I was cut from the same bigoted cloth.

August.

Sit-down.

The words smeared all my thoughts together like an old, dirty makeup sponge. I closed my eyes and took a calming breath and then another. Pretended I was at a head spa with a heated eye mask and someone spraying my scalp with warm water and that my email inbox was empty and that I didn't stare up at the ceiling at night wondering why being so busy didn't keep me from feeling so alone—

No, no! Back to the eye mask and the scalp massage! And also there was someone massaging my feet. And a hypoallergenic puppy snoozing on my chest. And someone to cuddle me for an hour afterward, because the only person I had to cuddle was my best friend, Winnie Baker (and, okay, her adorable baby too), but I was always working so much, and so I never saw her or the baby, and—

—this wasn't working.

How was I supposed to do the rest of this cruise with *August* hanging over my head? I needed to talk to my team, because maybe August was too soon. I mean, arguably it was too late, given that I was thirty-three years old, but it was coming up so fast, and I hadn't had any time to prepare, and maybe I just needed to push it back a quarter, rearrange the kanban board. Otherwise, I wasn't going to be able to pay full attention to Lemon Tree, and if Lemon Tree failed, *everything failed*.

Okay, yes, that was what I needed to do! I clapped my hands together even though I was alone, delighted with myself. I should have remembered that there wasn't a problem a revised schedule couldn't fix.

On my way to my bedroom, I noticed Krysta's door was closed, with not a single lumen of light seeping from under the door. Just in case she was still awake, I made a (nuanced, *restrained*) show of going into my room and closing the door and rustling loudly atop my covers, in case sounds could travel through our shared wall. And then I checked the clock. Ten forty-five. I needed to make my move sooner rather than later.

I quietly changed into jeans, a white T-shirt, and a collarless tweed jacket, slipped on my vegan leather tennis shoes, and crept down the stairs and out of the suite. And internally thanked Teenage Addison for her youthful indiscretions—I now had the dubious gift of being able to sneak out of any place, at any time. Sadly, there'd be no making out at the end of this foray, but such was the pain of being in your thirties, I guessed.

The ship, I was happy to see, was lively even at this late hour. The pools were splashing, the lazy river was full of half naked people soaking in the starlight, music leaked from the different clubs and bars as I made my way to the stern. I stopped to take a few selfies, complimented some influencers on their swimwear, and reached the hot tub right at eleven.

It wasn't as loud back here—there were only a few guests in the tub, gathered at the infinity edge to look out onto the dark waves as they drank and talked—and I couldn't hear any of the music. Just the wind and the water and the low murmur of voices.

I found a spot at the railing nearby and scanned the area for my would-be villain. But aside from an influencer making her friend take an unreasonable number of pictures of her, there were no obvious evildoers nearby.

I checked my watch, then took out the note and reread it. *11 PM.* That was now! Didn't potential blackmailers have schedules too?

I would wait thirty minutes. As much as I wanted to put this particular anxiety to bed, I also needed to put *myself* to bed, because the sunrise yoga class was happening whether I was there or not, and I needed to wake up with enough time for under-eye masks and an espresso shot. (A furtive espresso shot . . . I did a whole piece with Goop extolling the benefits of cutting caffeine and drinking dandelion coffee instead, and until my dandelion-coffee-sponsored posts were done, no public caffeine for me.)

I turned to scout the deck, thinking maybe my malefactor was hiding behind one of the potted lemon trees, and ran right into a wall of cedar-smelling hoodie.

I tilted my head back to look up at Krysta's unamused face.

"Hi!" I squeaked.

"What the fuck do you think you're doing?" she asked. Her voice was low but serrated. Pissed.

It was kind of hot, actually, but given that she was staring at me like I'd eaten a Nature Valley granola bar in her car, I knew better than to turn the moment flirty. I also knew better than to tell her the truth. She'd just make A Thing of it and refuse to let me fix this, and I had to fix it.

So. No truth for Krysta.

"I wanted to make sure everyone was having a good time tonight and that everything was running smoothly. Like a good hostess. I was hostessing!"

She stared down at me. "The rules," she said and nothing more.

I thought back to the short list I'd found in my email. *No sneaking off alone.*

"Okay, but can you even sneak out on a cruise ship?" I asked innocently. "Sneaking out implies a *mysterious* out, an out away from the *in*. But on a ship, they're one and the same! There's no other place! So really—"

Krysta had already taken my elbow at this point and was guiding me—firmly—away from the hot tub. I cast one last desperate look around to see if anyone new and dastardly had appeared, but Krysta was walking too fast, and I had to scurry to keep up. Her hand had moved to my upper arm, and her grip was so, so strong. The kind of grip that could pin both your wrists above your head.

Mmm.

"Look," I said, "if you're going to interrupt my hostessing, the least you can do is swing me by the twenty-four-hour snack bar for some fries."

"You can order room service," Krysta said, navigating me through the outdoor pool area with the blank-faced efficiency of a Secret Service agent.

I was aghast. "Order *fries* from room service?"

"Is there a problem with room service fries?" she asked.

"They won't be the right temperature! They'll be too cold!"

"So? It's the same ingredients. They are the same fries."

"How dare you! How very dare you! Room service fries *are not* the same!"

Krysta glanced over at the snack bar by the pool, which was admittedly very crowded and jostling and probably all the things a bodyguard wouldn't like.

"No," she said flatly.

I pouted. She ignored me and continued guiding me through the common area until we got to the suite. She locked the door behind us when we came in.

"So . . . how did you know I'd left the suite?" I asked. I tried to ask cheerfully so that she'd know I was willing to let bygones be fry-bygones.

She cut me a look but didn't answer. She had that expression again, the one of intense dislike, and her mouth was pressed so tightly together that the corners were white.

"Goodnight, Ms. Hayes" was all she said, and then she went into her room and closed the door with an irritated-sounding click.

Chapter Five

Mack Anderson paced in front of Pearl Purkiss, who was clutching a reusable cup of foul-smelling tea to her chest and staring at him with wide eyes. Mack's assistant—a bony, fair-skinned young woman with high-waisted trousers, giant round glasses, and a beret—stood behind him with a notebook, poised to write down any stray tidbits of genius he might dispense.

But I could tell we weren't currently in genius mode; we were in panic mode, and so I only paused for a beat in the doorway of the dressing room before I strode inside and took Mack's flapping hands in my own. A suited Krysta was behind me, and out in the hallway, our actors milled, fretted, and trilled vocal slides at each other while they waited for the lights to go down and the music to start.

"Mack," I said. "The show is going to be brilliant. The actors are ready. The music is flawless. And even if the show *isn't* brilliant, it will still be fun and campy, and the audience will love it."

Mack tossed his head in such a way that his wispy hair floated briefly in the air. "I thought you of all people would have understood the necessity of a perfect show."

"I do want a perfect show," I assured him. "But the mission statement of Lemon Tree Cruises is that we'll provide an unforgettable lifestyle experience worthy of documenting to the world. If the show is flawless, then our guests will be chattering about it on social media. If the show is a giant, hilarious disaster, our guests will be chattering about it on social media. Either way, a perfect outcome."

Mack didn't relax exactly, but he stopped trying to pull his hands out of mine. "I won't have my art mocked, Ms. Hayes," he said in the aggrieved tone of a misunderstood dog show judge. "Even if it's still okay for the cruise."

"They won't mock," I said soothingly. "They're ready to love it. Have you looked at the audience? Half of them are in baseball uniforms and floor-length black-and-red capes. So long as they get glittery skin and the wide-eyed baby doll, they're going to be delighted. Besides, do you even know you? There's no way Mack Anderson—*the* Mack Anderson—could create anything less than a masterpiece."

Mack sniffed once and then pulled his hands free to smooth his silk scarf over his rumpled blazer. It was an eggplant-colored scarf today. "You are correct."

"Mr. Anderson," his assistant whispered with the reverent tones of an acolyte, "it's almost time."

He smoothed his scarf again and, with a regal nod, left the dressing room to gather his sparkly flock. His assistant followed, taking notes, even though nothing had happened worth writing down. Which was actually great.

"Does anyone know her name?" I whispered. "I think she could teach Bailey a thing or two."

Pearl stood up, set down her tea, and did a stretch that made it look like her limbs were breaking and reforming in order to become a werewolf. "I think she's called Cassie. Or Capricorn." And then she left too.

When I turned to Krysta, her expression was still unfriendly, but there was some curiosity there now too in the lift of a blond eyebrow. "That was well done," she said.

"Mmm, what was?" I asked, already pulling out my phone to see if I could hunt down Cassie/Capricorn's information.

"How you managed the director's meltdown. Do you do that a lot?"

Aha! I found her cc'd in an email thread with Mack. *Cassiopeia Larchmont*. "Do what a lot? Soothe frantic theater people? No, I try to avoid them generally."

"No. Manage the people around you." Krysta paused, as if searching for a word. "Encourage them." The words were clipped enough that *encourage* sounded an awful lot like *manipulate*.

I couldn't decide whether to take that personally. On the one hand, I didn't love that she didn't seem to think very highly of me, but on the other, she was very tall. My sense of justice started dimming around the six-foot mark.

I knew it was a moral defect, but we all have them, okay!

"Well, I'm a decent actress and a decent singer," I said as I typed out a quick email to Cassiopeia to see if she'd be willing to meet with my cousin. "But I learned early on that I was *great* at making things happen for great people. Comfortable leggings, subtle but refreshing candle scents, a quarterly journal with aspirational living advice—you know. *Great things*. And making things happen is mostly just making sure the people around you feel seen." I finished the email and looked up at my bodyguard. The corners of her mouth were no longer white, and there was a slight gap between her lips. I could see the white glint of her teeth, and I wondered briefly what they would feel like on my neck.

"It's unusual," Krysta said. "For a celebrity to be the one listening."

I waved a hand and made for the door. "You're just used to Isaac Kelly moping around his mansion. We're not all monsters, you know."

"Isaac wasn't a monster," she clarified, "but I have known a few in my time."

"Ooh, really? I want names—" The show's psychic vampire danced past me in her ballet flats and pixie cut wig, and just then, I saw the house lights flash. It was almost time for the show. "We should get to our seats!"

Krysta nodded and, again with that firm hand on my elbow, guided me past someone putting extra tousle into our lead vampire's bronze-colored wig and a clump of ensemble performers in letter jackets and backpacks making sure their werewolf costumes were ready to go in the wings. We made it into the house and found our seats just as the lights began to dim.

Krysta sat down and stared doubtfully down at the blue-tinted eyeglasses she'd been handed as we'd come into the auditorium.

"It's necessary to the emotional journey of the play," I informed her. And then I twisted in my seat to look around. "I wonder if Bailey made it. I texted her that the show's debut was tonight, and all I got in response was a selfie of her covered in mud at the spa. I wasn't sure how to interpret that."

Meanwhile, Krysta had put on her glasses. She swiveled her head to look at me with a frigid expression, the brief thaw from the dressing room clearly over. But it was very hard to take her displeasure seriously when she had giant blue glasses on.

"You're right," I said. "She's probably taking a lil' mud nap. Oh oh oh!"

The curtain was lifting, and I hurriedly put my own glasses on. Instantly the stage and everything on it turned a moody, dreamy blue, and I watched as our slender human came onto the stage, nervously tucking her hair behind her ear as her mustached father showed her around his house.

"Juliet is amazing," I whispered about our lead actress. Without looking over at me, Krysta pressed a finger to my mouth so I'd be quiet. The gesture was as arousing as it was bossy, and I mentally chanted *she doesn't like you, she very much hates you* to myself so I wouldn't be tempted to nip at her finger and see what she did in response.

She dropped her finger, but I still felt the warm shape of it against my lips, the tingling skin she'd left behind. I hadn't—well, it had been a while since I'd, *you know* . . . Not that it mattered, really, it was just that it was natural to have a reaction like this after going so long without slaking my thirst. To borrow a vampire metaphor.

I really needed to arrange for a hookup the minute we docked back in Long Beach. If a single finger press was making it so I could barely sing along with the *whoa-hoa-hoa-hoa*s with the rest of the audience, that was probably not a good sign.

But I couldn't stop darting my tongue over my lower lip, like I was trying to chase away the lingering warmth. Or keep it there longer. And despite the high camp, acrobatic choreography, and frankly moving cesarean sequence, I also couldn't stop stealing glances over at my bodyguard. At what she looked like through the blue filter of my glasses, at the slope of her nose and the angle of her chin. At the long stretch of her throat before it reached the notch of her collarbone and the placket of her white button-down, unbuttoned only one professional button.

I wondered why she took this job. I wondered if she'd found me irritating from the start. I wondered if she had someone back home, and if not, if she wanted there to be a *someone*.

I wondered what she would do if I pressed my finger against her mouth instead.

And suddenly, it was the end of the show. The auditorium erupted in applause, cheers, whistles, chants for more, and the cast was glowing under their glitter as they came up to take their bows. I slid my glasses off and turned so I could take in the auditorium behind me. Beaming faces, laughter, joy. Most importantly, phones out and flashing.

Satisfaction rolled through me like a sweet, cool wave, that tasty feeling of validation, rewarded optimism, and shared glee with the people around me. It had worked—*The Lion and the Lamb* was off to a terrific start, which meant that Lemon Tree Cruises was off to a terrific start, which meant that the plan was working. And a plan working was my own personal brand of heroin.

Elated, I spun to Krysta and decided to hug her because I needed to hug somebody, and as I was grabbing for her, I decided to lift to my toes and kiss her on the cheek too, because this wasn't a hug-only moment, this was *celebration*.

Except right as I was about to stamp a kiss onto her cheek, she turned her head, and my lips made contact with her mouth instead.

She went still—so still—and now I had frozen too, my arms around her and my lips against her soft, moldable ones. They were unimaginably warm, unimaginably giving under pressure, and for a minute, I forgot that this was an accident, a mistake, a breach of etiquette and consent and God knew what else.

And maybe Krysta forgot for a moment too, because her lips parted, ever so slightly, like she was about to sneak a taste—

"Thank you! Thank you!" Mack's voice boomed over a microphone. Krysta and I leapt apart at the same time, and I was rambling an apology, and she was trying to take the glasses off her face, and then Mack was calling me up to the stage, and then I was giving an impromptu speech to the crowd.

And then it was time for dinner and an ad hoc cocktail party with the cast to celebrate their triumph, and Krysta said not a word to me the whole time, not even on the way back to our suite, when it was only us.

When I got into my room, vaguely horny and regretful, I saw a new arrangement of flowers on the table next to my bed. Tulips *and* carnations—ick.

There was a note wedged into a little plastic holder among the flowers, and I slid it free to see who was responsible for this bulbiferous monstrosity.

Two days. I'll give you more instructions soon.
And this time don't bring your muscle . . . or I'll do something rash.

Chapter Six

*D*oes that sign say 'daily foam parties'?" Bailey asked our private beach club concierge.

"Foam party wasn't on the vision board," I said under my breath, and to my surprise, Krysta didn't frown. In fact, I would daresay, she nearly smirked.

Bailey looked at me with pleading eyes, and I shooed her toward the concierge and the huge resort-style infinity pool.

"Generous," Krysta said as she did a brief patrol of the VIP cabana, which was removed from the action and overlooking the property. It was ideal for overseeing a good time without partaking in said good time.

There was a waist-high stone wall lining the cabana, and at the center of all the lounge furniture was a huge charcuterie spread and a pitcher of nonalcoholic sangria. (I'd done No Alcohol November last year, and it turned out I was way more productive without the steady stream of vodka. And, okay, *I guess* I was a tad nicer too. Sober Addison was here to stay.)

"Sometimes I wonder if Bailey gets in the way more than anything else," I admitted. "At least hiring her got my mom off my back for a little while."

Apparently satisfied that no murderers were hiding in the cabana, Krysta removed her black sunglasses and pushed them back over her head, channeling the vibe of a commercial for some sort of edgy hair product that only people in West Hollywood had heard of.

This morning, she'd walked out of her room in a look that could only be described as Bodyguard Mommy Goes to the Beach. Her black board shorts were slung low on her hips and her sports bra–style bikini top peekabooed from under her white sleeveless tank with armholes cut so wide that I could see the way her abs rippled from the right angle.

Since we'd docked this morning and disembarked, Krysta had been . . . different. Still a little grumpy and lurking in the shadows like a hot gay Batman. But she'd laughed once or twice since we'd done my scheduled pop-ins to the various curated excursions I'd planned for today's stop in Ensenada, Mexico. We'd done four-wheelers—well, observed them. We went to a cooking class and a local art market, and we even swung by the snorkeling excursion via a speedboat that nearly destroyed my sideswept fishtail braid.

"What's your mom on your back about?" Krysta said as she sat down and draped her arm over the back of the sectional. It was the most relaxed I'd seen her since we'd met, and the empty space next to her called to me like a magnet. "I can't imagine what else a mother could possibly expect of a daughter. You've pretty much created an empire and mastered every industry, one right after the other."

I gave in to the temptation of her arm and sat down beside her, half expecting her to pull her arm back, but when she didn't, I crossed one leg over the other and let myself lean toward her, ever so slightly.

Ever since our accidental kiss last night, I'd felt awkward. Perhaps for the first time in my life. By design, I was the kind of person who walked into a room and set the tone, but this morning I felt like a teenage girl who'd played spin the bottle over the weekend and now had to show up and face her crush on Monday in broad daylight.

And all the while, *August* lurked there at the corner of my mind. What if someone had seen us? The lights were low, but all it took was one snapshot. Context didn't matter. It never did.

I wasn't ashamed of my queerness, and despite what people might think after August rolled around, I never had been. Coming up through the entertainment business in the types of circles that referred to *purity* and *morality* as marketing buzzwords, I'd always detected the dishonesty inside the world I grew up in, and once I became a teenager and realized that I wasn't only attracted to boys, or even mostly attracted to boys, I didn't waste a single diary page stressing about it.

I'd known I'd have to be careful, that was all . . . and play the game right. And I had. Even as I grew more and more tired of being careful, of being in a game at all. Of my whole life being this visible distillation of manicured, Stanley tumbler–wielding success.

In the intervening years, I had strategically expanded my brand beyond the limitations of faith-based entertainment, and I did so successfully. It was helped in part by my mom's divorce from my dad in my early twenties. As she elegantly—and with enviable PR finesse—detangled herself from the judgmental world I grew up in, so did I. And that translated to my brand, which was in part her brand.

I didn't hold that against her. She'd worked just as hard as I had to turn Addison Hayes into a movement.

But . . . that meant she had opinions, and since the brand was me, that meant her opinions were about me.

And now August was nearly here. With its elaborate social media plan, its completed photo shoots, its impeccable podcast-tour strategy.

"Mama Hayes wants nothing more than two things," I finally said. "Firstly, for me to maximize my public coming-out, which is scheduled for this August via an appearance on Drew Barrymore's show and a feature piece in *People*. And then a grandchild, presumably because she loves kids, but also because kids are good for business."

"And she thinks a public coming-out is also good for business?" Krysta asked, her voice neutral.

I sighed. "She's not naive about it—the fallout or my safety. But she says she sees brand potential there too."

The corner of her lip quirked as she said, "So no pressure, then, huh? Just stage the perfect coming-out for public consumption?"

"You don't seem surprised," I observed. "About the gay thing. Well, *technically* bisexual with a serious inclination toward women."

She shrugged and tugged on my braid gently. "Would it be crossing a professional line for me to admit that I was hopefully suspicious?"

The air rushed out of my lungs long enough to render me silent, but before I could respond, Bailey rushed in, partially clad in hot-pink foam.

"You two have to go out there and join the party. Apparently, the foam is edible. Well, not edible exactly. But not dangerous to ingest . . . from what I've been told. Anyway, it smells like cotton candy. I really should have waited to drop out of college until the second semester. I would have been really good at spring breaking."

And then she was off again, blowing the foam off her fingers with a delighted shriek.

I turned back to Krysta, the bridge of her nose beginning to turn pink from the sun. "Did you forget sunscreen?" I asked. "Sun exposure is the leading cause of advanced aging."

What I really wanted to ask was what the hell she meant by *hopefully suspicious*, and also if that meant she wanted to kiss me again, and also why she'd spent the last two days acting like I was the most irritating principal she'd ever worked for. But skincare seemed safer.

"Am I burning?" Krysta asked, her finger brushing her cheek. "I'm wearing, like, SPF 90."

"You still have to reapply every two hours," I told her. "We have complimentary Wishes by Addison sunscreen scattered throughout the party. Just use that."

She looked at the light pink bottle nested in flowers on the table on the balcony for a moment before relenting. She got up, walked over to the table, and brought the sunscreen back into the cabana. She flicked the cap open with a strong thumb and squeezed the lotion into the palm of her hand with the kind of efficiency that made me think of lube and silicone.

And then she started rubbing the lotion into her arms and shoulders, lithe muscles popping, her shirt moving enough to give me glimpses of her corrugated stomach.

Oh, okay, this was not a bad view *at all*.

Krysta smeared lotion across her cheeks and nose, her neck and the crescent of pale chest exposed by her tank top, and then she closed the cap and went to set the sunscreen back in the basket on the balcony.

In the sunlight.

I swallowed back a gasp. I would have warned her if I'd remembered, but I hadn't remembered. So I sat there silently, mouth agape, as my bodyguard shimmered in the sun. Like diamonds.

The sunlight kept reflecting off her skin like the shiniest of shiny vampires, and it wasn't until she noticed her forearm glimmering that she froze and said, "Ms. Hayes. Did you fail to tell me that your sunscreen *has glitter in it*?"

I threw my hands in front of my mouth before she could hear me snort.

She groaned, but her voice was stern when she followed up with "And now I look like I just rolled around on the floor of a Claire's after a Saturday rush?"

I couldn't keep from smiling at my mean bodyguard mommy. "Well, not all of my sunscreen line is a shimmer formula, and I didn't even notice in time to tell you. But once you got started . . . well, it was just too good to make you stop. Besides, you look like Edward Cullen, and it's kind of doing it for me."

Krysta scowled and leaned back a little so she was slightly more shaded, but the shimmer ratio on my Glow Up Sunscreen was honestly one of its biggest selling points, so there was no hiding that she'd turned into a human disco ball.

"Is big scary Krysta embarrassed by a little glitter?" I asked.

"Embarrassment would require me to care what people thought, and that's simply not true." Her voice was matter-of-fact, not defensive at all. Like she was reading me a weather report.

I shook my head. She might have been skin-tinglingly hot, but that wasn't enough to stop me from calling bullshit. "I don't buy that," I said. "You give a shit. You care about rules and being good at your job . . . and . . . and having a really sleek bun and dark black sunglasses so no one can accidentally see into your soul."

"I care about what the people I love think about me," Krysta conceded. "I care about being good at my job, and yeah, maybe you're right about the sunglasses thing. But have you ever considered that you care *too* much about what people think?"

I stood and stepped into the sunlight and watched the crowd from behind the privacy fence. "That's really rich coming from someone who only met me properly forty-eight hours ago." I didn't actually mean it. I wanted Krysta to see right through me. I liked the feeling of it. "I care just enough to make the world care about me."

Other than the foam party, which would hopefully be winding down momentarily, the view was so aesthetically pleasing. Each cruiser who had chosen this excursion received their own Wishes by Addison x Lemon Tree–branded beach bag full of products that guaranteed the perfect carefree summertime look. A simple look that, in reality, was far from simple to accomplish. But that was one of those unattainable beauty standards, wasn't it? Try so hard to look like you haven't tried at all.

Beside me, Krysta slowly approached until her shadow cast over me. "That sounded like some kind of girlboss sound bite." Her voice was mild, without rancor, but also didn't give me any room to wiggle away from her observation.

"How would you recommend that I care less about what people think, then?" I asked.

She stood close enough now that when she inhaled, I felt her chest brush against my shoulders. "Last night was a good start," she said. "After the show. I didn't know you were capable of that kind of reckless joy. I'm sure kissing your female bodyguard in front of a theater full of people wasn't part of the staged coming-out plan, was it?"

"I don't think anyone saw, and it was a mistake anyway," I said. "Like when you're hanging up the phone with your doctor's office and accidentally tell the receptionist you love them."

"Sometimes mistakes are nothing more than subconscious intentions made manifest." Each syllable was hot on my neck.

"I said it was a mistake," I told her. "Not that I regret it."

From the corner of my gaze, I watched as she dropped a kiss on my shoulder. "That." She kissed my warm skin again. "Wasn't a mistake, just so you know."

Another kiss. This one was closer to the curve of my neck. I inhaled sharply and gripped the railing on the wall before I melted into a puddle of nonalcoholic sangria and cotton candy–flavored foam.

"Someone could see us," Krysta whispered against my skin. "Even through all these palm trees."

"I heard I should care less about what people think."

She traced the curve of my shoulder all the way to the tips of my fingers before her hand covered mine. I felt the strength of her and all the self-control she was trying to exhibit in the whites of her knuckles. If this was her version of restraint, my mind raced at the thought of what she might do when she let go of all the control she seemed to be clinging to. What might happen if I did the same?

"Tell me to stop," she whispered as her other hand coasted beneath the curve of my breast and over my abdomen. "Anytime. Just tell me to stop."

"If this is some hot game of chicken, you should know I never back down."

She laughed a little, her teeth nipping at my neck. "This whole image you create every morning is flawless. And all I've wanted to do for the last two days is undo all of it. I want to see your lipstick smeared and your hair tangled. I want to see this dress in a rumpled pile and this bikini yanked to the side so I can see your eager little pussy. It's eager, isn't it, Ms. Hayes? Wet."

Each touch was light. A whisper. A tease. "Then do it," I breathed. "Or are you a coward? All bark and no bite?"

Her fingers dug into my hip as she pressed me up against the wall. "What did you say to me?"

"Is the aloof bodyguard persona all an act? Is it just as pre-conceived as you think I am? Have you ever thought about that, Krysta? That maybe you and I are exactly the same?"

She rucked the skirt of my dress up, her fingers digging and clawing into my thighs. "There is *nothing* about this that was planned, Addison. I'm breaking my own rules right now."

I should pause this. I should figure things out. How she could go from barely talking to me to having her hands under my dress was a puzzle. And yet, I couldn't lie to myself. There was something about having a hot person who you thought hated you running their hands up your thighs. There was something about the way she'd said *Addison* instead of *Ms. Hayes*. Like I was already hers.

My whimper gave me away, and Krysta growled in my ear.

"Fucking do it," I panted harshly.

Her hand closed over my bikini-covered pussy like she owned it.

"Fucking do what, Ms. Hayes?"

"Fuck. Me," I gritted.

"Here?" she asked. "In front of all your loyal followers? Some-one could see. Even with the wall here, even with the trees. If they catch us at the right angle, they'll know."

"Good," I taunted.

She watched over my shoulder, and I followed her gaze as her fingers danced along the edge of my bikini bottoms before pushing inside the waistband. She was so close to my heat that I nearly purred.

Painfully slowly, she dragged one finger through my wet crease, and it felt like ice cutting fire. I was embarrassingly soaked. I knew how to make myself come. I could practically pencil it into my schedule for the exact amount of time it took, which was why I reached down to guide Krysta's hand. To take control.

But with her free hand she pulled mine back and then cuffed both of my wrists to the top of the wall with her fingers. "Do you want me to fuck you or not?" she whispered, her words sawing through me.

She pressed the pad of her finger to my clit, applying pressure in a way that made me feral. "You're dragging this out for too long," I moaned. "Someone will notice."

"They probably already have. They probably already know what a dirty little girl Addison Hayes is. How she practically mewls with need. Maybe I'll just make you fuck yourself on my fingers. Just hold still and make you pleasure yourself. Let you do all the work. There would be no hiding then." She slipped another finger in and began to circle my clit so slowly it made me dizzy.

"You're all talk," I told her, egging her on, begging her to punish me. "Shut up already and make me come." *Fuck.* This was definitely crossing the line of bodyguard-client decency. It was crossing many lines. It was jumping off the damn cliff.

"Brat." Her teeth sunk into my shoulder for a brief moment as a third finger sunk into the wet folds of my pussy and she began to abuse my clit with purpose now. "Right here and now in front of all of these people, this pussy is mine, and you will come when I say you can." Her third finger plunged inside of me as the other two continued to knead into the throbbing bud at my core.

One of the women from a bachelor party on the cruise nearly caught the anguished expression on my face before I could tilt my head to the side and close my eyes. But I must have appeared normal enough, because she was already looking away by the time I glanced back, waving her hand for another drink.

"Ah," Krysta hummed. "We might have an audience. Give the people what they want, Ms. Hayes. Come on my fingers like the filthy slut everyone knows you are."

A red flush crawled up my chest and neck until finally I broke right there on her fingers.

"So fast. So easy," she scolded, but I could already hear the satisfaction in her voice.

"It's your fault," I groaned, my glossed lips spreading into a smile.

She slid her hand free, gave me one hard swat on the ass, and then stepped forward next to me, leaning on the wall, dropping her bossy demeanor a bit. "Was that okay? Other than the fact that I just broke my most important rule and fucked a client."

My voice was breathy as I said, "Please, Mommy, may I have another?"

She shook her head and laughed softly. "That's the last time we break the rules."

I inhaled deeply for what felt like the first time in months. Like my lungs were finally working at capacity. Despite the heavy humidity and the constant cacophony of the pool DJ, the photo booth setup, the beach towel embroidery station, and every last perfect moment I had orchestrated for all of these strangers, never had I imagined that I could feel as uninhibited as I had just then. Least of all in a crowded place where I could be discovered at any moment.

Well, that was a new kink to unpack.

But what really had burrowed into my chest was Krysta herself. She didn't bow to me or back down. She was quiet and firm when my brain was a constant stream of chatter and to-do lists. She was my opposite in every single way, and I wanted her to consume me.

I certainly didn't have a bodyguard with benefits on my Lemon Tree Cruise itinerary, but the great thing about well-thought-out plans was that they were always adaptable . . .

Chapter Seven

*R*ight as Krysta finished sucking her fingers clean, Bailey crashed back into the cabana to tell us the director was calling everyone back to the ship. Which meant I couldn't wring a promise out of Krysta that she would forget her stupid rules and let me return the orgasm favor, and then it didn't matter anyway because a storm was rolling in, and there was no talking over the building wind.

I gave Krysta a horny puppy dog look as we went to board, but her eyes were on my legs under my short dress, her stare hot and interested. I could make out the faint imprint of her beaded nipples through her bra and top. I just needed to get her alone—somehow, immediately—but then I felt my watch buzz on my wrist, reminding me that I had twenty minutes to change for dinner and another exclusive influencer gathering after.

For once, my tightly planned schedule was a bad thing and not the singular freeing force from my existential dread.

Okay, okay. *After* dinner, *after* the exclusive gathering. I was having Krysta use my mouth like she paid for it, and then we were having a good long talk about why rules were made to be broken.

EXCEPT KRYSTA'S MOOD gradually but inexorably deteriorated throughout the evening. As the ship pulled back into open water and rocked over the waves, Krysta's expression mirrored the sky outside: turbulent and foreboding.

And when I accidentally-on-purpose grazed my fingers against hers at the influencer party, she reared back like I'd just burned her with coals.

Her eyebrows were drawn together, her mouth white at the corners again. "I'll be in the corner near the bathroom," she said in a tight, terse tone and then stalked away.

I watched her go, feeling wounded. Vexed, even! I wasn't expecting tastefully arranged sustainable flowers or anything, but surely fingering someone under their dress meant you'd graduated to *not running away from them*?

You know what? Fine. I didn't have the bandwidth to deal with this right now. Krysta's hot-and-cold act might have been sexy to someone who didn't have a virgin cruise to devirginify, but that wasn't the case for me. My calendar was too full for feelings! For emotional entanglements! This was why I preferred hookups from the discreet celebrity-only app I used from time to time. It kept things neat, simple, and, most importantly, locked down under ironclad NDAs. No hurt feelings, no stealing glances across the room to see if a tall person was still glaring at me. Just sex.

Maybe that was what I needed now, actually. Maybe everything that happened today was a natural response to having been too busy to make a washi tape–bordered time block for fornicating in my planner. In which case, maybe the sooner I reset to my normal routine, the better! The sooner I had sex with someone else, the sooner I could return my focus to *the plan*. The sooner I could prove to myself that I didn't care if my bodyguard went from screwing to scowling in the blink of an eye.

The prospect of making her jealous had nothing to do with how quickly I pulled out my phone and opened the app. It wouldn't even work anyway. She'd probably feel relieved that I was being so mature about the whole cabana-sex scenario and not doing awkward postorgasm things. Like catching feelings.

Which I definitely wasn't doing because we barely knew each other! And even if a real relationship *were* scheduled this early in the plan, Krysta wouldn't be my type anyway. I needed someone warm and consistent and who enjoyed smiling every now and again; I needed someone who would add brand value, not a bodyguard who considered being invisible a way of life.

The app's minimalist interface showed me that there were a handful of members aboard—mostly influencers with significant platforms. I debated with myself for a moment (influencers were messy prospects, even through the app—you could practically hear them thinking about content opportunities while you were fucking them), but then decided I owed it to myself and to Krysta to prove that I, *just like her*, wasn't at all hung up by a measly little orgasm.

One of the members was here at the party—if the geolocating were to be believed—a curvy woman with deep brown skin and tight curls in a halo around her head. Her profile note said that she only did hookups with her partner, who was included in her profile picture—a petite woman with olive skin and expressive eyebrows. When I swiped on them, my phone immediately chimed.

We'd matched.

I scanned the room and found the two of them near the open-air balcony, the influencer's partner trying and failing to take a selfie with the party in the background. Then her phone must have chimed too, because her mouth fell open and her partner giggled and kissed her shoulder.

Seeing the empty glasses on the high-top table nearby, I grabbed two flutes of champagne and glided over, making sure that I was showing off my legs in their lace-up heels to their best effect.

The influencer whose profile was on the app—Nova—tossed me a flirtatious grin. "Well, hello, there."

"Hello back," I said in my best purr. It was a pretty good purr, if I said so myself. Hookup sex didn't have to be devoid of seduction! "Bubbles?"

Nova took both glasses and then handed one to her partner. "This is Elena."

"Hi, Elena," I said, and a dark flush stained Elena's cheeks.

"Hello," she said. Any shyness in her voice was undercut by the way her eyes kept dropping to my mouth.

Nova grinned and lifted her glass to me. "I was hoping we'd match when I saw you on the app. So Addison Hayes is on the prowl—and for ladies, no less?"

"Dare I ask if you're surprised?"

"Ten years ago I would have been. But you're not the same Addison Hayes you were then, are you?"

I beamed, delighted that the painstaking endeavor of extricating my brand from its origins had worked so well. But I also added, "I'm the same Addison Hayes as I was ten years ago. Technology has just caught up." I waved my phone.

Elena and Nova beamed back, and I saw that we understood each other.

"So do you have to hang around the party long?" Elena asked, voice still a little on the shy side. "I know everyone is excited to see you."

I glanced down at my watch and then looked up to give her a wicked wink. She blushed even more. "I think I can safely move to the private-libations portion of the evening, if that's something you two might be interested in . . ."

Nova and Elena nodded eagerly. "As long as we aren't stealing you away from your adoring fans," Elena ventured.

Nova stepped a little closer and pressed her champagne flute against the skin exposed by the deep V-neck of my silk romper. I felt goose bumps erupt all over my chest. "But we'll adore you plenty to make up for it," she said in a low murmur.

"Excuse me," a voice said from behind us, and before I could process what was happening, Krysta had somehow inserted herself between me and my potential, *ah*, bosom buddies. Her expression was furious, her posture tense, and I was going to perverted hell, because the first thing I felt when her hand wrapped around my upper arm was a sharp, aroused thrill. Followed by a fleeting sense of victory.

Which was then followed by the realization that she was only doing her job.

Only bodyguarding. She'd seen a guest touch me and was here to address it.

Fuck, that was deflating.

"Krysta," I explained, "it's okay. This is Nova and Elena. Nova and Elena, this is my new bodyguard. She's a little food aggressive."

Krysta slid a look to me and then to the two women blinking up at her like they weren't sure if they should be terrified or turned on. She made a noise in her chest and then said, "It's time for Ms. Hayes to be getting to bed."

I opened my mouth to protest, but then thought better of it. Telling Krysta that I had been planning to go to bed—just not alone—seemed a little childish now. Plus, I hadn't had a chance to talk to Elena and Nova about what their boundaries were, and what they kept public and what they kept private, and I didn't know how much I could say. So instead, I gave them a rueful smile. "Krysta's right. I probably should get to bed tonight, since it's an early morning tomorrow. I'm so sorry! But maybe we can meet up again another evening?"

Krysta's hand tightened around my arm, but she didn't speak.

Nova and Elena glanced at each other, doing the silent communication of longtime lovers, and then looked back at me with smiles that seemed a little too knowing.

"Yes, of course," Nova said. "Hopefully we'll get to snag you for those private libations sometime."

"Definitely," I said. "And our next shore excursion is—"

But I was already being led away by a taciturn Krysta, pulled at a quick stride through the party and down a substantial length of the deck to our rooms.

I allowed her to guide me through the second-story door of the suite and lock it behind us before I yanked my arm away and spun to face her.

"What on earth was that?" I demanded.

Krysta's jaw was tight. "They were too close to you. It violates protocol."

"People have been giving me air-kisses and sideways hugs all night. You just thought Nova and Elena were *flirting* with me, and that's why you cared."

She didn't deny it, which I appreciated, but also: *arggggh!*

"You realize how ridiculous that is, right?" I asked, starting to pace. "You drop me like a half-finished chicken Caesar salad wrap after we have sex, but then no one else is allowed to touch me? How is that fair?"

Her mouth curved into a frown. Even with only the low glow of the wall sconces for light, I could still make out the lush pink color of her lips. "I didn't drop you after sex."

I once moderated a panel about gaslighting that had at least two licensed therapists on it, so I was something of an expert. "You did too! You reverted to *hating me*, like you have since the moment you stepped onto this ship, and I don't even understand why you took this job if you dislike me so much. I can't help it that my hair is this healthy, and that I'm so organized and driven, and that I can still tolerate gluten, okay? It's my cross to bear!"

The ship pitched to the side, and Krysta closed her eyes. "I don't hate you."

"You can't even look at me right now."

"That's not—" She huffed and then squeezed her eyes more tightly closed. "That's not what's going on."

"Then what's going on? Radioactive spider bite? Kryptonite?" I dragged my hands over my face, suddenly exhausted. "Look, I don't need you to like me. I know you're just here to do a job, but even you have to admit that going cold on me without so much as a heads-up—"

"I've never been on a cruise ship before, and I didn't know they could make you so seasick," Krysta said all in one breath, her eyes still closed.

My mouth was still hanging open, midrant, and it took me a minute to process what she'd said. "I'm sorry, make you what now?"

"Seasick," she answered through clamped teeth. "When we're at sea, I'm so sick that I can barely see straight. Every minute I've stepped away it's so I can vomit, and I haven't been able to keep anything down other than bananas and sparkling water, and I hate sparkling water, Addison, I hate it so much. I hate that it's just water that hurts your throat. I hate that other people think I'm in their bourgeois sparkling water club whenever they see me drinking it."

She finally opened her eyes and looked at me.

"But I don't hate *you*," she finished quietly. "I feel a lot of things when it comes to you, but not a single one of those things is hatred. Or dislike. Or anything close to it."

I thought back to earlier today, to how Krysta seemed like an entirely different person during our shore excursion, how her bad mood came on as the waves got rockier and rockier. I guessed it made sense . . .

"But why didn't you say anything?" I asked, half skeptical, half honestly curious. "I'm not a monster, Krysta. I would have let you take some time off."

Displeasure cooled her expression. "Bodyguards shouldn't need time off, especially not for motion sickness. And what could you have done anyway? Let me stay bedridden for eight days? The whole time I'm supposed to be working?"

"You know, for a former stuntwoman, you're not so great at emergency problem-solving," I told her, my mood gradually but definitely lightening.

I feel a lot of things when it comes to you.

She gave me a miffed look. "I don't know what you mean."

Smiling, I held out my hand. She took it with some suspicion.

"I have a better solution than being bedridden for a week. It's an antiemetic, and it will change your life."

AN HOUR LATER, Krysta and I were back from the ship's infirmary and sitting on the sofa on the upper story of the suite. Krysta's mouth had grown softer and softer, and so had her eyes, and now she was staring at me like I was the person who invented ranch dressing.

"Drugs are great," Krysta said wonderingly. "I feel like a human being again."

"Mm-hmm." I tried not to be too smug, but really. When would people learn that I had an answer for everything?

"I am sorry," Krysta said now. Our shoulders were pressed together, and the cuddle factor was increasing by orders of magnitude. The wet-panties factor was also increasing, because I could feel the firm warmth of Krysta's hip and thigh against my own, the pert swell of her breast against my arm. But I wasn't so far gone that I would shake down a nausea patient for sex.

Yet.

"Sorry for what?"

"Being an asshole. For not telling you why I was being an asshole."

"It's okay. I'm sorry too—I should have made sure you were doing okay. And I probably shouldn't have . . . well, in the cabana. I knew we were breaking your rules, and I did it anyway."

Krysta didn't answer for a moment. And then she sighed. "It's not your fault. I wanted to break them."

I didn't dare look up at her as I asked, "Do you still want to break them?"

Her voice was husky. "Yes."

I moved my hand—just to touch her knee, just to run my palm up her thigh—and she caught my wrist. "It's a terrible idea, Addison."

"But why?"

"It never works out well, a bodyguard and a principal. It's asking for mess and distraction, and I refuse to compromise your work or your security."

I groaned. "Forget about my work! I'll remember it enough for the both of us! Just break the rules with me!"

She laughed a little at my melodrama, and her laugh was a deep, gorgeous alto. I wanted to hear it again. And again.

"Is it not enough to have a long and happy cruise with me?"

"Don't understand why 'long and happy' precludes sex," I said with a long yawn. I rested my head against her shoulder and drank in the sharp, woodsy scent of her. "You made those rules. Can't you unmake them?"

"They're there for a reason." She paused. "My first client after I left stunt work was an heiress turned influencer turned model. She didn't want anyone to know she had diabetes, including me, and she also had a penchant for sneaking out. And then one night I woke up in my hotel room to a call that she'd been found in a park, hypoglycemic and nearly hypothermic. She'd slipped out of her hotel room to party, gotten disoriented after drinking too much, which meant her liver had fucked off making glucose, and then she'd stumbled off into the night. And when I got to the ER, I didn't *know* she had diabetes and it cost them crucial minutes to figure it out. She almost died because I didn't have all of the information. She almost died because she wanted to go off on her own. I couldn't keep her safe if she wouldn't let me keep her safe, and that's when I knew I needed the rules. I needed to trust that my client *understood* the rules, because it meant they understood me too."

Guilt was like an itchy blanket over me, and it was getting harder and harder to rationalize not telling Krysta about the threatening notes. About going off to meet my potential stalker. But surely Krysta only meant she needed to know about the things that someone couldn't handle on their own? Like a life-threatening illness or a chronic inability to charge a phone. Not something a client had completely and totally under control (probably).

Krysta stroked my head as another yawn took me and my eyes slid closed without me telling them to. "I promise it's better this way. Better with the rules," she assured me after a long beat, and I meant to argue with her, to tell her that if *this way* meant no sex, it definitely couldn't be better—but she was so cozy and the sea rain on the window was so soothing, and I'd tell her tomorrow, just after I finished resting my eyes . . .

Chapter Eight

I woke with a slightly stiff neck and a full bladder, but Krysta's arm was curled around my waist and it was one of the few times I could remember wishing I was the type of person who slept through alarms. We lay spooning together on the sofa despite my bedroom being just a few steps away. It was like neither of us wanted to break the cuddle trust even if it meant simply relocating.

But now I had to pee, and my bladder was unwilling to wait for anyone or anything. Even my schedule. Even horny cuddles.

I disentangled myself and tiptoed to the bathroom. You knew things were serious when I forgot to do my skincare routine and fell asleep with makeup on. As I flipped on the light, I braced myself for what the mirror would reveal.

At first, the harsh light was blinding. It was still partially dark outside from the storm. But then my eyes focused, and I coughed out a gasp. "What the actual fuck?"

My tube of lipstick—THEY REALLY LOVE ME, a true red from last year's fall collection—was squashed flat and the lid rolled around in the sink. On the mirror in a frantic scribble was a message. For me.

TIME TO FACE THE MUSIC
BACKSTAGE 6:30 PM

My brain was doing laps around every possibility. How did anyone even get in my room? This felt like an actual invasion. Dangerous, even. Someone was in here. Just feet away from me and Krysta.

Outside the door, something rustled.

Krysta. Shit. She couldn't see this. She'd go ballistic and handcuff me to her.

Okay, actually that sounded pretty fun. But I'd rather do it in more of an informed-role-play situation and not because I had a weird, threatening stalker.

Krysta yawned from the other room. "Addison?"

"Just a minute," I called back as I slammed the door and frantically looked for makeup wipes. Disclaimer: I could never admit to my aesthetician that I carried makeup wipes. After I launched some as part of my nighttime skincare line, she lectured me about how all they did was move dirt and makeup around your face and that she needed me to promise I would only ever use them in emergency situations. Julia's hands were actual magic, so I would have probably discontinued the product altogether if she'd asked.

I began to wipe the mirror and immediately saw exactly what she meant by just moving the makeup around. Red streaks smeared across my reflection, and I quickly abandoned the wipe for micellar water, which did a slightly better job.

"I'm going down to my room to get ready," Krysta said. "We disembark for our excursions in an hour. Should I order room service?"

"An acai bowl and an iced coffee, but don't tell anyone the iced coffee is for me, please!" My shoulders slumped with relief. Krysta wouldn't have a reason to come back up here before the housekeeping crew came through.

I had twelve hours to figure out how the hell I was going to escape Krysta and what I was going to say when I finally came face-to-face with this creep. Guilt swam in my stomach. I didn't want to break Krysta's rules (unless it was for a *horny* reason, like her riding my mouth harder than a roller coaster). After hearing about what had happened with her first client, I understood why Krysta had the boundaries she did. It wasn't a small thing to agree to hold someone's life in your hands, and maybe it was only worth doing if you knew the trust went both ways.

But. *But.*

But I had to handle this quietly. And I had a feeling Krysta's way of handling would not be quiet in the least . . .

I SPENT THE day in Cabo San Lucas making appearances at one excursion after the next. First was the water-adventure park, then the cenotes, then a beach party, and finally a food tour. Krysta and I hardly had a moment alone even when Bailey was wiggling her way into as many experiences as she possibly could. It was annoying, but impressive.

Still, there were selfies to be taken and fans to woo. But thankfully there was not a single foam party.

When we returned to the ship later that afternoon, I immediately began to get ready for my evening events. There were two shows and multiple private dinners I was set to appear at, including a small VIP event to soft launch my new line of nonalcoholic highballs. It was a night so tightly scheduled that it needed to be lubricated. (Couldn't blame a girl for being horny after a hands-off day spent with Bodyguard Mommy, could you?)

Krysta patiently waited while I primped and fussed, but finally I walked out into the downstairs living area.

Krysta swallowed and gave me one of those fierce looks of hers. She wore fitted slacks and a white button-down shirt that was undone a touch below the level of decency. It was fucking hot.

"If I were some toxic dude," she said, "I'd say I'm not letting you out of the room in that."

My dress was a short lavender sequined shift halter top with a low scooping back and a delicate chain across the back of my waist keeping it all together. And there was side boob. Tasteful side boob. Had I chosen the dress with the intention of Krysta ripping it off? Perhaps. Did her feasting eyes make me feel slick and needy? Without a doubt.

"While I love the sound of you not letting me go anywhere, I have to get to the theater and check in on everyone before the first show tonight."

"Has anyone ever told you that you do too much?" she asked as she opened the door for me to step out into the hallway.

"You say that like it's a bad thing."

IN THE THEATER, the whole cast sat in the first two rows of seats while Mack gave notes on their last performance. Apparently our vampire hero had a tendency to be so sad that it was no longer hot and our heroine wasn't blinking enough. To be fair, it was a tall order to ask the girl who used to play Patrick in *The SpongeBob Musical* on tour to let her eyes express constant angst.

But none of that mattered. People were talking about the show. It was starting to trend on TikTok, and future cruises were already booking up thanks to our vampire musical alone. It wasn't exactly the height of fine art, but it was a conversation piece and that was the exact linchpin I needed to take Lemon Tree Cruises from an Addison Hayes fan experience to a must-do viral experience. Also, who got to decide what fine art was anyway? Whoever they were, they'd clearly never experienced the raw pathos of a vampire giving his vampire bride a dental cesarean.

While Pearl and I observed Mack's hyperdetailed roasting of the cast, Gretchen and Krysta sat in seats a few rows back, whispering to each other. Krysta had her usual unyielding posture, her usual scanning eyes, but she was smiling. She even laughed at something Gretchen said, causing Mack to give some serious stink eye as he shushed her.

Krysta looked at me with a raised brow, like she was daring him to shush her one more time.

I gave her a wink, which Gretchen totally caught, and Krysta returned my flirtation with a stern gaze.

I glanced at my phone. Three minutes to six thirty. It was time to meet my stalker. I smothered my conscience with a fringed throw pillow and stood up.

"Be right back," I whispered to Pearl, who was riveted by whatever Mack was saying about blocking.

I walked up the aisle and waved to Gretchen as I leaned down to whisper in Krysta's ear, my breast brushing her shoulder. "I need to pee."

"Let's go," she said, all business.

"No, no. Stay. It's a single-stall bathroom backstage. I'll be right back."

"She's fiiiiiiine," Gretchen said. "Every time I've seen Addison walk into a restroom, she's always walked back out."

"See?" I said. "A resounding endorsement."

Krysta thought for a minute too long, so I leaned back down again. "You can trust me."

After a second, she nodded. "You've got five minutes before I come looking for you."

"That's all I need," I told her.

Hopefully, I thought to myself.

I slipped backstage and circled stage left and then stage right before checking the small fitting rooms off the main dressing area. A quick glance told me that my stalker was two minutes late.

Sitting at the stage manager's desk, huddled in the light of a small desk lamp with her back to me, was Mack's assistant, signature beret perched neatly on the back of her head, trousered legs crossed while she lightly bobbed a foot clad in an oxford. There had to be something keeping that beret in place, right? Bobby pins?

And God, what was her name again? Caroline? Catherine? Cora? Whatever it was, I needed her to scram. My stalker could be lurking right now, waiting for a moment of privacy, and I'd never know.

"Um, excuse me?" I said, searching my memory as quickly as possible. I hated forgetting people's names. It was bad for business. "It's . . . Callie?"

The girl didn't even bother to spin around or look over her shoulder. "Cassie," she said, clearly annoyed.

"Cassie, right. So sorry about that. Names slip my mind faster than you can say 'paid content.'"

"Hard to forget *your* name, Addison. It's everywhere."

I laughed as genuinely as I could manage. "Yeah, I can see how that might be annoying. But branding, et cetera, et cetera. Hey, I think Mack was looking for you? Something about a green juice and some missing props."

Cassie sighed and continued to pencil notes into her thick binder full of every last show detail. "Mack doesn't believe in vegetables, and I checked the props myself three minutes ago."

"Fine," I said lightly, like this was all some kind of inside joke. "You got me. I just need the backstage to myself for just a few minutes. I'm sure that sounds creepy, but I won't be long."

"No, you won't be," Cassie said as she slowly turned toward me. And then without a word, she opened something on her phone and held it up for me to see.

My lips parted but no words came out, which was truly a first.

Because it was me.

It was a video of me.

Chapter Nine

*I*n the video, I was wearing a green jumpsuit that I'd recognize until my dying day. I'd worn it for an infomercial that never aired because I'd killed it, buried it, hoped never to think of it again.

The video was muted, but I didn't need to hear it to know exactly what I was saying. It was three years ago and I was in the midst of launching my first skincare line. I was obsessed and so proud. The products and packaging were everything I'd envisioned.

The idea behind the segment was that I'd stand in front of a bathroom sink, talking to the mirror, except the mirror was the camera and I was talking to consumers. Video Me began to go through my skincare routine, and a heavy dread sunk through my chest and into my stomach.

No one had seen this video. It had disappeared from existence. My management team had scrubbed every last computer in the studio and everyone on set had signed an airtight NDA.

Cassie smiled sweetly as she began to drag her finger across the time bar at the bottom of the screen. "Don't mind me. I'm just skipping to the good part."

"What do you want?" I demanded.

"Shhh, shhh. This is my favorite." She shrieked quietly in a way that actually made me uncomfortable.

The video resumed normal speed except that for me, this moment would always feel like slow motion. On-screen, I opened the dropper bottle containing the overnight serum and dispensed a generous amount into my hands, then slathered it all over my face and down my neck.

"Don't ever forget the neck," Video Me reminded my viewers like we were best friends. "The neck and hands are always the true test of well-maintained skin."

Confusion had burrowed into my browline as my skin had begun to sting, but I'd powered through the application with a smile and then reached for the last and final step: moisturizer.

But I'd only just opened the cap before touching my skin on my cheek, which was swelling—and quickly, at that.

"Addison?" my manager had called from off-screen.

"Let's take a break," the director had announced.

But I hadn't heard him. My eyelids were already starting to puff and itchy hives were erupting up and down my neck and throat. "Benadryl," I'd rasped, my entire face and neck on fire. "Dear God, rub some Benadryl into my gums!"

Cassie giggled, then hit Pause. "You get the idea," she said.

I'd had an allergic reaction, one that was fairly rare. The lab had run endless tests and it was decided that the vitamin C added to the serum in the last round of tests was the culprit. I'd been furious with myself for not trying the new formula ahead of time, but vitamin C had sounded so innocuous! It was part of a complete breakfast!

But it didn't matter that this was an uncommon sensitivity and not a hugely serious one at that. Perception is everything. And the perception was that Addison's new skincare line was bad for your skin at best and medically threatening at worst. This video was career suicide.

After my legal team ran laps around every single possible scenario, we decided to go through with the launch after putting a warning on the packaging. Whether it was a good or bad decision didn't matter. An FDA review deemed all the skincare products safe, and after that, I decided I couldn't risk a multimillion-dollar venture just because it gave me hives. Did it feel dishonest to release a product I couldn't use myself? A little bit. Did tons of old white guys continue to profit off products like tampons and makeup that they likely didn't use themselves? You bet your Dow Jones ass they did.

But now, in this moment, there was no use in attempting to defend myself. Cassie didn't care about the truth and neither would the public.

I stood in a power pose with my hands on my hips. "What's your price, you Tumblr-browsing monster?"

"I don't want your money."

I didn't believe her. Good berets weren't cheap. "I'm not about to give you a sack of gold doubloons so you can flee the country or something."

"You don't get it," Cassie said. "You've had all of this handed to you on a decorative wooden cutting board. What would money do? Buy me things? Give me time to figure out my life?"

I flung up my hands. "Sure. Whatever. Do you think I care what nonsense you decide to do with a couple grand?"

"I'm telling you, I don't want any money. I know exactly what I want." Cassie grinned, which had the effect of pushing her giant glasses up her freckled nose. It was too bad she was a horrible blackmailing fiend, or she would have been adorable in a "dark academia Pinterest board" sort of way. "And you're going to give it to me. I want to play the heroine."

The heroine? *Cassie wanted to play the heroine?*

Of all the possible reasons she could have been blackmailing me for, this hadn't even crested the top twenty. "You're not the understudy." I tried to reason with her.

"That doesn't change anything."

I pressed my palms together and pointed my fingers at her. "Um, I don't know how to say this any more clearly, but you're not even in the show . . . at all. You're Mack's assistant. Your name isn't even on the program! Not even in the *thank-you* section of his bio."

"You don't have to remind me that I work for an irrelevant, thankless hack who's long past his prime. I didn't have the luxury of living on Mommy and Daddy's credit card while I traipsed around from audition to audition, so I took the job with Mack, and I guess I'm too fucking good at cleaning up his messes. Because somehow my ability to go to auditions disappeared, and then I opened my eyes and I'd been an assistant for ten years."

"Ten years?" I asked. "You look like you're seventeen."

She tossed her thick copper hair over her shoulder. "No thanks to your skincare line, I assure you."

"Ooooh," I said. "My feelings are so hurt."

"I'll make this simple. Give me the part, or else I'll post this video on every social media platform I can find. People will meme this. They'll remix your rasping voice until it's a fucking club song. You'll lose all legitimacy, and any time someone picks up a product with your name on it, all they'll see is the image of you clawing at your throat."

"You're a surprise," I told her. "I'll give you that." A zillion possibilities ran through my head. Not a chance in hell would I strong-arm her into the lead role, but I could give her a concession. Something to get her to shut the fuck up, and then I'd have my team scrub every piece of technology she'd ever touched followed by yet another NDA.

But then that was admitting I'd done something wrong to begin with when the truth was much more nuanced. The overnight serum was one of my bestsellers, with the kind of reviews that sold the product itself. The ingredients were clearly listed for customers to see, and each package and container had a warning about a potential reaction. If I'd known about my allergy to vitamin C in advance, then I would have known not to use it myself. But making sure every single consumer wasn't sensitive to any of the ingredients? That was impossible.

I wanted to fix this so badly. And I easily could. It wouldn't take much . . . just steamrollering over the director and cast members who'd put so much of themselves into our ridiculous show.

Krysta's words rang in my ears. Just the other day she'd told me I cared too much about what other people thought. And it was true.

But it didn't have to be. Krysta lived without worrying about everyone's perception of her, and she seemed remarkably well-adjusted, at least when she wasn't violently seasick. And abruptly, I wanted that. The way Krysta chose things for herself depending on what *she* wanted. The way she seemed anchored to herself no matter what happened.

I could have that. All I had to do was start choosing it.

"Nope," I told Cassie . . . and it felt like an immediate death sentence. I wanted it to feel good. Doing the right thing should feel good, shouldn't it?

"I'm sorry, what?"

"There you are," Krysta said as she stepped through the curtain leading into the house. "I gave you way more than five minutes."

Panic raced up the nape of my neck. If I couldn't have this video leak when I was on the cusp of expanding my empire, then neither could Krysta know about the *leaker*. Because then she'd know that

I'd been keeping secrets. That I'd been roaming off alone in potentially dangerous situations.

The thought of her disappointment was nearly as bad as the thought of my serum disaster tanking my Lemon Tree brand.

Cassie slunk back into her chair and tucked a loose piece of hair behind her ear, her shy-girl act back in full. I had to admit—the girl *could* perform.

"I was just catching up with Cassie, Mack's assistant. You remember Cassie, right?"

Krysta shook her head and held her hand out. "No, I don't believe we've met."

Cassie blushed and shook Krysta's hand before turning back to her binder.

The fucking quiet ones! You could never trust them!

"We need to get you to your first dinner," Krysta said softly. "Bye, Cassie! Nice to meet you."

Cassie glanced over her shoulder and ran a hand down her throat while Krysta wasn't looking. "You too," she said sweetly. "What a treat to get some *face* time with you both."

My heart began to stutter in my chest, and I felt my throat tightening again. Just like in the video.

Was this a panic attack? I didn't panic. There wasn't time in the schedule. It wasn't part of the plan. Panic attacks did not have their own roll of washi tape.

I yanked Krysta by the hand. I needed to get out of here. Away from Cassie. Away from the blackmail and the breathing, beret-wearing proof that I'd been keeping a very serious secret from her.

I pulled her through the crew door and down the stairs leading to the costume storage closet that doubled as the cast hangout room.

"Uh, the Korean barbeque restaurant is definitely not down here," she said.

"I need you to sit on my face right fucking now," I said as we walked through the first door and I turned the lock behind us.

The room was obviously a little home away from home for the cast. There were tons of personal photos held to the wall with magnets and mismatched tote bags full of street clothes and cell phone chargers.

But most importantly, there was a couch. I unclasped the halter around my neck and let my dress fall to the floor in a puddle, revealing the fact that I was completely nude underneath.

"The rules," Krysta said, but her resolve was already a hundred nautical miles away. Her hot gaze traveled from my lips to my pebbled nipples.

I shook my head. I was breaking all the rules. Krysta's. My own. I might as well have been tearing up my planner page by page at this point, and I didn't care. I couldn't even think of a single reason to care. I just needed this. Her.

"I have to taste you," I said urgently. *"Please."*

She ran a hand over her neatly arranged hair before rushing toward me and crushing her body to mine. Our lips found each other, hungry and open. I couldn't stop myself from moaning on her tongue.

We fumbled backward onto the couch, and I reached for the button and zipper of her pants, then yanked them down right along with her black boy shorts.

I straddled her lap and was only patient enough to take my time as I unbuttoned her shirt to reveal her pert tits. Then I moved so that her thigh was between my legs, giving me pressure where I needed it the most.

She cupped my face with one hand and gripped my hip with the other. "Show me how good it feels," she demanded. "So desperate to come that you can't even stop yourself from grinding on my leg." Her hand trailed down from my face and to my throat as she held me in place.

"I need you in my mouth," I whined.

"Show me," she said again.

I slid up and down her thigh as she took my nipple gently between her teeth and then nipped at the underside of my breast. I felt so desperate like this. Out of control. A burning tingle raced through my abdomen, and I looked down to see my wetness trickling down her leg. I was already about to climax, but *fuck*, not yet. I wasn't ready.

I curled my fingers around the wrist of the hand she had wrapped around my neck. "I'm going to make you come so hard you forget your fucking name." I sank to the ground in front of her, and her hand moved to the back of my head, reminding me that she could guide my mouth wherever she wanted it.

Reaching up, I held her breasts in my hands. They fit so perfectly, and the image of her wearing her shirt still with me between her legs, begging to worship her, was nearly enough to send me over the edge.

My fingers dragged down her torso, leaving red lines where nails had been. I parted her thighs as far as they would go and lifted one leg over my shoulder. With my arm hooked over her thigh, I trapped her in place and nuzzled against her silky curls.

The sweet smell of her pussy was too much. I parted her folds with my tongue and wasted no time in finding her clit.

"Oh my God," she gasped.

I lifted my head for a moment. "Your turn. Show me. Use me."

Her eyes darkened as she gripped the back of my head and pushed her cunt into my mouth. I moaned against her.

"Touch yourself," she commanded. "Come on those fingers and then slide them inside of me."

I stiffened my tongue as I continued to lap at her and made circles around the bundle of nerves at her center. My eager fingers found my own clitoris, and it only took a moment of masturbating while she rode my tongue before I was coming apart.

My head collapsed against her thigh for a brief moment as the fireworks faded. Then I plunged two slippery-from-myself fingers inside of her before addressing the soaking pearl with my tongue, sucking it as deeply between my lips as I could.

She writhed under my touch, her fingers lacing through my hair and tugging.

I slid a third finger in and mercilessly fucked her. Her juices dripped down my chin, and I greedily drank up every bit I could. My mouth and fingers made obscene noises that felt sensual and downright primal. I was vocal about what I wanted in bed, but with Krysta it felt like I didn't always have to be. Like she intuitively knew me, and it was ridiculous to even think, let alone say out loud, but it was as though she knew me just as well as I knew myself. We'd spent four days together and it felt like a lifetime.

And somehow not long enough. Not at all.

Her whole body stiffened as she came on my tongue, her essence running down my hand as the final aftershocks of her orgasm rolled through her.

Slowly, I removed my fingers and held them up for her to taste. She took them in her mouth and sucked each finger like they'd been dipped in sugar.

I laid my head against her abdomen as her fingers slowly traced along my shoulders.

It was so good. She was good. We were good. So good that I'd almost forgotten that soon I'd be facing one of the biggest scandals of my career. And while that still made my stomach twist into knots, what really made me ache with guilt was the fact that I'd lied about this whole blackmail scenario to Krysta. I'd kept it from her, and there was no way she wasn't going to find out.

Chapter Ten

*T*he next morning, I sat down next to Cassie in the café while Krysta got us both drinks.

"I'll do it," I said, "but I can only promise you the role on a future cruise. Not this one."

Cassie, who was wearing an oversize blazer even though it was July and we were sailing off the coast of Mexico, narrowed her eyes at me. "I want *this* sailing. The maiden voyage. This is the one everyone is talking about, and these are the performances that will go viral."

I glanced at the café line to make sure Krysta was still stalled out behind people ordering lavender oat milk lattes. "The other sailings will be just as popular," I said, trying not to sound pleading. "Look, there isn't a way—"

Cassie stood up and grabbed her satchel. "Do you know how much I want this, Addison Hayes? Do you know what it's been like to follow that man around and make notes on potential taxidermy ideas when I should be on the stage?"

"I get it," I told her, and I meant it. I did get it. "This business will exploit you up and down, left and right, and it feels like the only remedy is to exploit yourself before someone else can do it to you first."

"You're wrong there," Cassie said. "I'm not planning on exploiting myself. I'm planning on exploiting *you*. And if you can't deliver, then the world will see exactly how much Addison Hayes believes in her own products."

I took a deep breath. Pretended Krysta's fingers were tracing lines over my neck and shoulders, that she was standing behind me.

"Okay," I said. "So if I can't deliver, you'll leak the video. That's what will happen." The same dread and panic as before clung to every beat of my pulse. But weirdly, deep, *deep*, inside, I almost felt . . . relief. Like here it was, the damning blunder that could wreck *the plan*, that could derail years of progress. The thing that could be the beginning of the end of Addison Hayes as a brand.

And yet that tiny, tiny bloom of relief continued to unfurl in my stomach, like *thank God*.

Thank God it's finally here.

I no longer had to wait in terror for the asteroid to come crashing through the sky.

"I think I've made that very plain," replied Cassie as she slung the satchel over her shoulder.

"All right, then," I said. Took a deep breath. "Okay."

She pushed her glasses up on her nose. "So to be clear, this is you saying that you can't deliver?"

"Cassie, short of violent food poisoning for Lizzie and the understudies, there is nothing I can ethically do." I was willing to be ruthless in almost every facet of my business, but I'd decided last night that abusing my celebrity to get myself out of trouble was a kind of ruthless I didn't want to be.

Her head tilted to the side a moment, a gesture that made me feel like I was being sized up for a meal. She shrugged. "Then I hope you enjoy the memes and remixes at least."

"Can I at least ask how you even have that recording in the first place?"

"Disgruntled assistant of the segment's producer," Cassie said and then held up three fingers like she was about to recite a pledge. "Several of us unhappy assistants have banded together to create an underground PR militia—and a Discord—and we are sharing resources and taking what should be ours. And this week is the week when I wage war."

Ah, okay. So a disgruntled-assistant fight club. Great.

And then Cassie strode off as much as her short legs could stride, while Krysta approached from the other side with the drinks.

"Everything okay? Did the beret girl upset you?"

I forced myself to smile up at my bodyguard. The bright morning sun caught along the strong cords of her throat and lined the straight angles of her nose and jaw. The real concern in her eyes spoke of whatever we'd become to each other this week.

Friends? Lovers? Something more and less than both?

"Oh nothing, just a hiccup with the rehearsal schedule," I said, making a big show of grabbing at the hibiscus tea so I didn't have to look Krysta in the eyes. I was a decent liar, but the idea of lying to Krysta made me faintly ill. "Thank you for the drink!"

She searched my face, her now-free hand dropping to the back of my chair. It looked matter-of-fact, protective, but she whispered her fingertips over the nape of my neck in a way that wasn't at all businesslike. "Are you sure everything's okay?" she asked quietly. "You have that look like you're seven minutes late to something, and there's nothing you can do to make up the time."

Oh boy. Maybe I wasn't as good at acting as I thought . . . or maybe Krysta was learning my tells faster than anyone ever had before. But what could I say in response? *No, nothing's okay, because*

I've been hiding something from you this entire cruise. Nothing's okay, because the worst moment of my career is about to be leaked all over the internet unless I do something shady to protect myself. Nothing's okay, because the plan might get entirely fucked over, and that doesn't scare me as much as it should, and it makes me think that I don't even know myself anymore.

No. No, I couldn't say any of that. I didn't want to emotionally vomit on someone who was going to part ways with me in a few days anyway, someone who *had* to listen because I paid her salary. Someone whom I was lying to despite her request for honesty.

I reached up and tugged at her black jacket playfully. "I'm sure everything's great," I said with a perky cheer I absolutely did not feel. "Now, speaking of seven minutes late, it's time we check in with the director about the canopy zip-lining."

Chapter Eleven

*T*oday was our last excursion day, and it was a very special excursion, because it also happened to be an excursion *night*, spent at an exclusive resort composed of thatched villas, mountain-framed beaches, and small pools of shimmering cyan. As the busy day of zip-lining and touring historic Mazatlán came to a close, I retreated back to the villa I would share with Krysta, successfully tracked Bailey's location to the resort bar and received a proof-of-life selfie, and then kicked off my shoes and walked down the villa's shallow steps right onto the beach. The sand was soft under my feet as I made my way toward the moon-tinseled waves.

I could feel Krysta behind me, but she didn't speak, didn't try to stop me. Just bent down, rolled up her pant legs, and joined me in standing where the waves could kiss our ankles and lick up our calves.

"We'll be home in two days," I said, not sure why I was saying it. "It feels surreal. Like the whole week has been on fast-forward."

"It reminds me of a wedding," Krysta replied. "Months and months of planning, and somehow the event is over in the blink of an eye."

"Have you ever had a wedding before?" I asked curiously, and she laughed.

"No, no. But I have clients who have."

I looked out at the water, at the place where the dark waves and the dark sky became the same thing, differentiated only by the slices of reflected moonlight on the sea. "Have you ever wanted a wedding? To get married, I mean?"

I wasn't sure why I said this either—if I wanted this to be the kind of conversation you had with a new friend or the kind of conversation you had with a new lover. I just knew that I wanted to know. I wanted a glimpse at all those cards she held so close to her chest.

She swished her feet in the water a moment before answering. "Yes, I've wanted it. I want it still. Maybe not the big magazine-worthy weddings my clients have, but the rest, the vows and the dancing. A tall cake with different flavors in every tier. A honeymoon in a place where they put rose petals on the bed."

"So . . . you haven't met the right person yet?" I asked, knowing I was being nosy now and not caring. I was too curious. Being hookup only for . . . oh, sixteen years now meant that I'd met plenty of queer people who didn't find the idea of marriage appealing or remotely interesting. But it sounded like Krysta *did* want that, and it made me wonder what had stood in the way. Family? Internalized shame? The narcissistic hellmouth that was dating in the greater LA area?

Krysta didn't seem bothered by the cross-examination, but her voice was pensive when she answered. "You might have guessed this already, but being a bodyguard doesn't leave a lot of room for romance. For the last five years, my job has been babysitting a brokenhearted pop star while he refused to leave Malibu. My time existed only in relation to his; and yes, I rotated with other security for days off and vacation leave, but it was too far apart and sporadic to make a real relationship feasible."

"Is that why you didn't take a different job when Isaac Kelly moved to Christmas Notch?" I asked. "Um, other than this one, of course."

A sigh. "I used to be a stuntwoman, and every day used to be different. Used to be a challenge. I'd walk onto a set or to a location, and it would be something novel and thrilling, and then if I got bored, I could simply pick a different project next. I had freedom and variety and also time off when I wanted. So yes, partly it's because I want time to date, but I also needed something *new*, something that was tailored to me and what I like, and not tailored to what a grieving widower likes. Which is nothing, in case you were curious."

She stepped back as a cool wave washed a little higher than the last one and threatened to get her pants wet. She added, a bit shyly, "I'm actually hoping to start a stunt-consultancy firm this year— all the things I loved about stunt work, but without the part where I personally fling myself out of trains and whatnot."

"That sounds incredible," I told her. "It's so hot that you used to be a stuntwoman."

I thought she liked that, because she ducked her head a little, like she wanted to hide a smile. "It would be a fresh start at least," she said.

"I should say that I'm sorry I lured you away from that fresh start, but I'm not," I told her, and I let all the husky reasons that I wasn't sorry roughen the edges of my voice.

Krysta swept an interested gaze over me, her eyes finding my mouth as they so often did. "I'm not sorry either," she murmured. "I'm glad your manager hunted me down."

"Well, truthfully, I hunted down Winnie, who hunted down Kallum, who hunted down Isaac, who had your number on a Post-it and sent it in the literal mail to my manager without anything else in the envelope like a serial killer would. And *then* my manager worked his magic."

Krysta let out a laugh, as deep and velvet as the spaces between the stars. "Well, then."

"But I am glad you said yes."

She was still smiling, looking out at the ocean. Behind us was our villa, faintly lit by a handful of low orange lights, and behind that was a thick screen of trees. This villa was the most private of all the places on the resort, the most secluded, and I was glad, because it felt like we were in our own world tonight. Standing ankle-deep in our very own ocean.

"I wish I could say it was because your manager is just that good, but it's more boring than that," Krysta admitted. "I needed the money."

I was a little surprised. I'd always been under the impression that Isaac Kelly paid very well for the privilege of hiding away in his sumptuous tomb-mansion, but maybe I'd been wrong.

Krysta seemed to know what I was thinking though, and shook her head. "Isaac paid me just fine. But circumstances changed after I quit, and this was exactly the job that could help."

"I don't want to pry . . . but I kind of do. Was it a bad poker bet? An illegitimate love child? A century-old house with good bones that you couldn't walk away from?"

Another velvet laugh. "You're close with the good bones. It's my gran, actually. She's not able to live by herself any longer, but I couldn't bear to see her move into a place less awesome than she is."

"Your gran?" That was the sweetest, most adorable reason to go back to a job I'd ever heard. I gave Krysta heart-eyes as she continued.

"And then I found this place for her, and it's got a pickleball court and a juice bar and dueling pianos every Friday night, and I just really want her to be living her best life. And my folks are gone, and I'm the only child of an only child, so it's all down to me to make sure Gran's golden years are the goldest."

Ugh, my heart couldn't handle it. And as long as Krysta consented to it, I would make sure that Krysta's grandmother had everything she needed, because I wanted Gran to have dueling pianos too.

"So anyway, the deposit fee for this place is a little steep, but this gig takes care of it. So that's why I'm here."

I reached over to take her hand. It was warm, even amid the balmy night air.

"You're an awesome grandkid," I told her. "I hope you know that."

She rubbed her thumb over the back of my hand. "Thank you. And it turned out that the last-minute job wasn't such a sacrifice after all." Her voice got a little lower, a little huskier.

Heat pooled low in my stomach at the sound of it.

She raised my hand to her lips and kissed my knuckles. Her mouth was soft and warm and lingering, and then she flipped my hand over and lowered her mouth to the inside of my wrist. When she licked my pulse, I shivered, shocked at how such a small thing could feel so big. The thing about NDA-shielded hookups was that they tended to get to the point straightaway, and I'd never minded it, not really, because timeboxing was a proven strategy, and so why not timebox sex too? Why take detours, attempt multitasking, lose focus? You could still be flirty *and* goal oriented! Seductive *and* structured!

But oh, how Krysta's mouth on my pulse made me want hours of this, just this, silky flickers and warm breath, her gorgeous lips mapping every vein, tendon, and crease of my wrist. I wondered what other places on my body she could find to kiss, places that I'd never considered erogenous or noteworthy, places that would sing under her clever tongue. I wondered what places there were on her body that I'd never taken the time to touch or treasure on a lover. I wondered if I could make her shudder and gasp with kisses on the arch of her foot or on the back of her knee.

Krysta lifted her head. Her eyes were those of a starving woman.

"I'm going to break my rules tonight," she said quietly.

"Break them," I said. "Break them until we're sore."

She took a deep breath. "I want to see your tits," she said. "Now."

I didn't hesitate. I knew there was no one around, and actually at this point, I barely even cared. Forget August, forget the sit-down. *Addison Hayes Gets Railed by Bodyguard on the Beach* would be how the news broke to the world, and it would be worth it for the way she followed every infinitesimal movement of my hands as they worked open the ties of my halter dress and let it slip down my body to my ankles, where it got caught in the waves. I was only in a bikini now, and when I bent over to step out of my now-wet dress and toss it back onto the sand, I knew Krysta was drinking in the sight.

Before I even finished throwing the dress, she was in front of me, shoving the cups of my bikini top to the side and staring at my breasts, taking them in her hands and squeezing and plumping and then letting them drop again.

"I haven't been able to stop thinking about these since I saw them," Krysta said, the lust in her voice almost sounding like a threat. "God, even before yesterday. That jumpsuit you wore your first night, the necklace that hung down between your tits. I wanted you tied to a bed so I could play with these pretty things forever."

Her thumbs rolled over my stiff nipples, and I made a small noise, trembling a little. The heat in my belly moved lower now, filling the tender spot between my legs with urgency, and I reached down, just to stroke it a little.

Krysta caught my hand easily. "No, I don't think so," she murmured. "Only bad girls play with their pussies when they're not supposed to."

"Please," I whimpered, and she lifted an eyebrow.

"I think you need to learn some patience." She took both my hands now and put them behind her neck, and then before I could protest, she lifted me effortlessly in her arms, guiding my thighs around her waist and cupping my ass from below. And then she carried me deeper into the waves with sure, strong strides until the water was up to our waists.

"I always behave," I protested, faintly. She'd walked right into the water, still fully clothed, and the feeling of being held by her like this, still in her button-down and trousers, while my tits were shamelessly exposed and my pussy was against her hard stomach, was electrifying. There was no immediate point to this, to her bringing her mouth to my neck and kissing it as the ocean ebbed and flowed around us. There was no reason to do it except that it felt so good to have her holding me like she owned me, kissing me like she wanted me to forget that I'd ever been kissed by anyone else.

"You behave for the public, but in private, you are so sweetly filthy, aren't you?" Krysta purred before she bit my ear. I arched, which pressed my pussy even harder against her stomach. I tried to move, to get more friction, and the hands on my backside tightened. "See, this is what I mean," she crooned when I whined at her. "You need it so badly that you forget to ask politely. We can't have that."

"I said *please*," I complained. "What more do you want?"

She slid a hand from my ass up my hip to my waist and then up to a breast, which she squeezed. Hard.

"I want a new rule tonight," she said. The moonlight made her blond hair look like ice and her eyes look like the end of the world. She was stern and strong and playful and dirty and cold and full of secret tender spots that deserved licking and cherishing just like the inside of my wrist. She was nothing like a plan, nothing like a necessary release, nothing like anything I'd ever wanted for my life, and yet I couldn't imagine ever being able to let go of this. Of the moon glittering in her eyes and her mouth parted in hunger.

And I should have been thinking about the rules she already had, the rules I was already breaking, but I couldn't think of anything but her low voice and those strong fingers toying with my flesh, and I wanted to give her everything, everything that one person could give another and then even more after that.

"Yes," I finally breathed. "Any rule you want."

She smiled, cool and wicked. "Wonderful, Ms. Hayes. I want to be in charge."

"Aren't you always?" I asked coyly, and she dropped her hand back to my bottom and gave it a small smack under the water.

"Watch it, Ms. Hayes, or I will take you over my knee."

Oh fuck, that was hot. I caught her mouth with mine, getting the first taste of her since last night, and stroked my tongue against hers. "Only if you promise," I mumbled, and she nipped at my lower lip in warning.

I exhaled into our kiss as she waded us deeper. The water washed around our chests, caressing the turgid, aching tips of my exposed breasts, and it felt amazing, so goddamn good, like the ocean was having sex with me too, and then when she moved her hand to my stomach and slid her fingers into my bikini bottoms, I thought I would come right then and there.

"Oh. Oh *shit*," I moaned as she found the tight berry at the top of my sex and rubbed.

"You know how I know you need someone in charge of you?" she asked against my mouth. Her fingers explored me, farther, deeper, the fresh gap between my bikini bottoms and my skin meaning that the water was now kissing directly against my flesh, seeking and grazing everywhere that her fingers weren't. "You're rubbing against me like a cat in heat, even though I distinctly remember you riding your own hand to a writhing climax with your tongue in my cunt last night. That tells me you haven't been taking care of yourself. That you haven't been getting what you need."

She gave me two fingers at once, and I dug my fingers into her shoulders as my core clenched around her, sizzles of ripe, aching pleasure rolling down my thighs and up to my chest. I was not going to last long like this.

"And you're so fucking wet, Ms. Hayes," she murmured. "Wetter than the literal ocean I'm fucking you in. It's a good thing I'm taking over the care of this cunt, because I don't think you can be trusted with it. Not with the state it's in."

"It's yours," I panted as she returned to my clitoris and started working it with firm, commanding strokes. "Oh God, it's yours."

"Mmm. And those tits? With their pretty pink nipples?"

"Yours too," I gasped, trying to buck against her hand, trying to chase her touch.

"And that mouth? If I want to use it?"

"Yes, *fuck*, I'm so—"

Her fingers speared into the center of me again, and she shoved the heel of her palm against my clit so that every time she stroked, sparks of molten pleasure flew everywhere in my body. My head fell forward onto her shoulder, and she said, "Uh-uh, Ms. Hayes. Look at me."

I lifted my head. Our eyes were level like this, and so were our mouths, and she brought her lips almost to mine as she continued to fuck me under the water. I could feel her exhales against my lips, rough and short, like she was very, very close to losing control.

"It feels so good," I choked out.

"I know. Give it to me. Show me how well you can behave."

The climax ignited deep in my cunt, a rolling fire, an ocean of flames, licking and clenching and surging in hot, devastating swells. Krysta shuddered a breath against my mouth before taking it in a searing kiss, and the orgasm was everywhere, above and below, around her fingers and against her tongue, and in the restless embrace of the ocean, and oh my God, I'd never come this hard in my *life*. And I didn't want it to stop. I just wanted to be riding her hand for the rest of my days, feeling her kiss me like I was the last person on earth; I wanted this sprawling, messy, bossy sex every night and every morning, and I didn't want the end of the cruise to be the end of this.

The end of us.

Krysta held me as the hot, slickening quivers peaked and then gradually rolled away, her kiss no less possessive for how limp and breathless I'd become, her squeezing hand on my backside greedier than ever.

"I'm not done with you yet," she muttered, and then she started walking toward the shore, pulling her hand from my pussy and slipping her fingers between my lips as she did. I tasted salt and myself, and then as soon as we reached the shallow water, she set me on my feet and pushed me to my knees.

I landed on the sand, the waves just barely reaching us here, and looked up at Krysta, at the sinful cling of her wet white shirt, at her hands deftly working open her pants. The water swirled around my knees as she peeled the fabric down her legs and off her feet, and then she laced her fingers through my hair, tilting my face up to hers.

"I'm going to fuck this mouth now," she said. "And you're going to behave and let me use it, right?"

"Yes," I whispered.

"Good girl."

She guided my head to press my mouth to the wet center of her body. I tasted salt and need, and when I managed to lick inside her, my eyes fluttered closed. It was all her, all her sweet, earthy taste, and I speared my tongue into her cunt as deep as it would go.

"Fuck, I can't wait," she grunted and then tugged on my hair so that my tongue was on her clit now. She rocked her hips against it once, twice, and then ordered, "Suck on it."

I sucked. I pulled the bud into my mouth and swirled my tongue, fluttered against the glans, let go to tease her before doing it all again. My nose was pressed against her damp gold curls, her hands were just controlling enough to make me feel incomparably filthy, and every time I sucked, she made the *most* delicious noises. Noises I could get off to just remembering.

She came with a tightening of her fingers and a shuddering groan, pushing and pushing against my mouth, trying to fuck it as hard as she could while the pleasure tore through her.

She held me there for a long minute, breathing hard, and the moment her fingers relaxed, I angled my mouth to taste more of her, to run my tongue over the slick folds and wet opening to her body.

When I was done, she pulled my head back and leaned down to kiss me, unabashedly tasting herself. She broke the kiss, staring down at me, and we didn't move for a long beat, just there with the water and the moon and the thudding pulse of fading orgasms between our legs.

"More," she said after a minute.

"More," I agreed. And we gathered our clothes and went into the villa, where she pointed at the bed.

"Lie down, Ms. Hayes. Open your thighs for me and pull that slutty swimsuit to the side."

I was already squirming again, even though I'd literally just come, and I told her in a dazed voice, "I like this new rule of yours."

"Good," she said, her eyes on my cunt as she stripped off her white shirt. I could see all the flat, lean muscles moving under her skin as she walked toward the bed. "Because I have another one."

"Oh yeah?"

"Yes. You can't go to sleep until you come at least one more time."

I gave her my most innocent look—at least as innocent as I could look with my legs spread and my bikini bottoms pulled to the side. "That's one rule I can promise I won't break."

Unlike the others.

Chapter Twelve

*S*ince meeting Krysta for the first time several days ago, she'd always walked just behind or just ahead of me. Always clearing a path or watching my back. But as we exited the SUV that had taken us from the resort and back to port, Krysta stood by my side, our arms brushing, sending currents of awareness rippling up my spine.

This morning, I'd woken up with my mouth watering at the thought of what we'd done a few hours prior. We slept so heavily, limbs tangled. When I'd opened my eyes, I found Krysta wearing a robe and sipping coffee as she watched the early-morning sun shimmering along the water. Never mind the beach—that was a view I could wake up to on a regular basis. The thought of spending a single morning without her made every part of me feel hollow.

"I need to go back to our suite to get ready. I smell like orgasms and sea salt," I told her as we crossed the ship deck and walked down the hallway.

Krysta's gaze remained forward, but she smirked as she said, "I fail to see the issue with that, Ms. Hayes."

"You know," I cooed, "I might have a ten-minute gap in my schedule. You should see how much I can get done in the length of a productivity sprint . . ."

Krysta stopped short in front of our room. The door was cracked, and her posture stiffened as she went into mommy-bodyguard mode. "Stay here," she ordered.

"It's nothing," I told her. "I bet the cleaning crew just forgot to close the door all the way."

"I hope so," she muttered as she disappeared inside.

I stood there with our two overnight bags, glancing over my shoulder and then peering through the open door. There was the small table near the window with my planner and my zip-bag of pens and highlighters; there was the horrible tulip-and-carnation bouquet that I kept putting on the balcony, hoping that the Pacific wind would take care of it for me, the aesthetically offensive reminder of Cassie and her demands.

My stomach twisted into knots as the shine of this morning wore off and the abruptness of reality hit me. Last night it was all too easy to forget the looming disaster waiting for me on this ship.

I needed to come clean to Krysta. It couldn't wait a second longer.

"I'm coming in," I announced, but to my surprise, Krysta wasn't searching every last corner like a human German shepherd.

Instead, she stood over the table near the kitchenette with a small note in her hand. A note written on my own branded stationery.

"Addison," she said slowly. "What does this mean?"

I dropped my bag at my side and strode over to her. "Let me see that." As I took the note, I immediately recognized the handwriting. "Cassie," I whispered.

"Who?"

But I was already taking the paper from her and reading the words over and over again.

You had your chance. Time is up. Not only is your reputation going down the toilet, but so is your grand finale.

I was paralyzed with dread, unable to even inhale. The show? The cast. Oh my God. The cast. If Cassie was willing to destroy me to get her way, I could only imagine what she might do to stop the cast members from getting onstage. And how old was this note? How long had it been here?

"What does this mean?" Krysta demanded again.

"I have to go," I blurted. "I . . . This isn't just about me anymore."

I spun around and headed for the door, but Krysta took my hand and pulled me back to her. "What do you mean it's not only about you? What aren't you telling me?" Her brow was etched with worry and hurt danced in her eyes.

She was realizing I'd broken her rules, but it was more than that now. So much more.

"Someone's been stalking me since the cruise began and—and the point is that I'm being blackmailed," I said. Not even waiting for her to react, I continued, "But that's not what matters. I think some of the cast might be in danger." I yanked myself free of her. There was nothing I wanted more than to stay and beg her for forgiveness, but there was no time.

I ran out the door, cursing the stupid slippery sandals I'd put on this morning at the villa.

Footsteps thudded behind me. I glanced back to find Krysta, looking all business, and I suddenly remembered that this wasn't just her concerned for my well-being because she cared for me. Krysta was *working* and *I* was the job.

The elevator banks bustled with last-minute stragglers returning late from the overnight excursion. I hit the button, cutting in front

of more people than I could count. I wouldn't be surprised if one
of them posted in some Facebook group or comment section about
what an entitled twat I was for thinking I could overthrow the
elevator-line hierarchy. But I couldn't care about that right now! If
there was anything I'd learned as a baby mogul, it was that you had
to put out the actual fires first. Scorch marks and smoke damage
you could cover with paint and a decent in-feed apology.

I hit the button again and then again, like that might somehow
make it come faster.

Finally, the light above one of the elevator banks brightened just
as Krysta caught up to me.

"I need information." She wasn't even out of breath! What kind
of cardio did former stuntwomen/mommy bodyguards force upon
themselves? "Details."

The doors to the elevator parted to reveal a space crammed fuller
than my planner. "No!" someone called from the back as the doors
shut again.

"Fuck," I whispered.

But Krysta was already on the move. "It's faster if we take the
outdoor stairs. Fewer people."

I ran out past her, and she muttered something under her breath,
which I couldn't quite catch.

As I burst through the automatic doors leading to the deck, the
cool sea breeze hit me just as quickly as the beating sun.

Every sunbed and barstool was full of passengers. The pool was
full of bright swimsuits and frozen drinks. It was a party.

Or it should have been.

But instead, every last person was completely still, their attention concentrated on the jumbo screen above the pool.

I saw it happening. My face on the jumbo screen as I went through the motions of washing my face, applying moisturizer, creams, and then the serum. Shame expanded in my lungs with more efficiency than any deep breath ever could, and behind it, that cold, numb feeling that was almost like relief.

Because it was happening, it was done, and there was no taking it back. Not with several hundred cruisers recording it on their phones.

The most embarrassing moment of my career, the thing I'd done everything I could to hide, was exposed—and along with it, the lie behind the image I'd been building since I was eleven years old.

The world knew the truth now. I wasn't perfect. I wasn't always honest. And behind the GRWMs and the planners and the eternally bouncy hair was a messy, panic-filled catastrophe trying to outrun the lonely ache inside her chest.

Beside me, Krysta tensed as the on-screen version of me began to claw at her neck. "What is this?"

"It's me. Being a total, embarrassing fraud," I told her. But as I said it, a sense of clarity and certainty filled me. It didn't matter how embarrassing this was, how potentially career ruining it was. Image wasn't everything—making sure everyone around me was okay was far more important. "But I think this might just be a distraction. I think some of the cast might be in actual danger."

I took off again past the crowd of stunned cruisers and toward the spiral staircase, leading up to the fourteenth floor.

"Would you just wait?" Krysta called after me.

I glanced over my shoulder to tell her to catch up when the ship hit an especially rocky wave. I lost my balance and the toe of my cursed sandal caught on the edge of a step and I tumbled backward.

It happened so fast and so slowly all at once. My body crashed against the railing like a rag doll until I felt strong hands gripping my arm and cradling the back of my head.

I lay sprawled out across the bottom two steps with Krysta hovering above me. Her hands were warm and inviting and—

"OH FUCK," I howled. I'd moved my left foot just a bit and that was a bad idea.

"What is it?" Krysta asked, her voice heavy with concern.

I whimpered. "My foot. I fucked it up. Are people looking? Please don't let them see me cry." The thought was somehow worse than even the most damning video. Worse than an image being destroyed, because this was people seeing *me*. No veneer, no gloss.

And the potential snot of it all . . .

"Give us space," Krysta barked over her shoulder as she reached under my legs and around my back to lift me into her arms.

My cheek burrowed into her chest, and I hissed as she moved me.

"You're okay," she said softly. "I'm getting you to the infirmary."

For the first time in my life, I felt small. I felt like I could be hurt. I felt vulnerable.

"Thank you," I whispered as she used her body to shield me from prying onlookers and their cell phones. I should have said something more. I should have told everyone I was okay, but what had just happened would require a PR plan of attack. Or did it? Did I even care anymore?

"Don't thank me for doing my job," she said coolly.

"Mommy's mad," I said, trying to be playful through my tears, trying to soften her.

But Krysta's demeanor was unmoving as she backed into an employee entrance and, without even looking at me, said, "Yes,

Ms. Hayes. I'm pissed at you. You lied. You kept a secret. One that really mattered, both to you and your safety."

Ms. Hayes. That was not a sexy *Ms. Hayes*, not at all.

"Krysta—" I started.

"We're not having this conversation right now," she said sternly.

And then we were walking into the bright infirmary.

A woman with dark bronze skin and a dark curly ponytail rushed out from behind a partition. "Another case of food poisoning? What is happening with the kitchen today?"

Krysta shook her head and gently set me down on the exam bed. "No, she took a pretty bad spill. Complaining of pain in the left foot, and I don't think she hit her head, but she should be checked for a concussion."

"I definitely did not hit my head," I snapped, as though that was some kind of assault on my character. "My foot is a lost cause though. We should probably just cut it off."

"Addison?" a pitiful voice called from the other side of the curtain.

Krysta pulled the curtain back to reveal Frannie, our villain vampire. She was paler than a vampire from Alaska. Oh God. Had Cassie already gotten to them?

"Frannie, what's wrong?" I asked frantically. "Did someone hurt you?"

She threw her head back against her paper-covered pillow. "If by someone you mean the shrimp cocktail I had at our cast lunch, then yes. Teagan isn't looking too good either."

"Teagan?" I asked.

She gripped her stomach. "The understudy for Isabel. We were celebrating the final show tonight. A pregame celebration if you will."

The physician began to poke around and touched my now-swelling ankle.

"So I'm guessing you're a no go for the show tonight?" I asked. Cassie would love to hear that.

In response, Frannie rolled over and hurled into a bedside bucket.

Krysta stiffened. "I don't do well with—" She motioned to a sick Frannie and the nurse shooed Krysta away while the doctor went to town prodding me.

I stared at the ceiling and gritted my teeth all through the exam. Then I did my silly concussion test like a good girl. The diagnosis was: *go to a real hospital in Los Angeles in the morning, but here's a boot and some pain pills for now.*

As the nurse helped me up, Frannie curled onto her side facing me. "Cast members should be like the president and vice president. Never seen in the same room and definitely not eating the same things. The whole table ate that shrimp cocktail. There's no telling who will be next to drop."

The whole table.

"Fuck me," I said. "The show."

The nurse led me back out to the corridor with a folder full of paperwork to take with me to the hospital tomorrow. She opened the door, and I found Krysta sitting just outside like a guard dog with her arms braced on her knees.

"I'll get you back to the room," she informed me, not giving an inch of affection. It was unfair how much it stung to have her mad at me, and it was also unfair that all of the *dreading* of her being mad at me didn't make this moment any easier. Why was this the one thing that preparation couldn't help?

Why couldn't I go back in time and make a different choice? A less selfish choice?

And how could I explain that all the things that felt so important at the beginning of this cruise—the launch, my brand, *the plan*—now felt so much less important than they did just a few days ago?

"You and I need to talk. I messed up, I know. Okay? But first, I'm going to the theater," I told her despite her deepening frown. "I have a feeling some rogue shrimp cocktail is about to take out an entire show."

Chapter Thirteen

Krysta sourced a pair of crutches from the infirmary, and I made my way with noisy urgency down to the theater. Krysta went ahead of me, holding open doors and indicating to guests that I didn't have time to talk. She was polite, if cool, and professional, if clipped, but I could tell that she wanted to be anywhere but near me right now.

I felt awful, like the human equivalent of an olive oil coffee drink—greasy and unnecessary—but I knew I deserved to feel that way. I knew that the entire reason I was in this situation now, racing to the theater while the cast and crew started dropping like food-poisoned flies, was that I had tried to handle this on my own. If I'd told Krysta about the blackmail—and had let her do her job—I had no doubt that she would have handled it a lot better than me. Maybe she could have spared this ship a vicious shrimp-ocalypse.

But first, the shrimp-victims, the shrimp-scapegoats. The scape-shrimps. I had to warn them, if they didn't already know, and then find a way to cancel the show. It would be disappointing for the guests for sure, but better than having to watch a troupe of pirouetting vampires puke until their wigs fell off.

Krysta opened the backstage door to utter chaos.

Mack was darting from person to person, scarf flapping, while the two hair-and-makeup artists were trying to fit a few of the ensemble cast members with main-character wigs.

"Okay, which vampires are we missing?" Mack demanded. "Frannie, Noah, Austyn, Sam—"

"Austyn and Sam are werewolves!" someone called from the back.

"Teagan, the heroine's understudy," someone else added.

Mustache-dad raised his hand. "I'm not going to lie," he said weakly. "I don't feel so hot."

"Me neither," whispered another actor holding a golden onion.

Music filled the front of the house, and we could see the lights dim from under the grand drape. I moved to scan the wings for Cassie and suddenly realized that Pearl was *right next to me*, having appeared as silently as a ghost.

"Jesus," I gasped, my heart having jumped so far up my throat it was in my sinuses. "I didn't see you."

She gave me a serious look, her eyes shining in the backstage light. "A werewolf just threw up on my shoes," she said. I looked down at her feet to see that she was indeed barefoot, save for an anklet and several toe rings.

"Someone poisoned the shrimp at the party earlier," I whispered as the opening song began playing and the grand pulled back to reveal our heroine holding a cactus. "Are you feeling okay?"

Pearl nodded, and her silky hair waved like a gauzy curtain. "I'm vegan, and Gretchen only eats sustainably caught shrimp."

Was my shrimp not sustainably caught??? I made a mental note to look into that.

"Pearl, I think it's going to hit most of the cast before the show is over. I need to find the person responsible. Will you tell Mack what's going on?"

She agreed with a sigh—something about his turbulent energy—and then I moved as quietly as I could on the crutches to the dressing area, looking for Cassie. Krysta followed and then touched my arm. It was a perfunctory, nonloverly touch, and once again, I felt like an olive oil latte, like something no one had asked for.

"You stay here," she said quietly. "I'll check the director's room—"

She didn't have to. Cassie appeared that moment in a wig, jeans, and a long-sleeved T-shirt with a short-sleeved flannel shirt over the top. She was already in costume. She froze when she saw us and then narrowed her eyes.

"You can't stop this, Addison. It's happening."

"I know what you did, and we're not letting you get away with it," I said. And then I moved closer, hopping a little to keep my boot off the floor. "Look," I told her, gently, "a book I read once told me that you can't build a house on a foundation of sand. You can't build an acting career on top of Imodium and saltine crackers."

Cassie laughed. "That's rich, coming from the itchy-serum queen."

I let go of a crutch bar and waved my hand around to indicate she was making my point for me. "Exactly! I'm learning this lesson literally *right now*. Don't you think I wish I'd done things differently? Done things with less lying and arm-twisting? It's not worth living the rest of your life haunted by the terror that this will come to light. And Cassie, it's going to come to light."

"You wouldn't," Cassie said, red coming up underneath her freckles.

Wasn't it enough that I had to deal with a nemesis? Why did that nemesis also have to waste so much of my time? "You already leaked the video. I literally have no incentive not to."

"But—the launch." She cleared her throat, lifted her chin.

Looked like she was trying to project a confidence she didn't feel. "You wouldn't risk the PR damage to the show, to Lemon Tree."

I thought about it for a moment. Would I risk the damage? Did it matter? *The plan* was already out the window—and honestly, the only thing I cared about right now was getting my cast members some Gatorade and then apologizing to my bodyguard.

It turned out the plan wasn't the most important thing in my life after all.

"No, I think I'd risk it," I said. "All the victims of the shrimpening deserve justice. It's over, Cassie."

"Wait," she said. "*All* the victims?"

Before I could answer, Mack charged in from the wings, his eyes wild behind his designer glasses. "We just lost the psychic vampire and the problematic-history vampire," he hissed. "They both danced offstage and hurled onto the pile of JanSport backpacks!" Then he seemed to notice the strange standoff we were having with his assistant. He readjusted his glasses and blinked. "Cassie? Why are you wearing a wig?"

"She poisoned the cast members so she could have the lead role," I explained.

Cassie shook her head hard. "I only meant to poison the Isabels! Everyone knows they love shrimp!"

"It's a cruise! Everyone's eating shrimp!" I said.

Mack, for his part, was the most motionless I'd ever seen him. "I'm sorry," he said, "but are you *admitting* that you poisoned everyone?"

"I'm just *saying* that I only meant to poison two of them! And it's not real poison! I just set the shrimp out in the sun for a few hours and put some ipecac in the cocktail sauce for good measure!"

"Whoa," said a voice from behind me. I turned my head to see my cousin Bailey with her phone in one hand and a giant margarita in the other. She was recording the whole thing.

Gretchen Young, Pearl's girlfriend, was next to her, also with a giant margarita. Eyes still on the scene in front of her, she lowered her mouth to the straw sticking out of her drink and took a noisy sip.

"I'll need that recording, Bailey," Krysta said in the crisp tones of someone who had seen enough and was ready to move things along. "Cassie, you can come with me."

Cassie stepped back. "Come with you where?"

Krysta stared at her. Her expression was colder than I'd ever seen it, sharp with dislike. "To the security office, obviously. They'll hold you there until we reach LA tomorrow morning."

"Oh," Bailey breathed. "The *brig*! Just like in the movies!"

Cassie's mouth fell open. "I'm not getting locked up for this."

"All crimes against American citizens on a cruise ship are investigated by the FBI," Krysta stated, "and I think they'll be very interested to hear about how you 'only planned to poison two people.' They might also be interested in your attempted blackmail."

"You're wrong," Cassie said. Her voice shook. "You're so fucking wrong—you're—" Her hands twitched by her sides like she was going to throw a punch.

"Do it," Krysta said. Her face was a mask of ice. "I'd love to have an excuse."

But Cassie didn't swing at Krysta. With a scream, she lunged at me, hands out like she was going for my beautiful LASIKed eyeballs. I yelped and hopped back—but I needn't have bothered.

Krysta caught Cassie easily around the waist with one arm, and with a move that I wanted her to try with me someday, she slung Cassie over one shoulder. The assistant twisted and scratched, but she was no match for Krysta's effortless strength.

With no other fanfare, Krysta turned and carried a still-struggling Cassie toward the backstage door. Cassie's wig fell off and dropped onto the floor with a gentle, synthetic hiss.

"To the brig!" Bailey cheered, still filming.

Gretchen slurped more margarita and then said, "This cruise is amazing."

Krysta and Cassie disappeared through the door, and Mack swiveled his head to look at me. "I . . . trusted her," he said numbly. "Callie was the best assistant I ever had."

"It's Cassie, and you're a really bad boss," I told him just as Pearl floated in from the wings.

"It's almost the prom scene and the entire ensemble is currently outside the theater puking off the balcony," Pearl said calmly. "Only our leads are left, and Isabel is looking like she's in worse and worse shape."

We all stared at her.

"But it's only the end of Act One," Mack said weakly. "The rest of the show . . ."

"Will end at Act One, at the prom," I finished for him. "We'll make an announcement that the show is ending early, but that there will be complimentary drinks at the Lemon Bar for the rest of the night." I nodded at Bailey, who'd finally stopped filming. "Can you go tell the bar manager the plan? Tell her it came straight from me."

Bailey nodded as solemnly as someone who'd just pulled a sword from a stone. "You can trust me with the free drinks, Addison," she said and then left.

"Pearl, find a bucket for Isabel and Edmund in case they need it," I directed. "Mack, you tell the stage manager to raise the lights after the scene ends. I'll make the announcement the minute the prom dance is over. We can cross the finish line on this!"

Gretchen took one last sip and then set down her margarita glass. "Addison, we might need a contingency plan."

Chapter Fourteen

I was grateful for the contingency plan three minutes later when Lizzie/Isabel staggered back into the wings, unhesitatingly took the bucket Pearl offered her, and yakked into it. Gretchen took my crutches and helped me slip a white cardigan over the spare blue prom dress we had. I reached up to adjust Cassie's abandoned wig. It was already itchy. Big curls hung past my shoulders.

I gave it a final tug. "Does it look okay?" I whisper-asked Gretchen.

"No."

"Okay, well, here goes nothing."

She patted my shoulder. "I would say *break a leg*, but . . ." She gestured to the boot.

"Thanks, Gretch."

To the swells of the prom music, I made my way to the wings, where our hero was waiting to escort me out into what would be an empty prom scene. "You got this?" he asked in a low voice. The words had a quaver to them, and he was more than vampire-pale. The shrimp curse was coming for him.

"I got it," I replied quietly. There was no singing in this part, the dancing was mostly just standing on top of the hero's feet, and I had the legally-different-enough lines from the movie memorized by heart after sitting through so many rehearsals. "We're going to curtain after this scene. Just make it a few more minutes."

"I'm going to do my best," he swore, but then after about two steps onto the stage, he froze. "Sorry," he mumbled, and retreated backward into the wings, toward Pearl and her bucket.

Which meant that it was me alone, on the stage, just as people were realizing that I wasn't the same Isabel of just a moment ago. Whispers and giggles filtered from the crowd, and I started seeing phone lights popping up like fireflies in the dark, and oh God, on top of the serum video on the jumbo screen, I didn't know if I could take any more embarrassment today.

But then I thought, why the fuck not?

Last year I watched my best friend, Winnie Baker, become the world's most unexpected unwed mother, and a year before that, I watched The Hope Channel air a wholesome Christmas movie with porn star Bianca Von Honey as its lead. Who was to say what an image could survive? The important thing had been that Winnie and Bianca had been happy, making the right choices for themselves no matter what the rest of the world thought, and maybe I didn't know where I'd end up if I let go of the plan, but I did know the right choice for me right now, and it was on this stage, in a blue prom dress and a boot, giving this little musical that could a worthy send-off. I was in front of my guests, smiling and giving them a fun memory. And when I left this stage, I was going to my room to call my mom and let her know that I didn't want to do the *Addison Hayes is bisexual* announcement in some big, orchestrated PR way. I wanted to do it in the way that felt right, that felt honest, the truest to myself and not just to my brand.

I wanted to be more than my brand!

How wild was it that I had to fracture an ankle, face public humiliation, and have mind-blowing sex in the Pacific Ocean just to get to that very obvious conclusion? I really should try therapy sometime.

Shoulders back, epiphany in tow, I waved and smiled at the imaginary people who weren't actually on the stage—all the ensemble cast members who were supposed to be prom-goers and who were instead heaving shrimp into the ocean outside of the theater. And then I reached the middle of the stage and stood under the two-dimensional gazebo strung with lights. It was here that I would have danced with the hero and the characters would have shared their first kiss.

Well, I supposed the gazebo would be the backdrop for me announcing the end of the show and the beginning of the free drinks. I couldn't very well dance on my own—

A wave of noise from the audience drew my attention to the opposite side of the stage, where someone was stepping from the wings.

And it wasn't a vampire.

Krysta came toward me, her eyes only on me. And in her bodyguard uniform of a button-down, trousers, and blazer, slightly rumpled from her tussle with Cassie, she almost looked like a prom date. In no other way did she look like the vampire hero—her blond hair was still in its bun, showing the neat lines of her undercut, and her eternal sunglasses were propped on her head. And she was unmistakably *Krysta*, blue-eyed and plush-mouthed, with the long lines of her straight nose and finely carved jaw.

But she was coming toward me in a suit, and then she held out her hand, and before I knew it, I was in her arms, lifted so that my feet were on top of hers, and we were swaying from side to side.

I was supposed to say some lines now, but all of them left my mind because Krysta was holding me and I was looking up into her face and she was the most beautiful thing I'd ever seen.

"I'm sorry," I blurted out in a whisper. "I should have told you everything from the beginning. I shouldn't have broken your rules."

She searched my face, long blond lashes catching the stage lights above. "You know it's not about the rules, right? It's about trust."

Okay, I was definitely doing therapy when I got home. Add it to the vision board. It was happening. "I think I'm beginning to see that," I said, still speaking in a hushed voice so we couldn't be heard over the music. The crowd was silent now, and I was certain they were filming us, but I couldn't look away from Krysta's ocean-colored gaze to check. "I've made Addison Hayes a brand for so long that I think I've forgotten how to make her a person too. Because being a person felt lonely and disorienting, and it was so hard to be okay with not knowing what was going to happen next that I decided that I *had* to know everything that was going to happen next. And then that started to matter more than anything else, and I lost sight of who I could be without that knowledge. Until you."

Her throat moved, but she didn't speak.

"This week has been the messiest, most unpredictable, and maybe one of the worst weeks of my life," I whispered. ". . . and it's also been the most wonderful, the most magical, and the most life-changing. It's been the best week of my life, Krysta. Because of you."

Her lips parted. "Yeah?"

"Yeah. And if you can forgive me for breaking every rule of yours, I don't want this to stop when we get to the dock. I want more time together. I want . . . you."

She dropped her gaze to my mouth, her teeth catching her lower lip oh-so briefly. "I want you too," she said in a low voice, looking back to my eyes. "I don't want to stop either. You are stubborn and obscenely peppy and you have more pastel-colored sticky flags than anyone could ever need. And I'm completely fucking obsessed with you. I want to follow you everywhere. I want to watch you sleep. I want you to *smell* like me."

"Is this you saying that you forgive me?" I asked optimistically.

She sighed. But there was a smile tugging at the edges of her mouth. "Only because you didn't break my most important rule."

"What was that?"

More of a smile now. "No olives."

Natch.

"So what happens next? Do you still want to be my bodyguard? Even though it's a bad idea because I'm so hot that you can't stop thinking about me?"

"A terrible idea," she agreed, smiling wider. "But I think I have to. Someone's got to keep you safe from overgrown theater kids and bad shrimp."

Relief shivered down my spine. After having her so close this week, my own tall, bossy shadow, I couldn't imagine living without her. It just felt right somehow.

"I don't—" I paused, not sure how to say this next part. "I've never done the relationship thing before. I might not be any good at it. And I don't know what's going to happen when the world learns I'm queer. I don't think I even know *how* I want the world to learn now, only that I don't want to do it the way my mom and my manager want me to. But I do know that I want you to be part of it, if you want that too."

"I do want that. And it's okay not to know everything right now," Krysta murmured. She reached up and pressed her hand to my heart. "We'll figure it out together."

"Okay," I whispered as the music swelled around us. "I'd like that."

"Me too."

"You know," I breathed, unable to bear the gravity of her perfection a moment longer, "this is the part where I'm supposed to be kissed by a vampire."

"People will talk, Ms. Hayes."

"I know."

"Well, then."

As the music reached its peak, Krysta dipped me back with her strong arms. And under the twinkling lights of a fake prom gazebo on a cruise ship, she pressed her mouth to my neck, grazing with unbearable softness and heat until she found my pulse.

There she lingered, until the lights came up to uproarious applause.

Epilogue

A year and a half later

I startled awake in my bed, my thoughts as hazy as my vision as I registered someone watching me from the corner of the room. Someone tall. And blond. And hot.

Krysta stepped forward into the moonlight, holding an apple in one hand. She took a bite, regarding me as she did.

"Are you having a midnight snack while watching me sleep again?" I accused with mock heat as I sat up. The sheet slid from my chest as I did, and predictably, Krysta's eyes followed it down.

"I have a fast metabolism," Krysta said patiently as she came to the bed. "And you sleep naked."

"Hmm."

"And," Krysta added, setting the apple down on the nightstand, "we're about to leave home for Christmas Notch, and the rooms at the inn aren't as good for lurking."

"True."

And I did love the lurking.

I loved having Krysta with me always, right behind me, a cool, fearless shadow. I loved her strength, her loyalty, her honesty. I loved having her sly humor, her secretly soft and chewy caramel center that was gooey for baby animals and grandmas and planner-obsessed wives. I loved how she made me braver, more intuitive, able to face the world without knowing what exactly would happen next.

I loved her. And it didn't matter that it hadn't been part of a plan or that it happened too fast or that it probably wasn't a good idea to marry your bodyguard. I'd known she was it from the moment she kissed my throat under the gazebo, and there didn't seem much sense in pretending otherwise. I proposed a month after the cruise had disembarked, and a month after that, we were married at a sunny farm overlooking the Aegean. An *olive* farm.

I finally broke Krysta's last rule.

Krysta's grandmother was officially settled in her new spot, but to everyone's surprise, she'd foregone pickleball in favor of something called lawn bowls, where she was currently the league champion. We visited her every week and made sure to get her money's worth out of the juice bar while we were there. Krysta wouldn't accept my help with anything regarding her gran, so I decided to exploit our client-bodyguard relationship and increased her salary enough to end the discussion. It's the only fight she's lost to date, but Krysta would do a lot to keep her grandmother in lawn bowls championship pins, including sacrifice her pride.

Shockingly, the disaster that was my leaked serum video didn't derail the launch of Lemon Tree Cruises *or* end my skincare line. There were a few viral takedown videos, a handful of posts from people who'd had the same reaction to the serum, and a particularly mean article in *The Cut*, but mostly people seemed to forget about it within a few days. Vitamin C was a common enough ingredient, there *was* a warning on the label, and also that same week there were leaked DM screenshots from a Hollywood A-lister

who could only orgasm if he was role-playing George Washing-
ton at the time, and that dominated the online discourse for several days.

When the dust (and screenshots) settled, what remained was
a pleasant buzz around the cruise and—delightfully—the begin-
nings of a cult following for *The Lion and the Lamb*. The campy
songs, the bad wigs, the souvenir blue-filtered glasses—people were
hyperfixated. And the footage of Krysta kissing my neck at the
fake prom basically had its own fandom by the time I'd unpacked
my suitcase. Hashtags proliferated, cruise bookings soared, and
Lemon Tree Cruises was fully in the black within its first operating
year.

Even our cruise villain was flourishing, having made a series
of viral videos while cleaning the beach as part of her mandated
community service. Her impassioned re-creations of famous movie
scenes with sun-faded trash standing in for the other characters
ended up being enormously popular, and last time I'd checked,
she'd inked a decent deal with YouTube to keep making them. Apparently, having had a very public trial for food poisoning and celebrity stalking was good for engagement, and despite her relatively
short jail sentence, Cassie played up the world-weary felon angle to
great effect. Rumor was that she had a memoir deal in the works,
and that she was already attached to play herself in the adaptation,
although I hadn't heard anything concrete on that front yet. Probably because the conditions of her parole weren't quite to the *taking
meetings in New York* level yet.

Most importantly, when I'd gotten home and settled, I'd sat
down with my planner by my pool and spent an entire day thinking. And thinking. I'd opened up a brand-new planner (with
brand-new coordinating highlighters and pens, obvs), and started

writing along the edges of the pages, leaving days and even entire weeks blank.

I called my mother and talked to her for a long time. We both cried a little. I called my publicist. I fired my manager.

I canceled the sit-down interview.

I wasn't afraid to come out—at least not in the way that my publicist seemed to think—and I wasn't afraid of the world learning about me and Krysta (especially since *The Lion and the Lamb* fandom was already shipping the two of us). I did still want to be strategic when it came to our physical safety, to protecting my mental health and boundaries, to recognizing what would change for me and my career.

But I didn't want any kind of revelation or announcement to come from Addison Hayes™. I didn't want the persona to be the priority; I didn't want to couple something so indelible and intimate to my life with corporate partnerships and a Pride Month home-goods line at a big-box store. I'd kept this part of myself cordoned off for so long in order to protect the brand, and it hardly made sense to step into this new phase with *protecting the brand* still top of mind.

I wanted whatever happened next to be about me, and Krysta too, and about us as *people*. Not public figures or talking points or ideas—even though I couldn't control that we would be those things to many people. But what I could control, and what we could control together, was what we gave the world initially. Something honest and genuine and that came from a feeling of rightness, not a schedule vetted by a publicity team and dotted with Zoom meetings with different magazines and conglomerates.

Which meant that on our wedding day, floating on the scent of the Aegean and kisses from my new wife, I shared a selfie of Krysta and me, the bright sea behind us, her white tux like a beacon in the sun, her mouth nuzzled playfully to my throat. And then I'd turned off my phone and spent the rest of the day eating, drinking, and dancing with my favorite people in the world.

And I hadn't looked back since.

In the here and now, Krysta was tugging the sheet farther down my body, her jaw tight with restraint as she watched my nipples harden in the cool air of the bedroom. The only illumination came from the pool just outside of the bedroom, a moody blue light that reminded me of the filtered glasses we handed out at *The Lion and the Lamb*.

"Open your legs," Krysta said, and I did as I was told, happily, beamingly.

"Hungry for something other than your apple?"

Her eyes were on my cunt now, and *hunger* was the only word for what I saw in her face. Her eyes gleamed like dark stars; the bluish light caught the shine of her tongue as she licked her lower lip.

"I think so, Ms. Hayes," she murmured as she put her knee on the bed and then crawled between my open thighs. Like she usually did at night, she slept in a pair of boxers and a white tank top, and when she leaned her weight forward onto her hands, the front of her tank top hung down so that I could see her breasts and the firm lines of her stomach beyond.

She pressed a hand to my sternum to force me onto my back and then settled on her elbows and then her stomach.

The first skim of her lips over my pussy was enough to melt my smile, my laughter, dissolve everything into a shivering inhale. And then she kissed me again, every contour, every seam and curve, until all of me was touched, until every bit of me from top to bottom had been claimed. I knew Krysta adored me, respected me, but that's not what her kisses were right now. They were not the worshipful caresses of an awed lover, but instead the prowling, possessive marks of ownership, of raw lust. And the noise that came from my wife's chest when she finally took her first real taste was nothing but primal, almost brutal in its naked, exposed desire.

"Oh," I breathed, as she pressed her tongue inside me, seeking more of my secrets. "Oh God, that's so fucking good."

"Yes," she grunted. "Yes, it is." I could feel her speak the words against my flesh.

Her arms were wrapped around my thighs, and she pulled me closer, searching up my center until she found my tender peak under its hood. She teased at its ripeness with her tongue, sucked at it, pulling off at intervals to tell me how stiff it was, how it practically begged to be toyed with, how she'd never been with someone whose clit was so goddamn needy. How she could spend all day taking care of it, and it would still be swollen for attention the minute she looked away. And while she was at it, wasn't my cunt always so slick for her? Wasn't I ashamed that I was such a dirty wife, needing it pleased all the time?

Her fingers slid into me like I was made of butter. And then there was—

Pressure.

Heat.

Wet, urgent strokes.

I cracked like a frozen lake; I cracked like marble. A rupture, an ecstatic break from tension and trembling fullness. And Krysta reveled in the destruction, like she'd blown down the walls of a city, like she'd won a battle with nothing more than her mouth. She kept fucking me as I came, and then in the last, shuddering moments, she pulled back to watch. To witness my flesh wet and tight around her fingers, everything glistening, everything soft.

She got to her knees and then pushed her fingers into my mouth. I tasted myself and I tasted the apple from earlier, both sweet and both a little tart. After I sucked her fingers clean, she wiped them on my stomach and stood up, reaching behind her head and pulling her tank top off and dropping it to the floor. Her boxers came next. The blue-tinted shadows traced the faint grooves in her stomach and pooled in the muscled hollows of her ass. I could have sketched a medically accurate drawing of biceps, triceps, and deltoids just from watching her climb back onto the bed.

She shifted to pull open the drawer of the bedside table, and my clit—still pulsing from my last orgasm—kicked back to eager life. We had an armory in that drawer, beads and balls and Krysta's harness, which she'd used earlier today by the pool, railing into me with a lime-green cock until I'd clenched around it in a moaning, squirting orgasm. But tonight she pulled out our favorite wand massager, the big one that we could both use at the same time.

She arranged herself so that our cunts were nearly touching, our thighs tangled, and then she wedged the blunt head of the vibrator between us and turned it on. Immediate sensation bloomed through me, lush and tight, pulling at my core and the muscles in my thighs. But the best part was watching Krysta, the shifting muscles in her torso as she bucked her hips against our shared toy. The breathless part of her lips, usually held with such neutrality, such self-control, and the flush on her chest and neck. The quivering strength of her thighs. The bullet-hard tips of her breasts. Her neck, her fingers. The crease of her knee.

Sometimes I couldn't believe she'd chosen me, neurotic and chirpy and with baggage that refused to fit any easy category of faith or fame. I couldn't believe that she trusted me with all the parts of her that she kept locked behind scowls and sunglasses, her tendernesses and her devotions. Her greedy, unruly, hedonistic desires, and her unbridled obsession with fucking me. Her love, which she mumbled to me now, her eyes on our flushed, wet pussies, her hips jerking harder and harder against the toy.

"Fuck, I love you," she whispered, "beautiful girl. Fuck. *Fuck.*"

I went first and then she followed right after, her shoulders curling in and her stomach squeezing as the climax shredded her inside and out. It was the only time she had bad posture, during sex, and I loved it, loved every single indication that I had some kind of power over her, that I alone could make this strong, terrifying bodyguard weak.

I mean, who doesn't graduate Sunday school with a hint of a Samson and Delilah kink???

With her free hand, Krysta found mine, and I felt more than heard the subtle clink of our wedding rings as she held onto me like I was the last thing keeping her tethered to the ground. Gorgeous, fluttering contractions pulsed through me, and through her, and it was like it was the same release for both of us, rippling through my body into hers and vice versa, our panting exhales filling the room as we crested.

And then the pulses drifted apart, waves receding from the shore, and Krysta clicked the vibrator off. She collapsed next to me on the bed, legs open, one arm outflung. I nestled into her, relishing the warmth of her skin in the cool air of the room. She smelled like a very non–Wishes by Addison bodywash, like a bodywash that came in a gray plastic bottle and had a scent like Charcoal + One-Word Answers or something. But I could still catch the scent of her, something woodsy and cedar-like, and the delicious hint of sex underneath it all.

"Do we have to go to Christmas Notch?" I asked, twisting my legs around hers. "We could just stay here. I don't even know Teddy Ray Fletcher. I don't care about his wedding."

"But Steph D'Arezzo is your manager now," Krysta said, amused, looking down at me. "Plus, you told Winnie you'd help watch the babies so she and Kallum could stay through the reception. Also, how am *I* the one talking us into going out somewhere?"

I stared down her stomach to the swell of her sex, covered with pale gold curls. "I don't want to leave our bed," I fussed. I slid a hand down to her navel and then to her hip. "We could just spend this next week having sex instead."

"We'll have plenty of sex in Vermont," Krysta said. "We'll fuck in the hotel, in the mansion, in the dressing room of the ski outfitters, anywhere you need it."

"Is that a promise?"

"Even better," Krysta murmured. "It's a rule."

And then she turned to me and guided my hand to where she was the wettest. And as I explored the part of her that was never cold, never closed off, she pulled me close and found my lips with hers, sharing her exhales, stealing my inhales.

"I did promise to follow your rules," I breathed as I caressed her cunt.

"And I promise only to make good ones," she said and then parted my lips to slip inside for a deep, searching kiss. It was a kiss that was final, fixed, forever, as eternal as a vampire, as eternal as the sea.

And we fell into it like the moonlight fell into the waves, completely and wholly, with ripples and crests and surges up to a gasping, heart-pounding shore.

If you haven't read the Christmas Notch series, don't miss out! Here's a peek of

A Merry Little Meet Cute,

A Holly Jolly Ever After,

and

A Jingle Bell Mingle

Available now!

A Merry Little Meet Cute

**Cowritten by #1 *New York Times* bestselling author
Julie Murphy and *USA Today* bestselling author
Sierra Simone—a steamy plus-size holiday rom-com about an
adult film star who is semi-accidentally cast as a lead
in a family-friendly Christmas movie, and the former
bad-boy pop star she falls in love with.**

Bee Hobbes (aka Bianca Von Honey) has a successful career as a plus-size adult film star. With a huge following and two supportive moms, Bee couldn't ask for more. But when Bee's favorite producer casts her to star in a Christmas movie he's making for the squeaky-clean Hope Channel, Bee's career is about to take a more family-friendly direction.

Forced to keep her work as Bianca under wraps, Bee quickly learns this is a task a lot easier said than done. Though it all becomes worthwhile when she discovers her co-star is none other than childhood crush Nolan Shaw, an ex–boy band band member in desperate need of career rehab. Nolan's promised his bulldog manager to keep it zipped up on set, and he will if it means he'll be able to provide a more stable living situation for his sister and mom.

But things heat up quickly in Christmas Notch, Vermont, when Nolan recognizes his new co-star from her ClosedDoors account (oh yeah, he's a member). Now Bee and Nolan are sneaking off for quickies on set, keeping their new relationship a secret from the Hope Channel's execs. Things only get trickier when the reporter who torpedoed Nolan's singing career comes snooping around—and takes an instant interest in mysterious newcomer Bee.

And if Bee and Nolan can't keep their off-camera romance behind the scenes, then this merry little meet cute might end up on the cutting room floor.

Prologue

Teddy Ray Fletcher

A tusk?" he repeated, just to make sure he'd heard right.

"A *wooden* tusk," the voice clarified. Teddy heard the whoosh of traffic and the sound of a car door closing. Why was it that managers and agents were always going places when they called? Did they save all their phone calls for their commutes?

"Three broken arms, two broken legs, and five concussions between the four of them," Steph D'Arezzo finished over the hum of an accelerating car.

Teddy looked down at his desk, an acrylic thing his ex-wife had gotten him from IKEA before the divorce.

A very stressful production schedule looked back up at him.

He looked away from it, trying to focus on the picture of his two kids grinning from within his arms, their tiny hands clutching the tiny pumpkins he'd bought for them at the pumpkin patch that day. They used to be so little. And so inexpensive.

"Okay, so you're telling me that my entire costume and hair team went into the desert and stood under a wooden tusk, which then collapsed on top of them. And now they can't work on the movie, which starts *tomorrow*."

"Costume team, hair team, *and* your gaffer, Teddy. And there's no need to sound so judgmental about the wooden tusk. It was on a giant wooden walrus sculpture, after all. Don't you know anything about festivals? Haven't you been to Burning Man?"

Teddy squinted at the far wall in his tiny office, trying to imagine the fast-talking, suit-wearing, phone-addicted Steph D'Arezzo doing drugs in the desert. "Have *you* been to Burning Man?"

"We were all in our twenties once. No, don't take the five right now, are you even looking at your GPS?"

Teddy assumed she was talking to an Uber driver and ignored the last comment. "So they were at Burning Man?"

"No, this was *better* than Burning Man," she said. "It was UnFestival in Terlingua."

"UnFestival? I've never heard of it."

"Of course you haven't," Steph said dismissively. "It's exclusive."

"Ah," he said. "Invite only."

"No, Teddy, it's *un*invite only."

"Okay. Uninvite only to UnFestival. Where a wooden walrus fell on my crew."

"Just the tusk," she clarified. "Will it stop dinging at me if I put on my seat belt? Oh good. And the walrus was part of the Alice in Wonderland theme, Teddy. It wasn't just a random wooden walrus out on a mesa."

She scoffed as if *that* would be bananas.

"And how do you know all this before I do?" he asked.

"Ah, well, about that," Steph said, and it was in that brisk *I have some bad news* voice that all managers seemed to have.

Teddy's butthole clenched.

"I heard because it came bundled with another thing. I got a call from Winnie's agent, and she's going to call you later tonight when she knows more, but she wanted to put me and your male lead in the know, in case the story broke over social media before then. Winnie's in the hospital right now."

Shit.

Winnie Baker was a wholesome child star turned wholesome made-for-TV-movie actress, and she was going to be one of the leads in his first-ever Christmas movie production. More importantly, she was the star his director had specifically *chosen* to work with to make her directorial debut, and Teddy had to keep his director happy, because she made the Hope Channel happy.

And getting *Duke the Halls* distributed by Hope—and their new streaming platform Hopeflix—was the only thing that could turn Teddy's desperate Christmas movie gamble into real money. God knew his day job making cheap pornography wasn't paying for his son's art school tuition or his daughter's startup making carbon-neutral sex toys.

And Christmas movies couldn't be that hard to make, right? They were *almost* like porn. The scripts were on the flimsy side and the production times were shorter than a community college wintermester.

But now the wooden tusk. Now no Winnie Baker.

But Teddy wasn't a total asshole, so the first question he asked was "Is Winnie okay?"

"She'll be *fiiiine*," Steph said, in a voice that clearly conveyed how much she cared. "The word is that it was an ayahuasca ceremony gone wrong—also at UnFestival. Do you know how easy it is to get dehydrated on the mesa? Even before you start shitting yourself? Anyway, she's in the hospital now and hooked up to all sorts of IVs. Her agent thinks another few days and then a discharge with strict instructions to rest."

"So no movie for her," Teddy said numbly.

"No movie for her. By the way, if anyone asks, she's being treated for exhaustion. *Not* for puking in a tent full of vegans and DJs."

Right. No one would want sweet Winnie Baker's reputation tarnished—and Teddy definitely didn't want the movie tarnished by association. No, he needed his new production company to appear five thousand percent aboveboard, so that no one would dig too hard and find out that Teddy Ray Fletcher was the same man who owned Uncle Ray-Ray's, a porn studio specializing in—well, less stuff than it used to, now that his daughter was in her twenties and spent every family meal lecturing him about creating ethical mission statements. Last Thanksgiving, she and his son made him identify Uncle Ray-Ray's core values.

Core. Values.

"So if I were you," Steph went on, "I'd round up your director and get that shit recast ASAP. Sweet baby *Jesus*, did you see that? And on a unicycle! Only in Silver Lake, am I right?"

Assuming that Steph was talking to her Uber driver again, Teddy wisely chose not to answer, already stuffing everything on his desk related to *Duke the Halls* into his briefcase—another present from his ex-wife.

He was going to fix this. He was going to juggle Fletcher Productions and Uncle Ray-Ray's so smoothly that no one from the Christmas movie would ever, ever know about his career making porn. He had not figured out how to make separate IMDb accounts (*and* how to furtively use his great aunt Phyllis's address for a new LLC) for nothing!

I can fix this, he told himself as he forced the briefcase closed and bolted for the door. *I can still make this work.*

After all, how hard could it be to keep his two worlds separate?

THREE HOURS LATER, Teddy was sitting across from his director in an airport Chili's Too glowing with chili pepper string lights and mini Christmas trees at every table. He was trying to pull folders out of his briefcase while also choking down a molten-hot mozzarella stick.

"Are you okay?" she asked. "You're flushed."

Teddy fumbled some folders on the table and then dabbed at his forehead with his napkin, hoping he wasn't sweating too much. His pale complexion showed every degree of flush and every stipple of sweat. It made him self-conscious.

"This is stressful stuff, but nothing we can't handle," he said, trying to sound smooth and in control. He'd dealt with any number of porn catastrophes in his day, but unfortunately, the stakes were a bit higher here than having to recast a performer with hemorrhoids. "Obviously, it's less than ideal having to make this decision in the airport right before your plane leaves for Vermont, but ayahuasca is unpredictable."

"Words to live by." The director sighed. She was already pulling his folders across the table over to her side. Even as she sat in a booth made of vinyl and old crumbs, there was no hiding that indefinable celebrity aura she gave off. Gretchen Young had high cheekbones, flashing eyes, and warm medium brown skin—all of it finished off by long, waist-length twists, a nose piercing, and casual overalls that had probably cost as much as his watch.

"And how hard do you think it will be to get someone else to Vermont in time?" she asked, spreading the headshots across the table. "There were a few other women whom I liked at the audition, but with the shoot happening over the holidays and the short notice . . ."

"We'll make it work," Teddy said with a confidence he absolutely did not have. For one thing, the turnarounds on these Christmas movies were *tight*. Two weeks—three at the most. And with the actual filming set to begin in two days, he'd have to get their new actress out to Vermont by tomorrow, or the day after at the latest. While *Duke the Halls* wasn't exactly written in iambic pentameter, he assumed Winnie's replacement would want a day or so to read over the script and familiarize herself with the story.

And for another, *worse* thing, the little Vermont town where Gretchen wanted to shoot the movie—Christmas Notch—had only one opening in its little Vermont schedule: during the actual, literal Christmas season. And while they wouldn't be shooting on the twenty-fifth, they'd be right back to work on the twenty-sixth, meaning that whoever took Winnie's role would have to be okay with potentially missing Christmas at home.

Jesus. He needed another mozzarella stick. He shoved the breaded lava into his mouth and tried to remember that thing his son had told him about mindful breathing.

"*Fuck*," Gretchen breathed suddenly. "Who is she? We didn't see her at the audition, did we?"

"Uh," Teddy said through his mouthful of food, racking his brain.

"I don't think I've ever seen a headshot with nipples before," Gretchen added thoughtfully.

The horror slid through him in slow motion, as hot and gooey as the burning mozzarella lodged in his throat. He lowered his eyes to the table and saw what Gretchen was looking at: a picture that had most definitely *not* come from the *Duke the Halls* folder. He mentally rewound to three hours ago, when he had been shoving any and all folder-like objects into his briefcase, flustered and hurrying like hell so he could catch Gretchen before her flight.

And now here he was, looking at a still from Uncle Ray-Ray's latest porn shoot and not a headshot for *Duke the Halls*.

Gretchen traced a long finger over the woman's face. "She definitely wasn't at the audition. I'd remember her. Who is she?"

Teddy tried to put his hand over the rest of the folder—if she kept going through these pictures, she was going to see more than just nipples—and sound completely and totally nonchalant. Like this was no big deal. Like Gretchen didn't have her finger on a picture of one of the hottest alt-porn stars of their time.

"She's very talented," Teddy said, the nonchalance difficult to muster as he coughed down some stubborn mozzarella. "But she normally does edgier stuff. You know"—he cast around for the right nonporn word—"provocative. Artistic risks and stuff. Not really Hopeflix fare."

"She's exactly what I want," Gretchen said, still looking at the photo. "She's perfect for the part of Felicity."

"Uh . . ."

"I want her," Gretchen repeated, looking up at Teddy. "I want her in my movie. What's her name?"

He almost said her stage name and then caught himself at the last moment. "Bee Hobbes. But you haven't even seen her act yet," he protested weakly.

"Do you think she has a reel up on her website?" Gretchen asked. "I'll Google her."

Teddy had a sudden, queasy vision of her Googling Bee Hobbes and somehow landing upon Bianca von Honey. And Uncle Ray-Ray's.

"No need to Google," he said quickly. "I've worked with her before and she's brilliant. But maybe we should have some other backup options, in case she can't . . ."

"No, it needs to be her," Gretchen said, shaking her head, looking down at the picture again. "I want a degree of edginess; I want there to be something dangerous in the way the actors play Pearl's script."

Pearl Purkiss was the screenwriter for *Duke the Halls*—and Gretchen Young's girlfriend—and was in Christmas Notch now, preparing for a movie that didn't currently have a female lead. "We could find another edgy person," Teddy attempted valiantly, "if we just take a quick look at the other folder—"

"I hope," Gretchen said coolly, "that you're not balking because she's plus-size?"

"What? No!" Teddy worked with Bee all the time! She was gorgeous and filthy and great for business! But she couldn't be in a chaste-as-hell Christmas movie. For the flipping *Hope Channel*. What if she was recognized? What if Teddy Ray Fletcher was revealed to be a purveyor of porn and then *poof* went this fledgling Hopeflix partnership and his son the artist had to be a barista two years too early?

"I just think that we should maybe pick some alternates in case she's . . . busy," Teddy finally said.

"If we don't get her, then I don't even know," Gretchen said, closing her eyes in a way that sent alarm bells ringing through him. Alarm bells that shrieked, *Keep Gretchen happy so you can keep Hopeflix interested.* "I already lost Winnie. Another disappointment so soon . . ."

The alarm bells got louder.

Would it really be so bad? Teddy asked himself desperately. Would it really be so dangerous to have Bee in the movie?

She'd been begging him to cast her in something ever since he dreamed up this Christmas studio scheme last year, and she would have just as much to lose if her porn career came back to haunt her. And besides, how much did Hopeflix's audience really overlap with the feminist porn watchers? What tattooed, fair trade coffee drinkers with their body-safe silicone toys were also tuning in to sexless holiday schmaltz?

It might be okay, it really might. And if it was okay, if this *did* work, then perhaps he'd just stumbled upon an easy solution for any future casting problems. It was already giving him ideas for how to fill the holes in his production team created by the rogue wooden tusk.

"I'll reach out to her tonight," Teddy promised. "Why don't you, um, keep this folder here"—he carefully pushed the real *Duke the Halls* folder under her fingertips—"in case she can't."

"I hope she can," said Gretchen. "I get a really good energy from her picture. Very open, you know?"

Teddy stopped himself from making the obvious *very open* joke, stress ate another mozzarella stick, and then gestured for the check.

FINALLY, OUT IN the airport parking lot, he set his briefcase in the passenger seat of his minivan, did some mindful breathing that didn't help, and dialed Bee as he stared at a stray cat licking its paws on top of a Tesla.

"Hello?" answered Bee.

"I hope you're sitting down right now," Teddy said.

I know I am, he thought grimly.

Chapter One

Bee

I think six bottles of flavored lube might be overkill," I told Sunny.

She nodded as she plucked two from the bundle clutched to her chest and threw them on my bed. "You're right. Six is overkill. Four is the sweet spot. I'm cutting grape and French toast from the lineup. Honestly, what was I thinking including grape in the first place? No one chooses grape lube when there are other options. It's the Pepsi of flavored lubes. And French toast is really more of an acquired taste."

"S, I don't think I'm going to need any flavored lubes at all on the set of *Duke the Halls*. This is Hopeflix we're talking about. If my grandmother's stack of pioneer romance novels and megachurch energy had a baby, it still wouldn't be as squeaky clean as the Hope Channel."

Sunny plopped down on the floor in a sea of dildos, butt plugs, silk ties, harnesses, Ben Wa balls, pocket rockets, anal beads, paddles, ball gags, and vibrating cock rings. Shortly after I found out I was being shipped off to Vermont to star in my very first nonporn film as part of Teddy's venture into wholesome Christmas movies, I dumped out my suitcases, which just so happened to double as storage for my collection of toys, and started packing. And sure, two full suitcases of sex toys might be a bit much, but these are not only essential tools, they're also a tax write-off in my line of work.

"Bee, what if there's an emergency?" Sunny asked. "And you're lubeless?"

She had a point. "One," I said. "Sugar cookie flavored."

She rolled her eyes and tossed the bottle in with my toiletries. "Did you grab the fuzzy pink sweater out of my closet?"

This was one of the benefits of having a friend I could actually share clothing with for the first time in my life. I thumbed through the stack of leggings, jeans, and shirts I'd set aside. "Not yet. Uh, what time is it?"

She checked her phone as she stood and pulled the towel off her head, her damp black hair cascading over her olive shoulders. Colorful tattoos peeked from between the inky curls as she bounced back on the bed. "We've got forty-five minutes before we have to leave for the airport and I told my dad I'd be there in time to light the menorah, so get to packing, baby!"

Sunny was my best friend, roommate, and self-appointed shepherd through the endless hole-in-the-wall LA and surrounding area Mexican joints, and her grandmother was my chocolate chip challah bread pudding dealer. We met on the set of my first scene. Even though she did porn, she also worked as a makeup artist and was part of the crew on set that day. I was excited, but terrified. ClosedDoors had always just been me and my camera. That first day on set was the first time I'd let go of some control. She immediately calmed my nerves when she'd said, "This whole shoot is for you, Bee. You're the star of this show. Own it."

And she hadn't been entirely wrong. After I blew up on Closed-Doors, a paid subscription app that was basically a hybrid of Facebook and Instagram, but much more . . . naked, Teddy Ray

Fletcher reached out to me with an offer to sign a deal with his porn production company. I got lucky with Teddy. He was one of the good ones. The offer wasn't exclusive. I could work with other production companies and keep my ClosedDoors account active.

My first scene was the top performing video for Teddy that year and even won me a newcomer of the year nomination at the AVN Awards. (Of course, I didn't actually win. It would be too much to let the fat girl actually win. Sunny wrote a scathing Instagram post about body-size disparity in adult films. It was TED Talk levels of good.)

When Teddy landed the Hope Channel contract, I begged him for months to let me have a crack at one of his Christmas movies. I could play the dowdy sister or the dress shop owner. Hell, even Caroler Number 3 would be something.

But he told me over and over again that there would be no crossing of streams when it came to filthy porn and wholesome Christmas content, which is why I never expected him to call two and a half weeks before Christmas and tell me he needed me in Vermont in twelve hours to take on the role of Felicity in *Duke the Halls* and replace *the* Winnie Baker.

In fact, I almost didn't answer his call.

Teddy didn't know how to text. Or so he claimed. Sunny said she once saw him respond to a text from his ex-wife with the flame emoji, but that was no better than folklore in the unbelievable history of Teddy Ray Fletcher. Which is why I almost sent him to voicemail when I saw his face (a picture of him sleeping in a director's chair on set while people were literally fucking in front of him) light up my screen.

Teddy called for the kinds of things that could easily be communicated in a text: Because there was an accident on I-10 and he wanted me to take some confusing route through the hills, and he didn't trust my maps app to direct me around traffic. Or because he needed ideas for Astrid's or Angel's birthday. He called because he'd stopped for coffee and couldn't remember if I drank "cow milk or that vegan nut shit." He called because my moms were hounding him about sending DVD copies of my latest scene—not for them to watch, but for them to keep in their Little Bee Hall of Fame.

Teddy definitely did not call because he'd accidentally cast me in a Christmas movie as part of his attempt to diversify his portfolio/go legit. (Porn, by the way, was very legit. Just ask the retirement account I started at the behest of my mothers when I was only twenty years old.)

When he told me I'd be going to Vermont, I had to set the actual phone down while he continued to stress spiral on the line.

"Teddy," I said, finally picking up the phone again, "give me ten minutes. I need to think."

"Five," he demanded, the defeat in his voice palpable.

I wasted a whole minute trying to call Sunny, but she was on an early morning shoot and not in the . . . position to answer her phone.

Growing up, I'd always loved being onstage. In fact, I've spent a lot of time wondering who I might be today if I hadn't become instantly suburban famous in twelfth grade for posting my tits on Instagram before Tanner Dunn could beat me to it. That asshat. But now that the opportunity to not only be in *Duke the Halls* but to star in it was here, I felt frozen with indecision. What if I couldn't pull this off? What if my costar, Nolan Shaw, just walked right off the set after finding out I'd be replacing Winnie? I was a porn star—an adult film darling! Teddy must have been losing his mind if he'd actually cast me in his Christmas movie. Even if I'd asked—no, begged—him to.

And there it was. I *had* asked him. I wanted this in my gut. And if I'd learned anything since putting my titties on Instagram six years ago, it was that I should trust my instincts.

Exactly four minutes later, I called Teddy back. "I'm in."

"Okay," he said as he smacked on his nicotine gum so loudly I could practically smell the minty flavor through the speaker of my phone. "There's gonna be some rules. And not the kind of rules that you and Sunny break for shits and giggles. I'm talking real rules, Bee. The kind that could actually ruin me and this idiotic venture if they're broken."

"Okay," I told him, feeling my inner teenager rear her angsty head.

"I'm serious."

"I said okay."

"Fuck me," he muttered. "Not literally."

I bit back a smirk. In my business, that was a really important distinction to make.

TRUE LOVE WAS driving someone to LAX, and Sunny had proved her love for me on many occasions, but the traffic today was especially heinous.

"Shit," I whispered as I dug through my backpack. "I forgot my charger."

"Check your side pocket," she said calmly. "And the charger for your laptop should work for Rod too."

"Rod! I can't believe I almost forgot."

She nodded. "Leave no vibrator behind."

With chargers resolved, I slid the backpack down between my legs and leaned my head against the headrest, closing my eyes and taking a breather. Doubt washed over me the moment my brain began to quiet. This was an awful idea. I knew it deep down. My intuition was too good. I always felt the truth in my gut, even when it was the kind of truth I didn't want to face. And this was one of those truths.

I loved my job in the adult industry. It was a big middle finger to everyone who ever told me I had a pretty face or that no one would want a body like mine. But it was more than that. My job fulfilled me. It made me feel powerful. In control. It gave me community. Family, even. But Teddy's new venture with Hopeflix had reawoken dreams I'd put to bed before I could even verbalize them. I'd wanted to be an actress since first grade when I had my first speaking role in the school's production of *Charlotte's Web*. ("Look at that pig!")

It was a few years, though, before I was faced with the realities of being the fat girl with leading-lady aspirations. Eventually, my dreams faded. When it came to acting, it was easier to leave it entirely than watch from the sidelines. It was one clean heartbreak instead of lots of tiny cracks.

But now as an older, more sure version of myself, I wanted to take back the dreams that were stolen from me simply because some high school theater teacher couldn't imagine someone like me getting the guy or saving the day. And everyone in porn—especially women—had an expiration date. I couldn't help but think this might be good groundwork for future Bee. And yet, I had a hard time imagining how I would even pull this off.

"This is a bad idea," I finally blurted as we saw our first sign for LAX. "I need to call Teddy and tell him he'll have to find someone else. And Nolan Shaw! I haven't even wrapped my head around the fact that I'm supposed to be costarring with Nolan Shaw."

Sunny let out an excited shriek. "Do you think it's best to come clean about the INK shrine above your childhood bed before or after you finish filming?"

"Sunny! This is not something to joke about!"

"You used to jack off to the ex–boy band member you're about to star in a time-traveling Christmas movie with. Oh, and you're a porn star. That is prime joke material."

I let out a soft whimper as I gripped the center console. We needed to go home. We needed to turn this car around.

"Okay, okay," she said, pulling off on a random exit and into a gas station that had a big sign reading PARKING LOT KARAOKE SATURDAY NIGHT. She slid the car into park and took her seat belt off so she could face me and give me her full attention. "You once did a sex scene on a Jet Ski. With a life jacket on. You can do this, Bee. And I've seen those videos and pictures your moms showed us when you took me home for Thanksgiving that one year. Little Bee was a total theater nerd. Little Bee is liv*ing* for this moment."

"Adult Bee is too," I said softly. "But I'm scared. I'm scared I'll fail. I'm scared I'll meet Nolan and he'll be an asshole, or I'm scared he'll meet me and be one of those awful piece of shit guys who are like 'fat chicks need not apply'—"

"Okay, first off. Fuck that potential version of Nolan Shaw. You are a goddess and there are literal human beings in your inbox who would pay to clean your house for you."

"I know, I know, I know. But it's just . . . God, I loved him back in the day. I still have INK in my playlist rotation. But . . . he's expecting Winnie Baker, Sunny. Not Bee Hobbes, total unknown."

"To him," she muttered, and then in her this-is-all-fine-everything-is-under-control-these-nipple-clamps-aren't-stuck-they're-just-stubborn voice, she said, "Listen, I heard Winnie wasn't the only person taken out by UnFestival. Some crew members were there with her, and you're not the only replacement Teddy had to come up with on the fly. So there will be friendly faces too. That'll help. And you'll have me. I'll text so much you'll want to bury your phone in a foot of snow."

"Not possible," I said. "Okay, well, maybe a little possible. But what other porn people? Anyone I know?"

She shrugged as she put her seat belt back on and shifted the car into drive, deeming my crisis averted. "I'm not totally sure. I heard he was trying to get ahold of some people, but with Christmas coming up, the pickings were slim. So it sounds like it might be a mix of old- and new-school people."

"Okay, okay. That makes me feel . . . better."

She pulled back onto the highway and took the next exit for LAX.

"Oh no, wait. What are you going to do for Christmas?" I asked. "Fuck. What am I going to tell my moms?"

"Bee. Shut up. You know you're my favorite gentile, and I never even did anything for Christmas before I met you."

"False."

"Okay. I did do one and a half Christmases with Cooper before we broke up, but those don't count. His parents open presents on Christmas Eve. Who does that? Isn't Christmas Day the whole point for you people? And your moms—they'll be fine. Hell, maybe I'll go home to your place for Christmas and live it up as an only child."

"My helicopter moms would actually love that. I assure you."

The ginormous white LAX sign cast a shadow over the road as we pulled into the airport and took the signs for Terminal 4. My brain began to revisit the remaining list of all the reasons why I should not do this. "What if someone finds out I do porn?"

"Okay. This has two possible outcomes. The first and most likely scenario is that no one finds out. The people who watch those vanilla-ass excuses for movies are definitely not the same people who have *Bianca von Honey underwear for sale* in their search history."

"I don't sell my underwear," I clarified.

"Semantics," she said. "But don't pretend you're above it."

"Fair. Okay, what's the second, scarier, much more awful scenario?" I asked.

"The second scenario is that the people at Hopeflix find out about the job you openly do on the internet."

She said it so simply, but it wasn't quite that uncomplicated. There was Teddy to consider. And Nolan, even. The Hope Channel and what they might do when they found out. They were the kind of company that had morality clauses in their contracts, so I didn't think they'd super love finding out how creative I'd been with ropes and condom-covered cucumbers in the past.

"There's Teddy," Sunny said, pointing to a man waiting outside the terminal wearing cargo shorts and a Hawaiian shirt, with a briefcase wedged between his feet like he was nervous someone might steal all of his very important papers with all the same information he could easily find on his phone if he only knew how to use it.

He began to walk toward us the moment he saw Sunny's baby-blue nine-year-old Toyota Prius covered in unmistakable bumper stickers like MY OTHER RIDE IS A DILDO and DON'T YOU WISH YOUR GIRLFRIEND WAS PAGAN LIKE ME?

Sunny put the car in park, despite the crushing traffic behind us, and got out to help me with my bags, which barely fit in a trunk that was roughly the size of my back pocket.

"You're gonna kill it, Bee," she whispered over the honking horns. "You're a star. Don't forget it. Nolan Shaw won't know what hit him."

"I love you, I love you, I love you," I whispered back. "But you have to let me go before someone kills us with their Tesla."

"Fuck your Tesla," Sunny shouted over my shoulder to no one and everyone, and then to me, she said, "I packed an extra travel-size lube in your backpack. In case of emergency."

A Holly Jolly Ever After

From the authors of *A Merry Little Meet Cute* comes a steamy holiday rom-com cowritten by #1 *New York Times* bestselling author Julie Murphy and *USA Today* bestselling author Sierra Simone—about an actress and a perpetually single former boy band member reunited as costars on a steamy holiday film!

Kallum Lieberman is the funny one™. As the arguably lesser of the three former members of the boy band INK, he enjoyed his fifteen minutes of fame and then moved home, where he opened a regional pizza chain called Slice, Slice, Baby! He's living his best dad bod life, hooking up with bridesmaids at all his friends' weddings. But after an old one-off sex tape is leaked and quickly goes viral, Kallum decides he's ready to step into the spotlight again, starring in a sexy Santa biopic for the Hope Channel.

Winnie Baker did everything right. She married her childhood sweetheart, avoided the downfalls of adolescent stardom, and transitioned into a stable adult acting career. Hell, she even waited until marriage to have sex. But after her perfect life falls apart, Winnie is ready to redefine herself—and what better way than a steamier-than-a-steaming-hot-mug-of-cider Christmas movie?

With a decade-old Hollywood history between them, Winnie and Kallum are both feeling hesitant about their new situation as costars . . . especially Winnie, who can't seem to fake on-screen pleasure she's never experienced in real life. She's willing to do the pleasure research—for science and artistic authenticity, of course.

And there's no better research partner than her bridesmaid sex tape hall of fame costar, Kallum. But suddenly, Kallum's teenage crush on Winnie is bubbling to the surface and Winnie might be catching feelings herself.

They say opposites attract, but is this holly jolly ever after really ready for its close-up?

Prologue
Teddy Ray Fletcher

*W*hen Teddy Ray Fletcher's children were little, his fridge was covered in finger paintings, macaroni art, and paper mosaics framed with Popsicle sticks. He kept their masterpieces in his office and hung them in the hallways of his house; he made mouse pads and coffee mugs with their pictures and proudly showed them off to his friends, his performers, and complete strangers alike.

That said, Teddy rarely knew what those early pictures were supposed to *be*—occasionally one might be able to identify a flower or a cat, but for the most part, Teddy tried to see the pictures the same way his then wife talked about the abstract art at the galleries she was always dragging him to: as a display of movement and color.

Or something like that. Teddy hated abstract art.

But he didn't hate his *kids'* art, and so as a father, he promised himself he would never be handed an adorable mess and say, *Um, what is it supposed to be?* He just praised them for being perfect little geniuses, telling them that they were just as good as Picasso or Monet. Or the people who drew *The Wild Thornberrys* cartoons.

And so today, when his twenty-something daughter bounced into his office and plonked a shiny rectangle onto his desk—a rectangle with a cylinder attached by a still-twist-tied cord—Teddy didn't ask what it was supposed to be. He said, "Astrid, this is so great! Did you make it yourself?"

Sunlight winked off the medusa piercing right above her upper lip as she rolled her dark brown eyes. Her eyes, curls, and warm sepia skin were her mother's. (Her lactose intolerance and penchant for semi-regrettable body modifications were all Teddy's.) "It's a prototype, Dad. Obviously."

He lifted it up, giving his best all-knowing-dad expression as he did. "It's a great prototype, sweetie. It's very proto."

"Do you even know what it is?"

Teddy looked down at the thing in his hands—hands still sunburned from an outdoor MILF shoot near Big Bear. Astrid's contraption looked like a Walkman with a tiny microphone attached, except that everything was made of a matte plastic he suspected had something to do with being phthalate-free. "Is it for"—he mentally cast around, trying to think of where he'd seen tiny microphones before—"TikTok? Are you going to be a Tik-Tok star?"

"*Dad.* It's for Venus!"

Venus was Astrid's eco-friendly sex toy startup, and one of the reasons Teddy had expanded his operation last year to produce wholesome holiday movies along with regular non-wholesome pornography. (The other reason was his son's art school tuition, which Teddy tried not to think about without a glass of Jim Beam in his hand.)

"Ah," Teddy said. He still had no idea what it was for.

Astrid beamed. "It's a solar-powered vibrator!"

"I thought you were doing the nipple clamps first," Teddy said, setting the prototype down and looking up at his smiling daughter. He was a terrible investor—not because he didn't believe in

Astrid's climate-conscious vision, but because once she started talking about polyvinyl and thermoplastics, his attention started wandering to things like the new doughnut place in Westwood or if maybe he should text a certain pantsuited talent manager he couldn't stop thinking about.

"I'm still trying to source a carbon-neutral steel supplier for the clamps." Astrid sighed. "But I've been thinking about maybe doing more of a tassel-type thing with vegan leather instead— Oh, hi, Sunny!"

Teddy's eyelid twitched as Sunny Palmer bounded into his office. Her cat, Mr. Tumnus, had eaten some vital cord coming from the back of her computer last month, and ever since then, she'd been using Uncle Ray-Ray's equipment to edit her solo videos. Which Teddy didn't mind per se, but having Sunny here was like having a tiny kitten in the office. She got into everything, squawked at inanimate objects, and sometimes fell asleep in sunbeams before bouncing awake and coming to pester him while he was trying to squint his way through the latest edition of union bylaws for his performers. She was a lot. And Teddy preferred *a lot* when he didn't already have his hands full of Christmas movie bullshit, like he did today.

"Ooh, your proto-vibe came in!" Sunny squealed, reaching toward Teddy's desk and snatching it off the top like a tattooed Swiper the Fox. "This looks amazing! Will it charge on cloudy days? Do you think it would charge in space? Also, Teddy, there's someone here for you. She's finishing a call and then she'll be in."

"If she's making a delivery, tell her she can just leave it inside the front door," Teddy said automatically, turning back to his laptop. It woke up with an obnoxious *I'm an ancient computer please let me die* whirr.

"No, no," Sunny said absently, her attention on the solar-powered sex toy in her hand. "It's what's-her-name from Christmas Notch. The mean sexy woman. Steph something."

Time slowed down; Teddy's pulse sped up. It was thundering in his ears, and it matched the pounding in his chest.

Steph.

Steph was here.

Steph was here and he still had toasted BLT crumbs on his shirt.

Panicked, he tried to brush his shirt clean—along with his mustache—while also simultaneously straightening his desk and making shooing noises at his daughter and his performer to leave . . . which they characteristically ignored.

And then it happened.

Steph D'Arezzo, talent manager and the most perfect woman in the world, walked through his office door like she did it every day.

He hadn't seen her since they'd slept together seven months ago at a Fourth of July barbeque, but it didn't matter. His body remembered the press of hers like it was yesterday. And the impeccably tailored pantsuit she wore—cherry red with a black top underneath—would have reminded him if he hadn't remembered. It showed off those soft hips, those even softer breasts, and those long legs, which ended in black heels sharp enough to cut the five-tier wedding cake that appeared in his sappiest, most private daydreams. A single string of pearls hugged the base of her long, pale neck; her hair was down in dark waves.

She wore lipstick the same color as her pantsuit, and it made Teddy shift in his seat.

Say hi, he coached himself. *Say hi and then tell her you missed her. Maybe she's here for barbeque sex part two. Say hi. Say hi.* He managed to open his mouth.

Except then Sunny, who'd sidled up to Steph and was gazing up at the manager with a look somewhere between awed and horny, spoke first. "Are you my mommy?"

Steph seemed accustomed to the half-feral Uncle Ray-Ray's family after being on the set for *Duke the Halls*, because she ignored Sunny and walked right to the front of Teddy's desk and braced her hands on the top. Like he was a naughty student and she was a teacher, the prettiest teacher in the world.

His heart jumped right into his throat.

"Word on the street is that you have a script," Steph said.

Oh.

She wasn't here for barbeque sex part two. Teddy's heart burrowed mopefully down into his stomach.

"It was just finished last night," he managed to respond.

Teddy's company was producing the first-ever Hope After Dark movie this year—a film that would combine the unironic joy of the Hope Channel's usual fare with the soft-core raunch that he'd grown up watching on Skinemax. Even better, the movie was still a Christmas movie! *Santa, Baby* was about a soon-to-be Santa Claus sowing his wild Santa oats before he took over the proverbial reins to the sleigh. The young Santa would be played by none other than Steph's client Kallum Lieberman, former pop star (and present-day leaked-sex-tape star).

"Kallum should get it in the next week or so, if he's worried about having enough time—"

"I'm not worried about that," Steph interrupted. "I'm here because you still don't have a Mrs. Claus, do you?"

"Ah." Teddy squirmed. The truth was that despite the viral success of *Duke the Halls* and its meta-fusion of wholesome holiday fun and sex-drenched lead actors, he and his new casting director still hadn't found someone to star opposite Kallum for *Santa, Baby*. Or more so, they hadn't found someone that their director, Gretchen Young, *also* liked. "We're working on that."

"Gretchen hasn't found the right fit," Astrid said, coming to his defense. "It's not because he hasn't been trying."

"I believe you," Steph said. "And that's exactly why I'm here. Because I have an idea for who our Mrs. Claus should be."

"I'm all ears," Teddy said, and then added, "Not really. I'm only two ears."

Everyone in the room groaned.

"I appreciate the sentiment," Steph said, with a sharklike gleam in her eye, "because this idea is a little unconventional . . ."

Chapter One

Winnie

My name is Winnie Elizabeth Baker, and except for the one time I let a friend pierce my belly button, I have done everything right.

When my parents wanted me to spend every weekend auditioning for local commercials, I did exactly as they asked.

When they wanted me to upend my life at age ten and move to Los Angeles to star in a wholesome family sitcom, I did that too.

I hid my narcolepsy from the industry so well the tabloids still have no idea.

I married my childhood sweetheart when I was eighteen years old, and I didn't even kiss him until the day of our wedding.

I was a model daughter, a model wife: sweet, friendly, well-behaved. An icon for young women with purity rings everywhere.

So then why was I sitting in a therapist's office, holding up my phone, and gesturing at what was on the screen like I was the glummest Vanna White of all time?

"And then Dominic Diamond dredges up this old picture, and now all anyone can talk about—again—is how Winnie Baker lives to make a scandal out of herself." I dropped my phone in my lap, not wanting to look at the picture anymore, even to prove a point. I'd already seen it thousands of times anyway: a seventeen-year-old me, passed out in a car in front of the Chateau Marmont after that year's Teen Choice Awards. My head was lolled back on the headrest, my normally fair cheeks were flushed red, and my mouth was hanging open.

Picture-me looked drunk, and even worse, picture-me looked *sloppy*. Promiscuous, even, according to my parents. In many ways, the picture had been when everything changed for me; it had been the beginning of the end.

"Dominic Diamond is a gutter-dwelling sociopath," Renata said calmly. As a therapist to actors, models, and—if the rumors could be believed—a certain California-dwelling prince, Renata was more than familiar with Dominic Diamond. He was a gossip blogger turned gossip influencer who spared no one in his nasty content updates, and I'd believe in a heartbeat that he was the subject of many sessions here in Renata's office. "He's not allowed to change how you see yourself."

"But this is bigger than Dominic," I said, swiping my screen to show the next image on the post. It was a screenshot of a headline from a major news site: "Former Child Star Hospitalized After Drug-Fueled Music Festival in Texas, Says Anonymous Source." And then another screenshot, this time from an article published yesterday: "Troubled Actress Once Famed for Promoting Family Values Now Officially Divorced." "Everyone thinks I'm off the rails now. That I just randomly got a divorce for no reason. Like a hypocrite. Like a—like a crazy person."

"I don't like that word," Renata put in mildly.

"People on social media like it," I mumbled. My ex-husband liked it too, even if *lazy* was his preferred insult of choice. *If you weren't so lazy, you'd have better work than Hope Channel movies. If you weren't so lazy, you'd be healthier, and if you were healthier, you'd be pregnant by now.* And so forth. *Lazy* was a word that cut twice: once, because I considered myself to be disciplined, diligent, in control at all times, and twice, because my narcolepsy meant there were times that discipline and control were beyond me no matter how hard I tried.

"I did everything right," I said finally, telling her what had been running through my mind all day. "I thought I was a good daughter, a good wife, a good actor. But it didn't matter, did it? Michael cheated on me anyway. My parents still sided with him. And the *one* time I did do something for myself, something that was supposed to be fun, I ended up puking my guts out in a Texas desert, two hundred miles from a real airport. I missed the shoot for my next project, and the Hope Channel recast me, and now the entire world thinks I'm irresponsible. And I don't have a job and I can't repay the Hope Channel the money I owe them and everything is gone and I blew it all up myself—and it wasn't even a regular music festival! It was UnFestival, which is an exclusive desert experience and so much more than a regular festival could ever be!"

I sucked in a breath after that surprise monologue, blinking back the burn behind my eyelids. I wanted to cry. But I'd been raised better than that; I'd learned better after fourteen years of marriage. Being out of control wasn't welcome in my life, and had never been.

"You can cry if you'd like," Renata said, almost as if she knew what I was thinking, but before I could respond, a tiny alarm beeped from her watch.

Our session was up.

She sighed at her wrist as she silenced the alarm. "Next time, I'm going to remind you earlier that there's no need to hide your feelings here. But for now, I want you to remember what you told me during our second session, after I'd asked you to come up with a goal for our time together. Can you think of it?"

"Yes," I said, eager to be a good therapy student. "My entire life, everyone else has defined Winnie Baker for me, but now, I want to define Winnie Baker for myself. I want to be a new Winnie."

Renata nodded. "Maybe think about what that means in conjunction with what people are saying online right now, hmm? And what we can and can't control?"

"Okay," I said. With great confidence, because a new Winnie was not going to care about what people said online. Just like how a new Winnie was never, ever going to make the old Winnie's mistakes.

And Old Winnie had made quite a few, indeed.

COMING OUT OF Renata's building always felt like coming out of a womb, and I had to blink in the bright California sunshine for a few minutes until I could see again. And that was *with* my sunglasses on. In January.

"Finally," a sharp voice said next to me, and I nearly jumped out of my skin.

But when I turned to issue a panicked "no comment," it wasn't a paparazzo at all, but a tall woman wearing a knotted trench coat and a smile that was somehow bossy and reassuring at the same time.

"I've been waiting here for five minutes," the woman said, making *five minutes* sound like *twelve hours*. She stuck out a manicured hand, which I took. She had a quick, hard handshake. Michael would have hated it.

It made me like her immediately.

"Steph D'Arezzo, talent manager," she said briskly. "Nice to meet you."

Steph. Steph. The name swam hazily to the surface of my memories. "You're Nolan Shaw's manager," I said. Before I got sick at UnFestival and had to be recast, the former bad boy of pop Nolan Shaw was going to be my costar in *Duke the Halls*. I'd been nervous about working with him when I'd signed on—even after his years out of the spotlight, I couldn't picture him as anything other than the beanie-wearing boy-Jezebel I'd known as a teenager—but my distrust had been misplaced. He'd been fiercely supportive of his girlfriend, Bee Hobbes, when she'd been exposed as an adult content creator, and he'd also been nothing but a consummate professional since then, even helming a reboot of the reality show that had once made his career, *Band Camp*.

"That's right," Steph said. "Do you know how I made my name in this business, Winnie?"

I shook my head. Family and faith-based content was a whole other entertainment world, and where all of my career had taken place. I only had the faintest handle on the goings-on of the industry at large.

"I spin straw into gold. I take washed-up, scandal-ridden frogs and I turn them back into princes. Et cetera. Do you see where I'm going with this?"

"You rehabilitate celebrity reputations," I guessed.

"That's right. I do fixer-uppers exclusively, but if that fixer can't be uppered, I move on, because sometimes teamwork does *not* make the dream work, especially if half the team is a goddamn mess." Steph reached for her purse, stopped. Huffed at herself. I got the distinct vibe she was a former smoker. "But it turns out," she continued, "that sometimes a little scandal is good for business. I thought Nolan Shaw falling in love with Bianca von Honey was the end of his comeback, but it turbocharged his career instead. If

I'd had a hundred years and even more assistants grabbing me cold brews, I still couldn't have masterminded the boost he got from living his cute, messy life the way he did last year. You see what I'm saying?"

I didn't see. All I'd gotten for my brushes with scandal were broken contracts and estranged parents. And Dominic Diamond posts.

Steph seemed to know what I was thinking, because she crossed her arms and regarded me with an arched eyebrow. "They screwed you over pretty good, huh?"

"I—"

"Let me guess," she went on. "That Michael guy cheated on you, and you wanted to keep it private, and then he rewarded you by spinning the story to make it sound like you were the bad one. I'm guessing he was behind the leak last year about your hospital stay being for drugs instead of exhaustion?"

I flushed. That was exactly what had happened.

"'Winnie Baker's Fall from Grace,'" Steph said as if quoting a headline only she could see. "It's a good story. Because saints love to hate sinners, and sinners love knowing that the saints are all se-cretly sinning too. Everyone clicks that headline. Everyone."

"You don't have to tell me that," I said as politely as I could.

Steph nodded. "You're right. I don't." She leaned forward, a glint coming into her eye. "Doesn't it piss you off that he got to keep ev-erything? The good reputation, the gigs, the moral high ground?"

"Of course it does," I said. Breathed. "All I wanted was to move on. But he wouldn't let me."

"Because he's a chode and chodes think small, Winnie." Steph reached into her purse and pulled out a card. Her business card.

I took it, not sure what was happening.

"Have you heard of Hope After Dark?" she asked, snapping her purse shut.

"Um, yes," I said. Everyone had—the announcement that the Hope Channel was veering into racy content had been a bombshell no one had missed.

"The lead actor is my client. Kallum Lieberman, one of Nolan Shaw's former bandmates. I believe you two have met before?"

Met. Memories of that fateful Teen Choice Awards flashed through my mind: Blue eyes, a surfboard falling onto my foot. Hobbling around the after-party with my toes throbbing inside my kitten heel, narcolepsy clawing at my brain. Escaping the party at the Chateau Marmont to hide in the car, where I'd curled up on the seat and let drowsiness take me under.

And then the picture. The infamous picture. Taken by none other than Kallum Lieberman and posted to his MySpace that very night.

"Yes, we've met," I finally answered.

A nod. "Well, I think you'd do great opposite him in the first Hope After Dark movie."

For a moment, I thought I didn't hear her correctly. That I was mistaken. Then she gave my confusion a sharp smile. "Think about it. You have a Hope Channel contract you've never fulfilled, right? One in the process of being canceled because you broke their morality clause while you were at UnFestival?"

Ugh. "Yes."

"What if you didn't have to pay back the money you'd gotten from signing the contract? What if you could still satisfy that contract with a different Hope property?"

"I've already tried," I said. "Before my agent dumped me. They said with my reputation, they couldn't cast me in anyth—"

Steph interrupted me. "That was then, Winnie. This is now. After *Duke the Halls* and the way its stars have blown up after the Bianca von Honey scandal, Hope is seeing things in a brand-new light. And who better to head up their spicy new start than their fallen angel?"

"It would never work," I said, still utterly bewildered. "I can barely believe they're doing Hope After Dark as it is, but to work with *me* again? They'd never go for it."

"Oh, they already have," Steph said smugly. "And they loved the idea so much they begged me to get you to sign on, pronto. Which means the role is yours if you want it. A salvaged contract, a salvaged bank account, and who knows? Maybe a whole new direction for you."

"I can't be in a sexy movie," I murmured as I looked back down at her business card. The idea was ludicrous. I'd never even seen a raunchy movie. I didn't own a single sex toy, I'd never even . . . done things to myself, and I was pretty sure the only time I'd ever had an orgasm was while I was asleep and dreaming raunchy dreams that never seemed to star Michael. On the night my divorce was finalized, I'd drunk half a bottle of wine and Googled the word *pornography* for the first time in my entire life . . . and then I was so embarrassed by myself that I'd slammed my laptop shut and binged TikToks about spooky lakes instead.

And the thing was that I *wanted* to get rid of these walls in my mind; I wanted to watch porn and sexy movies and be the kind of person who could make dirty jokes. The kind of actor who could star in a Hope After Dark movie. But I wasn't. I was Winnie Baker and I was something much worse than a prude: I was a former prude who had no idea how to un-prude herself.

"Just think about it," Steph said. She patted my shoulder and strode off, trench coat flapping just above her high heels as she walked. I was still holding her card like it was a live grenade, half-tempted to lay it on the curving cobblestone path that led to Renata's tucked-away building and walk away. Forget this conversation ever happened.

But I didn't do any of that. I put the card in my pocket, squared my shoulders, and went home.

HOME WAS NOT the house I'd lived in for over a decade, nor was it my parents' house. The former was Michael's—bought for him as a wedding present by his mom and dad, who ran a faith-based media empire and had more money than every megachurch in Texas twice over—and the latter I was tacitly no longer welcome in. So I was currently bunking in an old friend's pool house. She also happened to be the only friend I had left.

I stopped by her back door on my way back to the pool house and saw her sitting at the kitchen island with her chef-made meal and a glass of something clear, which I knew wouldn't be water. Sure enough, when I slid open the door and stepped inside her minimalist kitchen, I saw a half-empty bottle of Grey Goose on the counter.

"Winnie!" Addison exclaimed, spinning on her stool and padding over to me in her bare feet. They were pale—she was due for a spray tan soon. "I had the chef make dinner for you too tonight."

"Thanks, Addy," I said, giving her a big hug. Actor, singer, and self-identified girl boss Addison Hayes had been on another show—a semiserious drama about a widowed pastor and his family—when we were both teenagers, and we'd been put together as manufactured best friends by our management teams. We had matching careers, matching blond hair, matching purity rings. I even did guest vocals on her first album, which had been the launching pad for her wildly successful crossover music career.

We'd drifted apart after the Chateau Marmont incident—all my time and energy was sucked into repairing my image after that—but had reconnected a few years ago, when we'd starred in a Hope Channel movie as long-lost sisters who fell in love with a pair of long-lost brothers. She'd been the only one to stay in touch through the divorce, much less to offer any help, and while we kept it hidden that I was living here so she wouldn't be tainted by association, she'd still welcomed me with open arms and even more open vodka bottles. I'd be grateful for that welcome until the day I died.

"How was the shrink?" Addison asked, sitting back down and picking up her fork to eat her tiny square of white fish.

I found a plate tented with foil on the counter and got myself a fork. "Fine. I complained about Dominic Diamond."

"He's a fuckface," Addison said. "Do you wanna vodka about it?"

Addison's willingness to (1) curse, (2) drink, and (3) talk about sex like we didn't grow up having accountability partners to make sure we weren't thinking about genitals *ever at all* had been really strange at first. And then it had become incredibly freeing, because I realized all the things I used to worry would make me a bad person . . . wouldn't? Or wouldn't necessarily? Because Addison was a lot of things, but she was also kind and loyal and a good listener, and she opened her home to me when I had no other place to go . . . and maybe when it came down to it, being a kind person was more important than having an empty swear jar.

"I might vodka about it later," I said. "But something else interesting did happen, actually . . ."

After I finished telling her about Steph and the Hope After Dark offer, Addison was staring at me, her perfectly contoured face gone ashen, like I'd just told her I'd picked up a hitchhiker off the road and that he was going to live in her backyard sauna now.

"And you immediately told her no, right?" asked Addison. "I mean, what the fuck? *The* Winnie Baker in a TV-MA movie? You have a brand!"

"Addy," I said, gently, tiredly, because I had to keep explaining this to people. "The brand is dead. There is no more *the* Winnie Baker. There is only Winnie Baker who got strung out at Un-Festival."

Addison sniffed in my defense. "Anyone should be so lucky. That's an exclusive desert experience."

"This is what I keep trying to tell people!"

"But baby girl," my old friend said, suddenly serious. "No brand is dead while you're still alive and pretty. You know what our circle loves more than anything? A good redemption story. And you have all your cards left to play when it comes to one. Make a big deal about how you've stopped backsliding and about how you're trying to work things out with Michael, because your heart has been changed. And then the jobs will come back, the money will come back. Hell, maybe even Michael will come back."

"But I don't *want* Michael back," I protested.

"Duh," Addison said, flipping her shining, camera-ready waves over her shoulder. She'd been on QVC every day this week selling leggings for her lifestyle brand, Wishes of Addison, and she hadn't messy-bun-ified her TV hair yet today. "But think of the optics, Winnie! Couple reunited! Love conquers all! You'll feed the narrative with a *People* story and joint public appearances at our church, and everyone will eat it up."

I made a face, and she gave me a look like I was being deliberately childish.

"I'm not saying *love* him again. Shit, I'm not even saying *only be with him*. Just get back together for publicity's sake and then secretly see other people. Famous couples do it all the time."

"You don't do that," I pointed out. Addison was a rare single woman in our sphere.

"That's because I have some mileage left on the whole 'living my calling' angle," she said, picking up her fork and gesturing with it like there was an invisible PowerPoint presentation she was teaching from. "I predict that in two years, Wishes of Addison will be anchored enough that I can transition into the 'I've just found the love of my life' phase of my career, and then by thirty-six, I'll start the baby phase. After that, Wishes of Addison will launch its new arm, Baby Wishes, and I'll sell the company and take a job as the chief creative officer. And then? Hotels." She nodded at her fork and then started digging at her fish again.

"You want to own hotels one day?"

"Fuck yes," Addison said through a bite of swordfish. "Do you know how much good I could do for the world as a hotel owner? First item of business: every hotel room bathroom has a proper, working fan. Every single one. And a bidet! Second item of business—"

"Is this really my only option?" I cut in, looking down at my own plate of fish. I still hadn't sat down yet. "Get back together with Michael unless I want to secretly live in your pool house forever?"

"Girl, no," Addison said. Now the fork was pointed at me. "I'm not telling you to be Michael's doormat. I'm just saying that you should *pretend* to be in public. And then do whatever you want in private. Play the game, but still have fun."

"Is that what you do, Addy?" I asked. For all the time we spent together, I didn't actually know what her romantic life was like. Given how open she was with me about everything else, it was a little strange that I didn't know anything more than that she sometimes slipped away at night.

The fork sank down a little, and Addison's gaze dropped with it. "I do my best," she said, but for the first time since I'd walked into her kitchen, she sounded a little uncertain.

And it struck me how ridiculous it all was. Here we were, thirty-two years old, household names, and still feeling like our entire lives had to be played by a set of rules that was handed to us when we were too young to choose for ourselves. And I was abruptly sick of it.

Not just *tired* of it and not just *sad* about it. But sick of it. Fevered, flushed, shaking. My body readying its defenses to fight off the past that corralled me, the bleak future that beckoned.

I want to define Winnie Baker for myself. That's what I'd told Renata today. Either I meant that or I didn't. And if I was going to mean it, then I needed to *mean* it.

I set down my fork. "Fuck it," I said and pulled Steph's card out of my pocket.

Addison's eyes went as round as Wishes of Addison tealights (only $12.99 at Target and on wishesofaddison.com) as she watched me reach for my phone.

"What are you doing?" she whispered.

"What has playing the game gotten me, Addy? A cheating husband, a public divorce, and therapy bills that I can barely pay. If the world thinks I'm a fallen angel," I said, dialing Steph's number, "then at the very least I want to choose my own wings."

A Jingle Bell Mingle

**From #1 *New York Times* bestselling author Julie Murphy
and *USA Today* bestselling author Sierra Simone, who gave us
A Merry Little Meet Cute, comes an extra spicy new holiday
rom-com—'tis the season for second chances!**

What happens when there's no room at the inn and you and
your potentially demonic cat become roommates with your grumpy
one-night stand?

Part-time adult film actress/one-time adult film director/makeup
artist Sunny Palmer has accidentally sold her very first screenplay
to the Hope Channel. That was six months ago. Fast forward to a
looming deadline: an uninspired Sunny has returned to the source
of her inspiration in Christmas Notch, Vermont, to immerse herself in the local Christmas miracle on which her fever dream of a
movie pitch was based.

Isaac Kelly, former boy band heartthrob and the saddest boy
in the music biz, is the latest owner of the town's historic mansion. After his years of heartbreak following his young wife's death,
Isaac's record label is done waiting for new music. What better
place to attempt his first holiday album than a snow-covered mansion where he can become a hermit in peace?

But after their best friends' wedding leads to them waking up
together in a freezing motel room with questionable wiring and a
broken shower, Isaac takes a chance and asks Sunny to stay with
him at his home. Surely the place is big enough that he'll hardly see
her or her unhinged cat. But when the two discover they're both

creatively blocked, they make a handshake deal: Isaac will help Sunny hunt down the truth behind the local lore, and Sunny will find Isaac a new muse.

And with these two opposites under one roof, there's no way this jingle bell mingle could go off script . . . right?

Prologue
Teddy Ray Fletcher

*W*hat's up, tampon strings?"

Protests erupted around Teddy Ray Fletcher as a curvy brides-maid appeared at the end of a pew, her inky black hair twisted into an elegant updo and her bright pink dress setting off the colorful tattoos on her light olive shoulders.

"Sunny Palmer, we're in a *church*—"

"I think that's Nolan's grandmother behind you—"

"And I," declared Jack Hart, former porn star, living Ken doll, and the only wedding guest to have brought a dog to the ceremony, "am a body-safe menstrual cup, at the very least."

Sunny narrowed her dark brown eyes, and Teddy sensed another outbreak of the long-standing war between the two, a war begun when Sunny took Jack's ex-stepmother home from his wedding six years back. Rumor had it that the feud had been interrupted only once, for a threesome starring the heartbroken pop idol Isaac Kelly, but Teddy had long ago stopped trusting Uncle Ray-Ray's rumor mill. Much as he loved his quirky little alliance of sexpots, misfits, and flexible adventurers with even more flexible attitudes toward public decency laws, the people employed (or employed-adjacent) by Teddy's porn production studio were prone to . . .

Well, there was no nice way of saying it. They were dramatic as fuck.

Besides, the notoriously broody Isaac Kelly and the plucky Sunny together? Teddy had seen a lot of things in his time, but that beggared belief.

"Is the trolley back yet?" Teddy asked, hoping to forestall yet another Sunny and Jack squabble. "We're starving." He had more important things to worry about than babysitting hungry porn stars. Like finding a way to propose to the pantsuited woman next to him, who was currently craning her neck to scan the emptying chapel. Even though they were here for the wedding of Bee Hobbes and Nolan Shaw—the adult content creator and the disgraced boy band member who'd met, fallen in love, and caused a scandal during the filming of a wholesome Christmas movie—the woman next to Teddy was still very much on the clock.

Steph D'Arezzo, talent manager, did not sleep on a chance to make money.

At least the distraction worked. Sunny huffed out a sigh. "Ronald is a slow driver."

"Ronald is a *careful* driver, and a goddamned pillar of this community," Jack countered. His decrepit dog—a half-blind critter with fur the color of old milk—growled weakly in agreement.

Teddy was inclined to believe Sunny in this, having been on a few of Ronald's trolley drives since he started side-hustling cheesy holiday movies here in Christmas Notch, Vermont. But before Sunny had a chance to retort, Teddy's son, Angel, appeared behind her with a panicked look on his face.

"The strippers," he said, breathing hard. "They're going to beat us to the trolley."

The whole pew stood at once in a clamor, shoving and grumping at one another to get out. Bee and Nolan's wedding had been beautiful, moving, stunningly designed, but the people were ready for food. And there'd been whispers of a nacho bar.

"Vixen will destroy those nachos before anyone else has a chance to eat them," Jack warned, and for once, everyone was in agreement with Jack Hart. They had to get to the trolley before the strippers.

Because Teddy was a gentleman, he offered his arm to Steph, who took it, but only so she could twist around and look one last time at the sanctuary while he guided them safely down the aisle to the door.

"I don't see him," she said anxiously.

"Who?"

"Isaac Kelly! I need to talk to him before he disappears again!"

Steph was desperate to collect the last jewel of the boy band INK for her talent management crown. She'd already successfully restarted Nolan Shaw's career and turned Kallum Lieberman into America's premier dad bod thirst trap.

And the last boy bander standing was Isaac, the heartthrob with a broken heart, the handsome recluse who'd been unable to write, sing, or record since his pop star wife died four years ago.

Of course, the problem with coaxing a recluse into becoming your client was that you had to *talk* to the recluse first, and Isaac Kelly was a hard person to talk to, even after he'd left his gated Malibu home for a Gilded Age mansion here in Christmas Notch. This wedding was the first time anyone had seen him in public for a very long time (a certain threesome two years ago notwithstanding).

"He's one of the groomsmen. I'm sure he's with Nolan and Kallum taking pictures wherever Sunny just disappeared to," Teddy soothed.

"But what if he doesn't come to the reception?" Steph asked.

"He'll be there," Teddy said confidently. "Even former teen idols wouldn't say no to a free nacho bar. Oh shit, I think the strippers are going to make it outside before we do."

Steph narrowed her eyes at the gaggle of bouncy-haired women in front of them, all tottering on inadvisably high heels and wearing the kind of minidresses that made it hard to move your legs.

"Not if we have anything to say about it," Steph said with grim pleasure, and then like a New York–honed knife through butter, she expertly cut through the crowd, dragging Teddy behind her.

It was Teddy's number one fantasy, being dragged down the aisle by Steph D'Arezzo, and so what if it was in the wrong direction? His heart was still a balloon floating in his chest by the time they made it to the trolley.

THE ICE-SKATING RINK was strung with lights and crowded with wedding guests when they arrived. The brick building that housed the skate rental counter and snack bar had its sliding glass doors flung open; inside were tables laden with food, drinks, and one extravagantly pink cake. Heat lamps edged along the outside of the rink itself, so anyone who didn't want to skate still had a reasonable chance of staying warm in the late December night. A mix of holiday music, old INK songs, and cheesy aughts hits played into the night while wedding guests wobbled around the rink.

Next to Teddy, his son gave a primal noise of relief. "I see the nachos," he whispered.

And that was all it took. Everyone who came on the trolley with them—including a clutch of boisterous triplets who were somehow related to Kallum Lieberman—began streaming toward the brick building and its promise of cheese.

"Surely the bridal party has to be done with pictures by now," Steph said as she allowed Teddy to tug her to the Nacho Promised Land. All of the Christmas Notch extended family were lining up to get a plate: Gretchen Young, who'd directed the movie that had brought Bee and Nolan together, and her screenwriter girlfriend, Pearl Purkiss; Isaac Kelly's former bodyguard, Krysta, and her wife, Addison; Nolan's mother and sister and grandparents; and Bee's moms, both beaming and showing off their matching MOTHER OF THE BRIDE satin jackets.

"If the parents are already here, the bridal party won't be long behind," Teddy said with the authority of having been behind the scenes of exactly one wedding in his life. A wedding for a marriage that had ended with a pity-hug outside of a lawyer's office and his then teenagers taking him out for ice cream like he'd been a kid who'd just lost a baseball game.

But damn if he wasn't ready to do this nonsense all over again.

By the time Steph and Teddy had loaded up their nachos, the trolley had arrived with a fresh batch of wedding guests—the strippers and the wedding party. Teddy watched as Kallum Lieberman helped his wife, Winnie, out of the trolley and they walked over to Kallum's mom, who was waiting with their daughter, Grace. Despite the fact that Grace still had the toddler version of new car smell, Kallum had announced at the combined bachelor and bachelorette party two nights ago that Winnie was pregnant again. And indeed, when Kallum pointed across the ice-skating rink to the nacho bar with excitement scrawled across his bearded features, Winnie went a delicate shade of green and vigorously shook her head.

Behind them, Isaac Kelly stepped off the trolley, the stiff Vermont breeze ruffling the loose pink bow tie around his neck. With his suntanned skin, shoulder-length blond hair, and square jaw, he looked like a living California stereotype . . . but there was a sadness clinging to him that no amount of sunshine and surf could brighten. It was in the haunted shape of his mouth and the indifferent way his eyes slid across the scene, as if nothing and no one could possibly make him smile.

Steph spotted him immediately.

"*Gotcha*," she drawled in that carnivorous voice that never failed to make Teddy's dick jolt. It was the voice of a hunter; it was like red fingernails dragging across his chest. It didn't matter if she was talking business or climbing onto him as he sat in the passenger seat of her Mercedes S-Class—that voice made him hot, and it maybe made him a little afraid too, which got him hotter.

What could he say? Some men liked whips and chains; he liked pantsuits and *I just signed a contract so big it'll make you piss yourself* smiles.

"Hold these," Steph said, shoving her nachos into Teddy's hand. She kissed his cheek, quick and hard enough to leave her lipstick above his scruff. "Wish me luck."

"You don't need it," he said honestly, and the most beautiful woman in the world threw him a smirk before adjusting her trench coat and then striding off. Teddy didn't expect her back soon; the hunt took as long as it took. Like any good predator, she'd stalk her prey, wait until he was separated from the pack, and then she'd pounce. Steph D'Arezzo got what she wanted.

But—Teddy sighed forlornly down at the two baskets of nachos he was holding—did she want *him*?

They'd all but moved in together, most of his Hawaiian shirts and all of his flip-flops in her closet next to her Stella McCartney blazers and the sheer things from Anya Lust that Teddy loved so very, very much. They brushed their teeth together, ate way-too-late dinners together, fell asleep after a single episode of an overhyped drama together. They spent long Sunday mornings with black coffee and honest reflections about marriages and divorces, about having adult children and how scary it was to love brilliant people messily making their way in the world.

And when Teddy woke up in the morning, he found that Steph had wrapped her arms around his chest and tangled her legs in his, like she was afraid he'd leave her while she slept.

He knew that there was no one else for him, that there was no going back. At some point between all the stolen trysts in Christmas Notch and Mercedes-sexings and Sunday mornings where sunlight glinted off Steph's cobalt eyes as she lowered wall after wall, Teddy had fallen harder than a shoddily mounted sex swing.

And like all the shoddily mounted sex swings he'd dealt with over the past twenty-odd years, there was no fixing it. There was only dealing with the bruising reality of it all.

He was a lost cause for Steph D'Arezzo.

After a few minutes of marinating in his feelings, Teddy made his way to the wall separating the actual rink from the rink-adjacent spaces and balanced the nachos on the ledge. A clear plastic dome on a mat had been set in the middle to make a dance floor of sorts, and people were already dancing inside while skaters circled around them. Kallum's triplet nephews—newly into ice hockey, or so he'd heard—were carving a path of chaos through the wedding guests, and his own kids were out there: Astrid, his daughter, medusa piercing flashing and natural curls bouncing, and then Angel laughing beside her.

Teddy's chest squeezed to watch them, the two best people in his life, happy and healthy and full of the energy that only chasing dreams could give them. He might not have been the most impressive father, but somehow he'd wound up with the most impressive kids, and because of that he'd never stop feeling like the luckiest bastard alive.

Someone came up next to him and braced their arms on the ledge. They had their phone out.

Teddy looked over to see the pink bridesmaid dress, dark hair, and trademark eyebrows of Sunny Palmer.

"No nachos?" Teddy asked and watched her thumbs fly over the screen of her phone.

"Yes nachos. I've already nacho-ed. I'm post-nacho." She looked over at his two baskets of chips and cheese and then up to his face. "Double-fisting?"

"Steph's on the client prowl," Teddy explained. "Isaac Kelly."

Dark slashes of red appeared on Sunny's cheeks. "Oh," she said. "Neat." She said *neat* the way most people would say *I think my clothes just caught on fire, please help.*

Hmm. Maybe there was something to that threesome rumor after all.

Astrid and Angel skated by—competently, if not without a wobble or two—and Angel tugged at Sunny's cape as he passed. His kids had always been fond of Sunny, but Angel and Sunny had grown even closer since she'd played a role in his happily ever after with Teddy's former costume designer Luca. (A happily ever after via a *Pretty Woman* porn remake and an accident involving a rosebush, no less.) Sunny was getting something of a reputation as a matchmaker, or at least as a cupid of romantic chaos.

Which gave Teddy a really, really smart idea just then.

"Tell me how to propose to Steph," he said, turning to face her.

Her eyes were back on her phone, and she was swiping on a hookup app. The blush lingered on her cheeks.

When she didn't answer, Teddy decided she needed more information. "It's been nearly a year that we've been officially together, and three years since we started being an unofficial *something*, and I love her, and I'm going to love her forever, and *she* loves *me*, and I think we're a once-in-a-lifetime fit, you know? Soul mates."

"Oh, I love that," Sunny said, glancing up from her phone.

"And I don't think anyone has to get married to their soul mate, necessarily."

"I agree."

"And I don't even know if I believe in marriage anymore, anyway. But I believe in her and I believe in us, and goddammit, I want the whole thing, even if it is bullshit, even if it's the wrong thing to want. I know it's our second time around, I know we're probably too old and too jaded, but I don't want to be jaded when it comes to this. I want to be fresh and full of hope and give her my whole life."

Teddy stopped, suddenly out of breath. He didn't usually say so many words at once.

Sunny's finger was still hovering over her phone screen as she regarded him. "You going to wear that suit when you propose?"

Teddy looked down at his suit, his only suit. He'd worn it to weddings, to the AVN Awards, and to traffic court. He thought it was pretty spiffy—it was from Men's Wearhouse and it hadn't even been on sale when he bought it. "Well, yeah. Why?"

Her face softened. "No reason. And you know what, Teddy, I think you should just tell her everything you told me. Steph is a direct woman, and she won't want a grand gesture or some over-the-top surprise. She'll want you to come to her with a deal, with your best offer, and then she'll want to negotiate the hell out of it. Give her that, and I think she'll be all in."

Teddy's heart was a balloon again. "You're right. You're so smart. And so romantically wise. No wonder the Hope Channel hired you to write a Hopeflix movie for them."

"Ugh, don't remind me," Sunny said, going back to her phone. "I'm blocked as hell."

"You could always direct more films for me at Uncle Ray-Ray's," offered Teddy.

"Don't think I won't take you up on it." *Swipe. Swipe.*

Teddy put his arm on Sunny's shoulder. Instead of a coat, she'd opted for a fake fur cape in jet black. The breeze had tugged a few tendrils of hair free to flutter around her high-cheekboned face. With the hot pink dress, the fur, and the tattoos peeking out around the stole, she was an alt-girl stunner. One of the reasons he'd hired her years ago.

(The other reason being that she had her own car.)

"Now let me give you some advice," he said in a fatherly tone. "This is Christmas Notch, Vermont, population twenty-five hundred. You can't swipe forever without running out of lumberjacks and lumberjanes."

She sighed. Nodded.

"Whoever you pick will be blown away by you," he told her honestly. "You're pretty and smart and a literal porn star. Just accept that Christmas Notch has slim pickings and embrace this for the messy, bridesmaid-dress-wearing hookup it will be."

"Thank you for the hookup pep talk, porn dad," she said with a smile, and then briefly rested her head on his shoulder. "Also you have a jalapeño in your mustache."

Teddy was trying to comb it free when a cheer broke out around the rink. Bee and Nolan had arrived, with a triumphant Luca in tow. Bee glittered like an ice princess in her custom Luca-designed dress, with soft brown waves around her shoulders, her lips a pale pink, and her new septum piercing glinting with tiny diamonds—a collective wedding gift from the Uncle Ray-Ray's gang. Nolan's tousled hair hung over his forehead, and his crooked grin was fixed permanently to his face as he stared with unabashed adoration at his new wife.

Just past them, Teddy could make out the person who would hopefully be his wife chatting animatedly with Gretchen and Pearl, the directing and screenwriting power couple who were currently remaking the Hope Channel's pristine image into something edgy and fresh. Next to them, Isaac Kelly was on his phone, his brow creased and his lower lip tucked between his teeth.

It looked like he was swiping too.

Chapter One

Sunny

I held a perfectly greasy cheeseburger in one hand and my cell phone in the other. "Oh my God," I said with a moan. "This is the best thing I've ever put in my mouth."

"And that's saying a lot coming from you." Luca took a bite of his burger and nodded furiously. With his mouth full, he added: "All weddings should have a second dinner."

"It's like a hobbit wedding, but with shoes."

He lifted his burger in agreement.

Bee and Nolan's reception had been chef's-kiss perfection. They'd rented a clear plastic dome tent and had set it on a huge mat in the middle of the Christmas Notch ice-skating rink. Some guests gyrated on the dance floor while others took laps around the ice.

It was really fucking charming, to be honest. I didn't test my fate on the ice though. I was a Southern California girl through and through, and the only ice I was interested in was the kind that chilled my beverages. Especially the little pebble kind from Sonic that Bee had introduced me to. How was it so incredibly superior?

Luca dabbed delicately at the corner of his mouth as though he weren't absolutely housing his concession-stand burger, which had been brought in as part of a heap of burgers on a sterling serving tray like my own personal fifth-grade fantasy. "I saw you swiping on your phone . . . Is Sunny Palmer on the prowl tonight? Missing Jack's stepmom?"

"That was one time," I reminded him. "One glorious time." It truly had been glorious. Jack had only just begun to forgive me for boning his stepmom, but I could never be sorry for the good time I showed Rebecca.

Bee plopped down beside me and her skirt poofed up so that it rivaled her boobs for attention. "We have a situation," she said.

I dropped the burger and stuffed the phone into my bra. "What is it?" I asked. "Paparazzi? Handsy drunk uncle? Is Winnie double-pregnant somehow?"

With terror in her eyes, my best friend said the four words she'd been dreading since her first wedding-dress fitting. "I have to pee."

I punched my fist into my palm like I was ready to step into a wrestling ring for this girl—and I would. "We're going to smash this," I said just as Luca said, "You're sure you can't hold it?"

"Luca," I said, "there are serious medical complications caused by holding it." I stood and held a hand out for Bee as I pulled her to her feet. "We need Bee's puss in full working order for her upcoming honeymoon."

Luca threw his napkin to the table with a slight bit of outrage. "I don't trust you two to handle this delicate matter on your own."

Of course, Luca loved Bee. In his own way. But the dress he'd designed for her walk down the aisle was truly his pride and joy. And if he had to choose Bee or the dress, I couldn't be sure which way he'd sway. Plus he'd once seen her drunkenly pee on one of my ex's mailboxes, and her aim hadn't been great.

The thing about holding your wedding at an ice-skating rink is that the bathrooms are just frigid little concrete buildings where nuts and nipples shrivel and the floor is constantly damp.

With all six of our hands full of tulle, we held Bee's dress up from the ground before even walking inside.

"Guys, I really need us to hustle here," Bee said with a whimper.

"This is an act of precision," Luca told her as we backed into the handicap stall. "This garment was not designed to absorb urine. I told you to wear an incontinence diaper."

"Yeah, that didn't really feel very sexy," she said.

"Okay," I said as we approached the porcelain throne. "Here's our game plan. Luca and Bee, you two hold up the layers. I'm going in."

"I trust you," Bee said as I dropped into a squat and dove under her dress in search of underwear.

"For what it's worth," I said, "diapers can be very comfortable."

"Do I want to know what experience you have with diapers?" Luca asked.

"Just believe me when I say she knows what she's talking about," Bee told him.

"I've got the panties," I said as I tugged down on the light blue lacy boyshorts I'd bought Bee to wear today. "The dress is in the clear. You can sit—or squat. Whatever you prefer."

I stood up to help with the skirt, and Bee eased down with a sigh as she began to let go and let God.

In my bra, my phone vibrated as it chirped with my Spark app notification.

"I know what that sound means," Luca said. "You've got a match."

Bee let out a squeal. "No one goes home alone from my wedding, baby!"

THE RECEPTION WENT on for another hour or so. I even got Teddy out on the dance floor, and he surprised everyone by knowing a popular dance from TikTok, even though it was a few years too late. That man was full of secrets, and I would fight to the death for that fact to be on his headstone one day.

The remaining guests who had made it to the very last dance lined the sidewalk outside the skating rink as we waited for Bee and Nolan to take off to the mansion on their getaway trolley.

"Here they come!" one of the strippers—Dancer, maybe—whispered beside me.

On my other side, Jack Hart wore Miss Crumpets in a baby sling where she was peacefully snoozing as we all held our sparklers up, and the wedding planner—an older woman who ran a ship so tight it almost turned me on—barked at us to keep our arms straight.

"Mommy?" I called after her as she passed us by.

"There's something frightening about that woman," Jack said.

"I know." I nodded as I watched her bully Tall Ron into submission so that he didn't accidentally block the photographer's shot. "I like it."

And then suddenly Bee and Nolan were walking hand in hand down the tunnel made by their loved ones. Their eyes glistened, and as they passed us by, Bee reached out a hand for me, but it was too fast for a hug or a kiss on the cheek.

An unexpected sadness settled in my chest, just holding me down for a moment before it disappeared. I was so happy for Bee, and nothing about her being with Nolan or getting married, or someday even having babies, made me feel distant from her. But I couldn't ignore this feeling that she'd found something that I might never find.

The moment was gone as Luca called, "Wait for me!" He boarded the trolley behind them, because of course he didn't trust Nolan to properly undress Bee with his creation intact.

I rechecked the Spark notification on my phone and I did indeed have only one match in all of Christmas Notch. His name was Todd and the only pictures on his profile were of landscapes and a huge Saint Bernard. There were worse red flags, right? Though it did go against the community guidelines not to show your face in your profile.

I'll be at the Dirty Snowball if you want to meet up.

He wanted to meet in public! How bad could he be? Serial killers didn't meet in public.

Well, I guess they did sometimes for the whole luring part of the kill. But still, I'd be surrounded by wedding guests and Christmas Notch locals; this was a safe space.

After a quick walk down the street, I reached into my dress to reposition my boobs before walking into the bar tits first.

Okay, landscapes-and-giant-dog man, where are you?

I scanned the room for horny loners on their phones, but it was all wedding guests without shoes and loosened neckties.

Then there was Isaac, sitting by himself at the bar. He wasn't actually by himself. He was in the outer orbit of Kallum and Winnie and a few others who'd also wound up at the local dive. But he was by himself, because no matter where he was or who he was with, Isaac Kelly was always alone.

God, his sad-boy energy really gave me a lady boner.

And I'd been to the Isaac sad-boy promised land.

With Jack Hart, which had not been ideal. But I couldn't say no to a sad-boy threesome in the moment. Isaac was so sad! And horny! And okay, Jack was pretty great in bed too. So I did the thing. I boned the fuck out of him, and oh my God, did he give it right back.

But then he passed the hell out while Jack and I were cleaning up—separately, because he was still my sworn frenemy. And then it got awkward, and when things get awkward, I get gone.

So this wedding weekend was the first time I'd laid physical eyes on Isaac since that fateful night.

As I was still searching, Isaac peered over his shoulder, like he was hiding, but also scoping, and all I could see were those dark blue eyes gazing over his arm. Then my stomach dropped to the damn floor as he flashed me his phone, showing landscapes and a huge-ass Saint Bernard.

I stormed over to him and said, "Well, well, if it isn't sad Isaac."

"I'm not *only* sad," he said defensively.

I took a sip of his umbrella-studded piña colada and held up my phone. "You don't even own a dog!"

"It's aspirational," he said with a shrug as he pulled out the barstool beside him and slid his drink back, taking a sip after me. I watched his Grammy-winning mouth as he put the straw back between his lips. There was a faint sheen of wet on his lower lip that I knew would taste amazing when we kissed. I meant *if*! If we kissed!

I half climbed the stool and perched with my feet dangling. Show me a plus-size woman who can sit comfortably on a barstool. I must learn her ways, because there is nothing more unsexy than me trying to fidget my way onto this thing like a toddler.

"You catfished me," I said.

"I can't just go on dating apps," he said. The undone bow tie around his neck along with all that tousled, jaw-length hair made him look like a men's fashion shoot come to life. "Plus, isn't catfishing when you get a downgrade? I think it's fair to say I'm an upgrade from a faceless sunset man with a comically large dog."

"But it was an uneven match. I have my face and my name on my profile, *Todd*. You knew it was me. You could have just walked across the reception and asked me out for a drink."

"You're here, aren't you?" he asked as he dragged his thumb around the edge of his glass. His tuxedo jacket hung from the back of his chair and his sleeves were rolled halfway up his forearms, so I could see that vein. The one that curved around his arm and pulsed when he came. That time there was no shirt though.

Every time I blinked, the memory of my night with him was there. Me on top, Jack kissing his neck as Isaac's hands roamed up my hips to my waist. The image of his hand clasping with mine as he thrust into me from below, completely guiding the moment and controlling me with each buck of his hips.

But fuck. I could not do this again. Our lives were too intertwined at this point. We'd likely be the godparents to whatever spawn Nolan and Bee created, and I was not about to make every holiday and birthday party for the rest of my life awkward AF.

"God, I love this song," Isaac said as he closed his eyes and slowly let his head sway from side to side. The opening notes to "Hopelessly Devoted to You" played, but it was Kallum's drunk sister behind the mic on the karaoke stage singing instead of Olivia Newton-John. That didn't seem to bother Isaac though.

In one smooth motion, he hopped off the barstool and held his hand out for me. "Dance with me, Sunny."

I looked down at his open hand and back up at him. This felt too much like romance.

"Come on," he said. "It's just one dance."

"You're under the misconception that I can dance," I told him. "Not all of us are products of the pop machine."

"You can move your body, Palmer."

I took his hand and stumbled off the stool. "You know what my grandmother always said: if you can fuck, you can dance."

He looked taken aback. "Did she really?"

I shook my head. "No, but she did always tell me to wear clean underwear in case I died and someone had to see what I was rocking down there."

"Good advice."

I shrugged. "If you decide to wear underwear at all."

With a quiet laugh, he led me to the makeshift dance floor with tables pushed off to the side. A few other couples danced alongside us. He wrapped his arm around my waist and held my hand in his as we moved gently from side to side.

"Did you really buy the infamous mansion?" I asked.

He nodded. "It's pretty quaint, don't you think?"

"Yeah, super subtle," I said. "The marble floors and columns just have this humble air about them."

"Well, it's not much, but it's home." He tucked a loose piece of hair behind my ear. Okay, he was definitely not playing fair here. "Except for tonight," he added. "Tonight, the place belongs to Bee and Nolan."

"Oh, really? So you're crashing at the Mistletoe Inn?"

He frowned. "No room at the inn."

"I've heard that line before," I said.

"Well, I just figured I'd crash in whatever warm bed the Spark app presented me with."

"Quite the gamble, mister."

He turned his head to watch our hands and shifted his fingers so they intertwined with mine. A perfect fit.

Heat gathered in my chest and between my thighs.

His fingers tightened their grip.

Fuck it.

What was one more one-night stand with Isaac Kelly? At least this time I wouldn't have to share him with Jack Hart.

I cleared my eyes and looked up at him. "A warm bed, you say?"

About the Authors

It all started with a series of tropes: just one bed, forced proximity, and a dash of enemies to lovers, and now ten years later, **Julie Murphy** and **Sierra Simone** are best friends and co-authors of the *USA Today* bestselling *A Merry Little Meet Cute, A Holly Jolly Ever After,* and *A Jingle Bell Mingle.* Sierra is the *USA Today* bestselling author of *Priest* and *American Queen.*

When they're not writing, Julie and Sierra enjoy forcing their families to go on vacation together and eating an array of pies while watching delightfully bad movies.

Snow Place Like LA

By Julie Murphy and Sierra Simone

A Merry Little Meet Cute
Snow Place Like LA
A Holly Jolly Ever After
Seas and Greetings
A Jingle Bell Mingle

Snow Place Like LA

A Christmas Notch Novella

JULIE and SIERRA
MURPHY SIMONE

AVON

An Imprint of HarperCollinsPublishers

SNOW PLACE LIKE LA. Copyright © 2023 by Bittersweet Media LLC and Sierra Simone.

SEAS AND GREETINGS. Copyright © 2024 by Bittersweet Media LLC and Sierra Simone.

Originally published separately in ebook format as *Snow Place Like LA* and *Seas and Greetings* in the United States by Avon Impulse in 2023 and 2024.

Designed by Diahann Sturge-Campbell

Christmas palm trees © Radiocat/Stock.Adobe.com

Library of Congress Cataloging-in-Publication Data has been applied for.

ISBN 978-0-06-344312-9

25 26 27 28 29 LBC 5 4 3 2 1

To Dana Hagen, who loves *Pretty Woman*

Snow Place Like LA

Prologue

I would never forgive *Love Actually*. How dare they make me think airports were romantic places?

I smoothed the front of my coat—a tangerine wool number I found in a Las Vegas thrift store—and tried not to look at the tall, handsome man next to me. At his artsy glasses, at his lean frame. At those high cheekbones and that narrow, light brown jaw currently rough with stubble.

If I looked at him being all handsome and creative looking, I was going to speak, and if I spoke, I just *knew* it would be something embarrassing. And Luca né Jeffrey Derosa was many things, but he was never embarrassing!

The Burlington airport hummed and moved outside of the little nook where we were waiting. Outside the windows, snow fell in giant, fluffy flakes, just as it had for the past two weeks while Angel Fletcher and I had shacked up in a ramshackle rental just up the street from the Hope Channel's offices. Two weeks of nothing but sex and pancakes and being really clumsy at using a wood-burning fireplace—not to mention the two weeks before that when we'd started our *liaison amoureuse* on the set of *Duke the Halls*. Which meant Angel Fletcher and I had been sort-of-maybe-kind-of-together for a month.

A month.

And okay, yes, working for the wholesome AF Hope Channel wasn't exactly the most sensual milieu for a budding romance. And fine, maybe we hadn't actually *talked* about being together, but that's only because there hadn't been anything to say. We'd been dancing around each other for the two years since I started working for his dad (Teddy Ray Fletcher, LA's premiere producer of top-quality pornos, also the producer of the very non-porno *Duke the Halls*, it's a long story). And finally, among the snow and Christmas lights, the thing between us had caught fire. A heartrending saga two years in the making, now complete with stubble-burns all over my neck and a happily ever after.

Except . . . except now it was time for us to fly home, and I guess I'd assumed this moment would come with more orchestral crescendos. And less awkward silences.

Why wasn't Angel saying anything? I snuck a glance over to see him typing rapidly on his phone, switching between his email app and the airline app. A series of snow-related cancellations had meant we'd gotten rebooked on two different flights home, but we were both headed back to LA and to the rest of our great love affair, and so shouldn't we be beaming secret smiles at each other right now? Shouldn't we be searching for an abandoned gate with a convenient make-out corner? How could we go from playing house—while mostly naked—to barely able to make eye contact?

No, I was imagining things. I inarguably had an incredible imagination (which is why the wedding fashion world tragically lost its brightest future star when I was forced to drop out of fashion school due to cashflow—or lack thereof) and sometimes my imagination ran away with me, that was all. We were in this together, and anyway, there was no way he could miss how I felt.

I'd willingly extended a stay in a Christmas-themed hellhole for him! I'd let him see me in the morning! Multiple mornings! In my twenty-four years, I'd never let someone I wanted to kiss see me before I had time to dab flawlessly matched light olive concealer under my eyeballs!

But I couldn't shake the feeling that, like a gorgeous but fragile movie costume, my great love affair might not survive a change of scenery. The last month, with all its midnight kisses and toe-curling sighs, might become nothing more than a memory, and the memory might start right here in a technically international Vermont airport.

I cleared my throat, not sure what to say, but knowing it would come to me. I was nothing if not an improviser, and I would find exactly the right way to tell him that this last month had been everything.

Angel looked up from his phone, his sepia eyes glinting almost bronze in the lights of the airport. His eyelashes cast faint fan-shapes on his cheeks, and for a moment, I was so hypnotized by the shape of them that I forgot I was supposed to be talking.

"Yes?" he asked softly, hesitantly. Angel wasn't a hesitant person, but we'd been in each other's orbits for a long time now, and I knew he was a *thoughtful* person. Probably came with being an animator—half artist, half computer genius. So I wasn't really hearing hesitation, I decided. He was probably just thinking about everything we needed to do when we got back to LA. He had one more semester of art school left, and his sister, Astrid, was trying to launch an eco-friendly sex toy empire, so there wouldn't be a shortage of demands on his time.

Of course, I'd be the most interesting and sexy demand on his time.

"Do you want to come to Vanya's birthday party this weekend?" I finally asked. Vanya was my best friend in Los Angeles, and the pickiest person I knew (aside from myself, of course). I only introduced people to her who I knew were special, perfect, chosen—partly for Vanya's sake, and partly for my own. If someone met my platonic soulmate, then that person was inside the very deepest layer of the onion, a layer so deep you couldn't even make onion rings with it, and there was no undoing that. I felt the face-tingling thrill of doing something this bold for me. "I'd like to see you there."

Angel blinked once, twice. "This weekend?" he asked.

"The very same," I said, but of course, right then the thrill shifted into something closer to panic. I'd never invited someone I was romantically entangled with to meet Vanya, and oh God, what if Vanya hated Angel? Or what if Angel heard stories about me from before I'd reinvented myself as a sexy, eyeliner-wearing swan, and lost interest? Oh God, oh God—

Angel opened his mouth, but I interrupted him before he could speak.

"I mean. Only if you want to. Or have time." I tried to make my voice as casual as possible, like this wasn't the biggest thing I could offer him short of getting a tattoo on my unmentionables. "Just let me know."

Angel's tongue dipped down to lick his lower lip, which was extremely unfair, because now all I could think about was his tongue. And licking. And the kilt I was wearing under my tangerine coat was great for many things, but hiding erections was not one of them.

"Luca, I need to—"

Just then the boarding announcement for my flight came over the intercom. I turned to see people lining up at my gate, and I knew I needed to get myself and my fantastically long legs settled so I didn't have to do the awkward aisle shuffle when I got to my row.

I turned back to Angel, seeing him in all his stubbled, bespectacled glory, his strong throat working, his high forehead furrowed like he couldn't figure out the answer to some important problem, and he was so adorable and hot—and adorably hot—and I couldn't help myself, I surged forward and kissed him.

His lips were warm and supple, and when I ran my tongue along his upper lip, he parted for me with a groan. The inside of his mouth was hot, silky, soft, his tongue unbelievably wicked against mine, and the memory of a thousand other kisses burned inside me. Kisses in the bed, on the floor, in the shower. Sideways while I was bent over a kitchen table or the back of a couch . . .

His hands found their way inside my coat, fisting the thin sweater I wore, and I cupped the nape of his neck to kiss him even harder. Found the lapels of his coat to tug him closer and closer and closer. I knew we were mostly sheltered from sight in our little nook, and all I could think about was shoving him back against the wall and grinding my hips against his until we both felt better.

"Flight number 2287, nonstop to Los Angeles, boarding now," called the fatigued voice over the intercom. "Group one, please board."

I broke away from the kiss, noting with some smugness how stunned Angel looked right now. "Will you think about the party?" I asked.

His eyes were glazed, and with the air of someone shell-shocked, he reached down to adjust himself in his jeans. "Yes," he managed to get out.

"I can't wait to see you in LA," I whispered, and then I gave him another lingering kiss, leaving him slumped against the wall, his hand holding his hand-painted denim coat closed over his hard-on.

I was smiling to myself the whole way back to Los Angeles.

TWO DAYS LATER, and I was not smiling.

Angel hadn't called, hadn't texted, hadn't DM'd. A piece of me larger than I was ever willing to admit boarded that plane expecting to see him just hours after we landed, already sprawled across my bed the moment I walked through the door.

That first night I got back to LA, I waited hours for a text, but eventually I fell asleep with my phone in my hand. When I woke up in the morning without any contact from Angel, it felt like someone had filled my throat with gravel.

I'd learned long ago what silence meant; my parents had taught me that, along with my childhood friends and the first boy I'd ever kissed. And I'd only ever reacted one way to silence—by leaving. If someone didn't have the gumption or the guts to say what they wanted to say to my face, then they didn't get my face at all any more. Why would I stick around just to be ignored?

Except . . .

Except maybe, the *teensiest* bit maybe, Angel deserved the benefit of the doubt. He had spent an entire evening in Vermont cooking me steamed dampfnudel because we saw it on an episode of *The Great British Bake Off* after all, and had even made the vanilla sauce to go with it.

So I relented and did the whole benefit of the doubt thing: I texted first, telling him the time and place of Vanya's party.

And still, no response.

The night of Vanya's party, I spent way too much time getting ready, ultimately choosing the perfect skintight leather pants and my favorite black tunic sweater with thoughtfully placed shreds and holes. It was like a comfort blanket. A truly fabulous and devastatingly hot comfort blanket.

And then I went to Vanya's warehouse/domicile, completely prepared for my artsy Prince Charming to show up and sweep me off my feet. He'd tell me that he'd been so busy, so overwhelmed, but that he was still consumed by the memory of firelight on my skin as we'd made love in front of the fire in Vermont.

Never mind that we never actually got the fire to light long enough to also have sex while it was burning. It was the *vibe* that mattered.

He would apologize and then he'd kiss me and then he'd apologize to Vanya for turning me into an insecure mess for the last three days and then Vanya would graciously forgive him and ask him what he thought about her latest canvases (and it would be a trick question, because she *hated* her most recent work) and then even if he got it wrong, he'd get it wrong so sweetly and cutely that it wouldn't matter. And then we'd both get tipsy from violet femme cocktails and go back to my apartment and have the kind of sex that required towels.

And I was ready for The Moment. I posted myself far from the door and made sure to be mid-laugh as many times as possible, so when Angel walked in, he'd have to search for me, and then when he found me, I'd be utterly unconcerned with his tardiness and surrounded by a crowd of people who were completely charmed by me.

But the first hour of the party passed without my Prince Charming walking through the door.

And then the second. And then the third.

By the fourth hour, I'd had five drinks and had to convince Vanya several times not to issue her version of a CIA burn notice. With an inadvisable amount of gin circulating through my system, I did something I had never done, and would never again do if I could help it.

I texted someone who hadn't responded to my last text.

Aaaand I got no response.

Again.

By the fifth hour of the party, I was sitting glumly on my best friend's bed watching the rest of the guests get on without me, or the indie-music soundtracked moment I'd been waiting for. Vanya sashayed over in a chartreuse caftan and boots with multiple goldfish in the clear platform bottoms, her long pink hair catching on her rich brown shoulders. She sat on the bed next to me and handed me a fresh drink in one of those Gatsby-looking glasses she liked so much.

"Is this him?" she asked, showing me his Instagram account.

"Yes," I said automatically, having become an expert in Angel's social media over the last three days and already knowing every post, caption, and comment. I tapped through his profile through sheer force of habit, not expecting to see anything new, and that's when I saw it. A tagged post, shared just a few minutes ago.

It was a picture of Angel with an unmistakably Parisian cityscape behind him. Angel had his arm around a tall blond guy that looked like a long-lost Hemsworth brother. And the Hemsworth had his arm slung over Angel's shoulders and his fingers tangled casually in the lapel of Angel's coat. A familiar gesture. A possessive one.

The caption was just a baguette and a heart.

"That's his ex," I said numbly. "Blake."

"He's with his ex in Paris," Vanya said to drive the point home, but there was pity in her voice too. "Babes."

My hand was shaking. I couldn't look at this picture anymore. I couldn't look away. Angel was in *Paris*. Letting his ex touch the lapel of the same denim coat I'd used to pull him closer to my mouth.

Had Angel known then he wouldn't come to the party? That he'd be in Paris? With a guy named Blake who never missed leg day? Was that why he hadn't responded to my texts?

"You know what you need to do," my best friend said, as seriously as anyone wearing goldfish shoes could say anything. "Burn. Notice."

She was right. I handed the phone back to Vanya, tossed back the rest of my purple cocktail, and handed Vanya the empty glass. And then I pulled out my own phone and tapped open my text messages.

When Vanya saw I'd texted him twice with no response, she sucked her teeth.

"Burn notice," she repeated, and then made an approving noise as I opened up his contact info and then tapped *Block This Caller*. I pulled up one of his social media accounts and blocked him, and then another and blocked him there. On and on until the only place left was his Instagram, where I had to see him canoodling with Blake once again before I could block him there too.

And now he wouldn't be able to call, text, or DM—and even better, I could pretend that Angel Fletcher, my lowkey crush for two years (and highkey obsession for a month) had never existed.

Just a hypothermic hallucination while freezing my nips off in Christmas Notch. Just a hazy dream brought on by too much

Grinch Punch at my favorite Christmas-themed strip club, The North Pole.

Angel Fletcher thought he could ghost me? Well, I could ghost him better.

Boo, bitch.

Chapter One

Seven Months Later

A backyard barbecue was deeply off-brand for me, and I made sure Bee Hobbes, my friend and the star of *Duke the Halls*, knew so when she invited me to her new Los Feliz digs.

"Pretty please," she'd begged over FaceTime. "I need someone to hang out with Sunny while I'm playing hostess."

Sunny was another adult film star in Uncle Ray-Ray's stable, and since I'd been doing costumes for Teddy Ray Fletcher and his band of performers for years, I'd known her as long as I'd known Bee. Which was why I knew the truth. "You just want me to keep Sunny and Jack from getting into a fracas at your barbeque."

Bee made a face, her full mouth screwing up into a pout as her septum piercing glinted on the screen. "I can't babysit them while I'm also refilling punch bowls, you know? I need a wingperson."

I'd pinched the bridge of my nose. "Can't your floppy-haired boyfriend do it?" Nolan Shaw was the former boy band member who'd inexplicably captured Bee's heart while they were filming *Duke the Halls*, despite him being a human disaster who'd single-handedly (or, *fine*, mostly *inadvertently*) ruined my favorite ice skater's career. But I guessed Bee had a soft spot for tattooed boys who looked good in tight pants, because now they were a disgustingly smitten couple and did things like acquire houses together and then throw meat-themed housewarming parties for said houses.

"Luca!" Bee had exclaimed. "Just be there! Or," she'd added in the voice of a threat, "I won't tell you *a secret*. A very special secret that Sunny and I learned."

"What secret?" I'd demanded. People didn't hide secrets from me; I hid secrets from *them*.

"Come and you'll find out," she'd sang, and then hung up.

. . . which was why I was now at a barbeque in Los Feliz, even though I could have been doing any number of more interesting things, like taking a bath or catching up on my favorite true crime podcasts.

But no, I was here to babysit Sunny Palmer when she was the one who'd made an archnemesis of Jack Hart in the first place by sleeping with his stepmom at his wedding. Which I understood, because Rebecca definitely had *mommy* energy, if you get my drift, but still. Sometimes you had to soak in your own dishwater, and in this case, the dishwater was having a very flexible porn star as an eternal enemy.

Summoning up the sense of loyal, unruffled duty that I was sure I was famous for, I stepped out onto the patio overlooking the pool in Bee's new backyard and looked around for my curvy, tattooed charge.

Movement near the edge of the pool caught my eye. A lanky form in a vintage cardigan and jeans. Hair shaved close on the sides and left long on top. Big, wire-framed glasses, and before the person ducked their head, I saw thick brows, a long nose, and a very, very kissable mouth.

I froze, my heart liquefying into a toxic sludge in my chest. I couldn't seem to inhale properly, my chest stuck in exhale-mode, as sparks danced at the edge of my vision.

Angel.

He was back from Europe.

Angel was back from Europe, and no one had told me.

"Breathe," said someone next to me, and I turned to see Bee approaching, her face creased in worry. "Breathe, baby."

"Angel is here," I whispered. "You didn't tell me Angel would be here!"

"I didn't know!" Bee said and held up both hands. "I mean, I suspected there might be a teeny, tiny chance he'd come because the invite was pretty open, but—"

I glared at her.

"Okay, look," Bee said, changing tack. "You told me that you were completely, one hundred percent over Angel. In fact, let the record show you've made a point to announce you're *so very over him* at least once a week. Is that the truth or not? Am I going to have to start hosting two parties for every milestone in my life now? Do I need to have a shadow cabinet friend group and then a real friend group?"

I was still glaring, but she did have a very small point, which was that I had been slightly declarative about the fact I was over Angel breaking my heart in the most callous and ungentlemanly way. Which I was. I was over it.

Obviously.

"There's no need," I sniffed. "I've already forgotten about him."

"Good." Bee put a reassuring hand on my shoulder. "And anyway, what are the odds you'll see him again? LA is huge."

I NEVER DID get that secret out of Bee, a fact I realized the next day as I was on the set of the latest Uncle Ray-Ray's masterpiece, a porn remake of *Pretty Woman*.

While it would be a stretch to say that costuming is the tentpole of any adult entertainment production, Teddy Ray Fletcher did have a soft spot for remakes, and part of selling any good porn remake was a decent facsimile of the costumes. Of course, the budget was never great and the timeline always super compressed, but in a way, it was no different than being in fashion school. And it also helped me creatively. When the budget was juicy and the time to make something was endless . . . well, then it was hard not to want something to be perfect. And the more I wanted something to be perfect, the less I was able to actually work on it. It was weird. Or maybe it was undiagnosed ADHD. Only Dr. TikTok could tell.

Luckily, the call to perfection was very rarely a problem at good old Uncle Ray-Ray's. Although I was pretty proud of the costumes I'd been working on for this one, and especially today's: a faithful recreation of Vivian's streetwalking outfit, complete with thigh-high boots and a beret.

I was pulling the outfit out of a small tote box in the cheap rented mansion that would double as the penthouse when the director—none other than Sunny Palmer—bounded up beside me.

"Hey, hi, heyyyy," she said. "Are we ready to roll? Mackenzie's naked in the next room. Like 'ready to get dressed' naked, not 'ready for fucking' naked."

"Tell Mackenzie to cool her tits," I replied as I carefully reshaped the beret, which had gotten a little smashed in the tote.

"Mackenzie doesn't have much tit to cool, but sure," said Sunny. She was bouncier than normal, up on the balls of her feet and practically vibrating.

"Are you feeling okay?" I asked and then narrowed my eyes. "Are you drinking that energy tea again? You know the FDA has formed a committee to work on banning it, right?"

Sunny shook her head emphatically. "I'm on one hundred percent, raw, organic nerves right now. It's my first time behind the camera, you know."

Sunny was a bit of a porn polymath—she fucked, she sex-fluenced, and she did professional makeup on the side, most recently for *Duke the Halls*. But she hadn't ever directed anything until now.

"You'll do fab," I told her, and I meant it. I didn't give out compliments lightly, but Sunny was the real deal. Smart, hilarious, and with an ass that would have knocked Rubens dead.

"Merci." But from the way she was clutching her headset, I didn't think she felt that reassured.

Mackenzie wandered in like a naked baby deer, lost-looking and spindly-legged. "Um, hi? Does anyone know where my Julie Rogers dress is?"

"The younger generation," I said in low tones of condemnation, even though Mackenzie was probably only three or four years younger than me. "Okay, missy," I said louder. "Let's get you ready for your big moment."

WITH MACKENZIE READY, the last performer I'd need to dress was the guy playing the Richard Gere character, who'd been listed in the email as *TBD*. It wasn't that unusual in the porn world—sometimes a performer wasn't even officially cast until the day of the shoot—but it did make my job a little harder, since the trick to making a suit look good was the tailoring, and I couldn't tailor without measurements. But I was used to working wonders with ironing tape and a portable sewing machine, so I'd make it work.

Or so I thought, because the actor who walked into the room that was doubling as my wardrobe department was very familiar. So familiar I thought surely I was imagining him. Surely I'd fallen asleep and was having a nightmare and so it wasn't really Angel's ex-boyfriend Blake walking into the room right now. It wasn't really a Hemsworth lookalike pulling off a hoodie and kicking off his sneakers before even saying *hello*.

I stared as he yanked down his pants and then turned and faced me, his penis swinging around like a beige windsock. "Hey, I'm Blake," he said in a deep voice. "I hear you got a suit for me?"

"I do," I managed to say, spinning around to fumble for the suit. I'd known that Blake did porn—he and Angel had met at some Uncle Ray-Ray's holiday party a year and a half ago while I'd sulked in the corner and watched their chemistry blossom.

But he'd been off the scene for a while, and I'd put him in the coffin showroom of my brain. May he never rest in peace.

But here he was. Muscled thighs, windsock dick, and all.

After forcing my eyes up, I yanked his pants off the hanger and threw them in his general direction. "Try those on and we'll see if we can make them work. I'll be right back."

I marched out of the room and slammed the door behind me as I roared, "Sunny!"

Weaving in and out of crew members and cast members, I pushed down the hallway into the room doubling as the hotel suite. "Sunny," I called again. "We need to—"

I stopped right there in my special edition Doc Martens tracks.

Right there on a stepladder, positioning lights, was Angel.

Sunny looked up from where she was perched on her director's chair with her laptop balanced precariously on her thighs.

I opened my mouth to shout—at anyone—but Angel spoke first, shaking his head as he dismounted the stepladder. "You didn't tell me he was going to be here, Sunny." His voice was tight, furious, and his hand as he pushed his big glasses up his nose was shaking.

Without another word, he stormed out of the room, his shoulder brushing mine just enough for it to sting, and I staggered back, my hand going to my deltoid like I'd just been hit with a cannonball.

Which was possibly not *entirely* warranted, since Angel was as lanky as they came, but *still*.

I swiveled my head back to Sunny, Sunny the Betrayer, Sunny the Summoner of Cute Exes with Glasses. She threw her arms up as if this wasn't all her fault.

I made a frustrated noise in her general direction before stomping back to wardrobe.

By the time I made it there, Blake was gone. I supposed he'd used the two spark plugs in his brain to find the rest of his suit, so I slumped down on the white leather sofa to text Bee and tell her, We should put out an Amber Alert for Sunny.

Bee responded almost immediately.

BEE: Why? Where is she? Did she not make it to work this morning?

LUCA: She's here now, but I'm about to kill her, and if you want any help finding the body, you'll need help from the authorities.

BEE: I'm guessing you ran into Blake.

> **LUCA:** And Angel.

> **LUCA:** Wait.

> **LUCA:** You knew?

BEE: 🫣

BEE: LA is a small town and porn is an even smaller business, hun.

Hun! Hun? How dare she *hun* me?

I threw my phone in the adorable little upcycled Dooney & Bourke bum bag Vanya had got me a few years ago. She'd hand painted flowers that looked strikingly similar to vaginas all over it, making it the perfect 911 bag for porn sets. It had all the necessities. Needle, thread, pasties, and even a plant-based menstrual disc because I was a good friend to uterus-having people, despite the fact that two of my favorite uterus-having people were making an actual attempt on my life at the moment.

As I popped in an earbud, Harry Styles "Daylight" remixes playing, I began to sort through costumes for the next scene, my hands shaking just like Angel's had been earlier. I flexed them once and then rubbed them together. As much as I appreciated what an incredible music video this would make right now—the lonely beauty in his kilt bravely hiding his agony at seeing his cheating, Eiffel-Tower-loving ex—I wasn't going to give Angel music video power over me. It had been seven months! I could easily handle however long this took . . . right?

I quickly did the production math in my head. Some porn shoots happened in a day, but the bigger budget remakes Teddy had a soft spot for could take anywhere from one to two weeks, and with this being Sunny's first movie, I wasn't sure what to expect.

Which meant I could be on set with Angel, Blake, and Blake's windsock dick, for at least the next week. Possibly two. Or—God, no—three.

That was doubtful, of course, but it was better to brace myself now.

There was a knock at the door and then Graham, a pale twenty-something with Big Tweed Energy, and Sunny's assistant for the shoot, poked his head in. "Would you believe me if I told you Mackenzie broke her costume?"

I threw my head back with a groan. "This day!"

I followed him downstairs to where the crew was in full panic mode, trying to get cameras rolling before the light shifted again.

But it was fine. Everything was fine. I'd fix Mackenzie's costume, because that was a problem I knew how to fix. Unlike Angel being here with his very naked ex.

Unlike my life, which sometimes felt entirely too much like a music video—the same scenes, over and over. The perfect aesthetic with no real substance behind it.

Anyway, we'd start rolling on this shiz and before I knew it, we'd have one day down. And that's how I would survive this. One day at a time.

Part of me still wanted to call Teddy and demand he take me off this shoot due to his hot, mean artist son being here, but I'd been ecstatic about the as-yet-untitled *Pretty Woman* parody since Sunny first pitched it. So why should I let Angel and Blake ruin this for me?

"Right down here in the last bedroom," Graham said as he walked faster than a nurse in a pair of Crocs leading you through the office to your appointment room. You always knew they meant business when that little loop was pulled up around the heel. It was like sport mode for Crocs.

I dug around in my bag for my sewing kit as Graham opened the door and then stepped back for me to walk ahead.

The door shut behind me just as I looked up to see Sunny pushing a reluctant Angel through the door of a bathroom, which was conjoined to the next bedroom over.

I gasped.

I'd been tricked. Bamboozled!

"Graham!" I shouted as I rapped my fist on the door. "You lied to me!"

"Not technically," he protested. "I asked if you would believe me if I told you Mackenzie broke her costume. I didn't say she actually did."

"I don't have time for your drama on my set," Sunny said through the other door.

"Me neither," I yelled back, as Angel slid down the wall and onto the floor.

"And I'm not about to choose between you two," Sunny said. "So work it out."

"You're dead to me, Graham," I called back to him.

"Don't listen to him, Graham," Sunny shouted. "You haven't lived if you've never been dead to Luca."

"Can confirm," Angel mumbled.

I let myself really look at him for the first time as he ran his fingers over the shredded knee of his jeans.

"And please keep the yelling to a minimum," Sunny said. "We're trying to make a movie out here."

I tugged on the doorknob just to confirm that yes, we were indeed locked in like some TV episode where everything is resolved in eighteen minutes.

A sigh that sounded more like a whimper slipped from me as I rested my forehead against the door. My back burned at the feeling of Angel's gaze on me.

But why would he even be looking at me? He certainly couldn't bother to tell me he was skipping off to Europe with his exboyfriend. There was nothing he could possibly say in the next hour that would make me forgive him. The best Sunny and Graham could hope for was that I would be calm and gracious enough to work alongside him for the rest of the shoot without airing his tagged Instagram laundry.

And I was calm—without him. I'd moved on. But how could I possibly be expected to stay calm over someone who reappeared without any kind of warning or explanation?

I pulled myself as upright as I could go, as though my spine was made of steel. I turned to face him with as much aloof poise as I could manage.

He stood too, ruffling a hand through the styled curls at the top of his head. The move pulled the hem of his T-shirt up, exposing a slice of lean stomach with a trail of dark hair leading into his boxers. My eyes were pulled there, and then they lifted back to his long fingers in his hair, to his teeth digging into his lip as he slowly dropped his hand.

"Well, are we doing the talking thing?" Angel asked, his voice low and smooth.

And with my best Vivien Leigh eyebrow lift, and with all the violet femme-flavored agony I felt the night of Vanya's party, I replied.

"I don't talk to ghosts."

Chapter Two

*F*ine," Angel said as he stepped closer to me. "We don't have to talk. There are plenty of things we're good at that don't involve saying a single word."

I hated this feeling. This feeling of being angry and hurt and rejected—and like I wanted nothing more in the world than to pull him to me until he was as close as my own shadow.

Angel moved toward me, his foot between mine.

"Dammit, dammit, dammit," I muttered, as I stared down at the paint-splattered toe of his boot.

He hooked a finger under my chin, lifting my eyes to meet his.

Everything flooded back all at once, because it was never actually gone. The last two years of wanting from afar and then our frenzied Christmas romance . . . it was all there just below the surface, and now my throat was dry and my skin was warm and all I wanted was just to run my fingers through his hair.

So I did.

And that was all the permission Angel needed to wrap an arm around my waist and form my body against his.

His chest to mine, his stomach to mine. Our hips pressed nearly together, the slight difference in our heights meaning I could feel the lengthening part of him just above the lengthening part of me as his lips dropped to mine, hovering there.

I could smell him—fresh soap and the tiniest nip of turpentine, and that wonderful scent that was just *him* underneath it all— and I could feel his breath warm and sweet against my lips. His chest swelled against mine as he shuddered in a long inhale, and I remembered that shuddering breath from the cabin, the same breath he'd take before he pushed all the way inside me until he was buried to the hilt.

It was like music, that breath, the kind of music that inspired ten minute music videos directed by the artist and starring cute people from hit TV shows. A song that changed you the first time you heard it, and every time thereafter. If it were on Spotify, I'd build a whole playlist around it. If it were a hymn, I'd start a church, become the director of its bell choir, and ring bells to it.

His styled curls were tousled and longish under my fingers, and I couldn't resist tugging a little as I tangled my fingers in his hair. It was Angel's little secret that he liked things a little rough—looking at him with his giant glasses and paint-stained clothes, listening to him talk about his favorite Studio Ghibli film or the various pros and cons of 3ds Max and Maya for computer animation, you'd never think *oh, this one's a biter*. But Angel fucked like he made art: like he couldn't come up for air until he'd finished. And it was heady, being at the center of that kind of storm. Knowing that you were the one who turned a good-natured genius into a grabbing, biting wall of hunger . . .

I lifted my chin even more, licking my lower lip, and Angel groaned, finally relenting and slashing his mouth down over mine.

His kiss was hot, hard, searching, and he delved into my mouth immediately, his tongue seeking mine and then stroking against it. Unlike me, he could keep a shave when he wanted, and his face was smooth, lovely, like heaven against my lip and cheeks. His lips worked mine open until I was panting against him, and his fingers dug into my waist, pulling me closer, our dicks grazing against each other's. He walked me back against the door, his kiss turning rough and hungry as my back hit the wood, and our feet slotted against each other's so we could keep rubbing ourselves below as we kissed above, and then his hand slipped down to my hip, and then my ass, and a needy groan tore out of my chest. I needed him, and I needed him now, and I didn't care about anything else—

I broke away from him, tripping back against the door, my lips burning and my chest heaving. I stared at him with wide, panicked eyes, lust and fury pounding in my bloodstream. I'd been bamboozled a second time!

"I can't believe I fell for your mouth!" I said, and then remembered how all this heartbreak had started in Christmas Notch to begin with. "Again!"

Angel brushed a thumb against my cheek, and I could feel my body falling under his hypnosis all over again. Before I absolutely drowned in his touch, I swatted his hand away just like I'd learned in the self-defense class Bee's moms gifted to her, me, and Sunny for Christmas the year after Bee had moved to LA.

I spun around to try the door again, but that was locked, so I shoved past him to try the adjoining bathroom door Sunny had pushed him through, but that was also locked. Of course. Sunny Palmer was many things, and thorough was definitely one of them.

Fuck me.

I eyed the huge brocade drapes covering the windows on the other two walls and tore the nearest set open.

"You're going to escape through a window?" Angel asked, doing a poor job of hiding the laughter in his voice. "Luca, come on. We don't even have to talk."

I flipped the lock on the window and pushed up on the bottom, but I could only get it open a few inches. "Not talking didn't really pan out for us all of two seconds ago." I shoved at the window again, and the glass rattled in the frame, but the sash only budged another few inches.

"The window's jammed," Angel said.

"Thank you so much for pointing that out," I said. "I thought this was just how windows worked and that they were there just to look pretty and not actually function. Who wants to actually escape a fire? Or an ex?"

The second that last word left my mouth, a knot formed in my stomach. We'd never actually defined the relationship, and there was nothing more mortifying than being the one to define a relationship that had never even existed.

"It's not like they're going to leave us in here all day," Angel said. "Eventually someone is going to need a light adjusted or a costume changed."

Continuing to use my self-defense moves, I punched the screen out of the window and peered down. The first floor of the house was more elevated than I had expected. It was at least a five foot drop, but there were bushes to break my fall.

"Luca," Angel said, and this time my name was strained on his lips.

I had to get the hell out of here, so I began to do what any reasonable human being would do and shimmied out the narrow gap between the window and the frame, my legs kicking and my hips wiggling.

I'd always thought stuck porn was incredibly unbelievable, but in this moment, it began to make sense. Of course, admitting I was wrong had always been a tough pill to swallow, but I made a mental note to let Teddy know I'd had a change of heart, especially after our argument over plausibility on the set of *Stuck Step-Mommies 8*.

Fuck. I couldn't wiggle my luscious ass through the window.

"You're going to hurt yourself," said Angel.

Nothing—and I mean nothing—could hurt more than being stuck in this McMansion with him, Blake, and Blake's windsock dick. With a grunt, I pushed as hard as I could, my body tipping over the window frame to freedom.

"Oh, fuck," I swore as I realized I had zero control of how my body was about to fall.

Okay, maybe the ground was more like six and a half feet away. Or eight. How tall was a standard house story again?

A shriek tore through my chest as my body broke through the bushes, my shirt snagging, until I found myself cradled precariously in a tangle of leaves and branches and—*ouch*—thorns. Who landscaped an LA mansion with thorny bushes? Didn't rich people have special rich people plants that were made of skin-enhancing snail mucus and yacht insurance policies???

"What the hell?" I shouted as I tried to push myself up and out, but I was surrounded. My arms were bleeding and—

"My hands! My beautiful hands!"

I couldn't work without my hands, and now they were riddled with cuts, many of which had thorns now lodged inside of them. Blood welled along a few of the wounds, a deep, deep scarlet.

Angel peered out from the window above me. "Don't move! You fell in a rose bush."

He disappeared, and I stared helplessly up at the blue sky, entirely offended by how bright and cheery it was in the face of my suffering.

Could this day just end? Could I just exit out of this browser and do a hard reset on my life?

And then I felt a warm hand reach for me. It wrapped with comforting strength around my forearm. "I've got you," Angel said. "This might hurt."

With one hand wrapped in his jacket, he cleared the branches and stems just enough so that he could haul me out of the bush and to my feet.

I stumbled forward a little and into his chest, dropping my mangled hands before they could get smashed between us. "Sorry," I said under my breath and then looked around to the wall of windows behind us. "How the hell did you get out here so fast?"

He was already wrapping his hand around my upper arm and guiding me somewhere. I should resist, I knew I should, but my hands hurt so much, and I was always a total goner the minute he turned bossy. "The door," he said as we turned the corner around the back of the house.

Which was when I saw the balcony with its wide, easy steps coming down from the second floor. Along with the huge sliding glass door leading straight to the room we'd just been locked inside of.

"There was a third door?" I asked. "You have to be kidding me."

"It was hidden behind those Olive Garden–looking drapes," Angel said.

I looked down at my hands and whimpered at the sight of the blood and thorns.

Angel clicked his tongue sympathetically. "Let's get your dumb ass cleaned up."

"I didn't *know* it was a bush full of thorns," I grumbled as we walked down the backside of the house to the pool house where craft services was set up. Teddy hired a nurse for every major shoot, and she usually posted up near the doughnuts and sub sandwiches. (Craft services also served fancy crushed ice and Metamucil smoothies for all the performers who, for anal reasons, might not have been eating much that day. Teddy Ray Fletcher was a thoughtful man.)

Angel just looked back at me with a dry expression. "The roses didn't give it away?"

I wanted to tell him that not all roses showed their thorns. That not all artists-slash-animators displayed the fact that they'd leave you for Paris and an ex named Blake.

But as always, I opted for the high road, and lifted my chin to stride past him to where the nurse sat eating a doughnut while handing a tube of hemorrhoid cream to a performer.

Chapter Three

*I*t burns," I hissed.

"Not the first time someone's said that on set," Fiona, our on-set nurse, tutted. We were in the McMansion's pool house now, a shockingly tacky space decorated with a Tuscan-themed mural and bowls of fake grapes set on marble-topped tables. I was sitting next to an oversize rooster made of wrought iron while she doused my hands in rubbing alcohol.

Well, perhaps doused wasn't the correct word. But she wasn't exactly gentle as she pressed her alcohol-soaked swab into every cut. And there were many.

Behind her, Angel stood with his arms crossed over his chest, watching her every move.

Fiona's phone chirped and she looked away from her sadistic swab-based work on my hands. "I've got to run over to the main house. One of the camera guys had an allergic reaction to the cantaloupe on the breakfast bar."

"Because it's a horrible and useless fruit?" I asked.

"I can handle it from here," volunteered Angel.

Fiona heaved a heavy sigh. "You've got to go in with the tweezers and pull out any remaining thorns." She turned to me. "It'll hurt."

I sniffed. "I am very familiar with Angel causing me pain."

She shrugged and rushed out the door as Angel sat down on the little stool in front of me.

"I'll be gentle," he said.

"Don't start now."

He paused and looked directly at me, his gaze practically pinning me to the wall before reaching into Fiona's kit for a long pair of pointed tweezers.

I flinched slightly.

"Don't look," he whispered. "It's easier if you're not anticipating it."

I didn't trust him, of course, but he did make sense. So although it pained me to listen to his advice, I closed my eyes.

He started talking, his voice soft and cheerful. He was trying to distract me from what he was doing to my hands. "Mackenzie's Julia Roberts hooker dress"—he plucked a thorn from my palm with a quick, graceful jerk and I gasped—"was uncanny . . . not that I've actually seen the original movie."

My eyes shot open. "I'm sorry. What?"

He held up the tweezers. "Eyes closed."

I obeyed. "You have some explaining to do."

"I'm sure it's a great movie, but it came out a decade before I was born. Plus I was more of an anime gay than a 'divas of the past' gay." He pulled out another thorn, which seemed to hurt less than the last one.

"I resent the fact that you would refer to Julia Roberts as a past diva," I told him.

He laughed softly as he continued to work. "Just a few more," he promised.

We sat there in silence, the only sound in the Tuscan nightmare room our breathing and the occasional clink of the tweezers.

The sun pouring in through the windows caught on his eyelashes and made his small diamond studs wink against his earlobes. It had never escaped my notice that Angel spent all his waking hours trying to make art when he *was* art already. All he had to do was smile or move or breathe, and he showed the world some ineluctable revelation about being alive.

"Okay," he finally said. "You can look."

I opened one eye to find him smirking as he tore open a new alcohol swab and started cleaning the cuts for a final time.

As he worked, I noticed a speck of color on his biceps peeking out from the sleeve of his T-shirt.

"That's new," I said, pointing with the hand not currently being tended to.

He glanced down, slight blush gathering in the apples of his cheeks.

I took the liberty of lifting the hem of his sleeve and laughed for what felt like the first time in months. "Is that . . . a reindeer . . . on ice skates?"

Right there on Angel's arm was a vintage-looking mint green reindeer wearing an ice skate on each leg. Its legs were sprawling and wobbly looking, like it was skating for the very first time.

"It's a character I developed," he said, tugging his sleeve back down. "I . . . uh . . . the studio I was interning with this spring decided to use it for one of their children's holiday specials."

"Really?" Inside I was beaming with pride, but on the outside I maintained my nonchalance-bordering-on-disgust. "That's sort of a big deal, isn't it?"

He returned to his diligent work on my hands. "For me it was."

"Is that why you were in France?" I asked quietly. "To intern with them?"

He nodded.

"Was it top secret or something?"

He shook his head. "I only found out when we were sitting there at the airport. I applied late . . . so I found out at the last minute."

"And you just couldn't tell me?" I asked.

He looked up from beneath his heavy, sun-drenched lashes. "I tried."

"Did you?"

"I wanted to, and I'm sorry I screwed that up." He shook his head. "At the airport. I was trying and then I couldn't find the words and we were kissing, and you had to get on your plane. And then I was a total mess when I landed in Paris. When I showed up to my new place the day I landed, the pipes were rusted in the apartment Astrid had helped me find. She'd literally taken a tour via FaceTime while I was in the air. Luckily, my ride from the airport was willing to take me out for the day while my apartment was de-flooded. Not to mention that my phone wasn't working because I couldn't connect to a French carrier right away."

"I guess the internet doesn't exist in France then. I wouldn't know. I've never been."

Angel gave me a look. "By the time I got my phone figured out and settled, you'd blocked me everywhere."

I narrowed my eyes, remembering that I hadn't blocked him before I saw Blake's post of them together at the Eiffel Tower. Blake must have been the *ride from the airport*, which was also kind of galling on its own, because an ex you trusted to battle an airport arrivals lane for you??? That was barely an ex! That was someone you might still adopt a pet with one day!

And flooded apartments and phone carriers aside, he'd still boarded a plane to another continent without telling me first. It was ghosting of the highest order. Mon beau fantôme!

"*And* you can't even remember your own email address," Angel added to his last reply.

"Email addresses are pointless," I reminded him. "There are a million other ways for people to get a hold of me. Texts. Calls. Direct messages. And I do know my email address. It's written down somewhere."

"God, you're worse than my dad. He keeps a Post-it with all his passwords in his wallet."

"I would never put a Post-it inside my Hermès wallet. The adhesive could compromise the leather."

He grinned the same way he always had when he thought I was being adorably ridiculous. His hands slid up my forearms as he checked his work. Goose bumps followed his touch, which was all the warmer for how cold my alcohol-dabbed hands were, and I hated that it felt so good when I was still so upset with him.

How could he not tell me that Paris was on the table?

How could he just *leave the continent* with no word at all?

And *why* had Blake been there too? There was no way that windsock motherfucker had been interning at an animation studio too.

"You'd be shocked by how many people don't realize they have a melon allergy," Fiona said as she sashayed back through the sliding glass door of the pool house. "Oh, Angel! You've got him all cleaned up and ready for his bandages! And he was such a fussy patient. I'm impressed."

"I'm sorry if acknowledging my pain is fussy," I said in a venomous tone that rolled right off her as she shooed Angel out of her seat.

Angel watched intently as Fiona wrapped my hands in enough gauze and bandages that they were even more useless than they were before.

"How am I supposed to do anything like this? Especially my job!"

Fiona continued wrapping as she said, "Well, while you're on set, you should be all bandaged up, but at home, let your hands breathe when you can. But be gentle with them! No heavy lifting. And be sure to apply triple antibiotic cream twice a day." She patted my hands, which I couldn't even feel. "All set."

Slowly I lifted my bandaged hands. "My hands look like clubs," I said. "My precious, genius hands. I can't sew like this. I can barely even pick up a hanger." The bandages were so thick that my fingers could barely move.

Fiona shrugged with indifference. "I can't imagine a lot of clothing is actually involved on the set of a porn."

I was on the verge of hyperventilating. Most days my job included thongs and ball gags—which were sometimes the prop department's problem, depending on the scene. Also sometimes I was the props department. But with this movie, I had the chance to do something so perfectly suited to me. No one was out here trying to give me an award or any kind of recognition for my costuming, but this one was special. This one was something I could truly be proud of. But how could I possibly work without my—

"I'll be your hands," Angel said. "It can't be that hard."

There was no hiding the outrage on my face.

"No, no, no," he backpedaled. "I just meant that the hard part is what you do in your head. It's your taste and your vision. That's the part you can't teach me. But the sewing and the hanging and the organizing. That's stuff I can do—with your help, of course."

Fiona's brows arched. "He's got a point."

How did I go from being so completely over Angel to being stuck with him on set to actually needing him? I racked my brain for every possible alternative. Vanya was in Costa Rica for a breathwork retreat. Sunny was running this whole show, and Bee was on the set of her mainstream gig, *Nun of Your Business*.

I wanted more than anything for there to be another answer, but the thought of even holding a needle with the countless cuts in my hands made my eyes water.

"I guess I don't really have any other option, do I?"

Angel shook his head. "You and me at the end of the world," he said.

Chapter Four

Angel Fletcher loved apocalyptic movies. It was his favorite genre of movie. He watched them for comfort in the same way I watched ice skating compilations on YouTube or rom coms from the '90s and early 2000s. Or *The Little Mermaid* and *Mulan*.

(*The Little Mermaid* for Ursula, my inspiration in all things, and *Mulan* for Li Shang, the hottest cartoon character of all time.)

But nothing soothed Angel more than a blockbuster end-of-the-world movie. He especially loved the sad ones where the world really did end. So yesterday, when he looked all earnest and told me it was me and him until the end of the world, I wanted to kiss him and punch him at the same time.

Of course, I had a painfully hard boner all night, *and* I couldn't even tend to it with my new mummy-hands.

Today we were shooting on-site, using a run-down strip mall in Sherman Oaks for our Rodeo Drive store, except in our version the iconic scene would end in a dressing room ménage between the two leads and the bitchy sales clerk.

Last night, I got a frantic text from Sunny asking me to load up my trunk with "fancy lady shit" to fill the store set. When I asked why the set department hadn't taken care of that, I was met with silence, which was so rich of her considering she had yet to apologize for locking me in a hostile environment with the enemy.

However, when I walked into the dilapidated former Jean Sue's Hallmark card store, it wasn't a good look.

"Cody thought I meant a rodeo store when I told him a *Rodeo Drive* store," Sunny said frantically.

I looked around at the wall lined with dusty boots surely found at thrift shops—and not the good kind. There were racks full of the kinds of jeans that had back pockets imprinted with dip canisters and threadbare pearl snap shirts with sweat stains.

"Please tell me you brought the goods," Sunny said, her hair piled on top of her head in a knot and the cobalt blue strap of her bra hanging off her shoulder. And this was only day two.

"You're asking me to turn Mountain Dew into wine here." I felt a little too righteously proud of myself for choosing not to hold her accountable for her actions yesterday at this moment. "And yes, my trunk is full. But first we have to get this stuff out of here. It smells like a serial killer's storage unit in this place."

Sunny nodded. "Not sexy. Not sexy at all. Cody!" she yelled. "Take this shit back to the hellscape from whence it came."

"Please note that it was no easy task to load my personal collection of fine goods without opposable thumbs," I told her as I passed off my car keys. "Cody and his crew can unload when they're done clearing this out, but they must handle my things with care and use latex gloves."

"We're all about gloving it up here at Uncle Ray-Ray's," Sunny said.

"I don't need them getting their grimy sebaceous oils all over my goodies." And it was true. I'd never had a lot of money, but sometimes in the fashion game, time trumped money and I'd spent thousands of hours of my life combing secondhand shops for the kind of collection most LA stylists would kill for. So much of it I hadn't even used, but the only thing I loved as much as I did creating beautiful things was collecting them and surrounding myself with them.

After leaving Sunny with my keys, I went to what was the old employee break room.

I braced myself to find Angel waiting there for me, but he was nowhere to be seen. However, the day's wardrobe was already unpacked and neatly labeled. Maybe if he continued to help me out while managing to remain unseen, we'd survive this shoot after all.

"Lucaaaaa!" Mackenzie said as she teetered through the door, her makeup half done and her red hair in curlers. "Can you run my line with me?" she asked as she attempted to hand me a single sheet of paper that I, of course, could not grasp with my bandaged hands. This morning, I'd had to brush my teeth by holding the toothbrush between my gauze paws. It had been the second clumsiest thing I'd ever done, aside from a regrettable footjob I'd once given a cellist.

Mackenzie watched me struggle until finally I said, "Let's just put it on the table."

I sat as she placed the paper down, patting it on each corner like it was a good girl.

After a quick glance, it became clear that most of the page was blocking save for Mackenzie's one single line. I cleared my throat. "Um, ready when you are."

She closed her eyes and stretched her mouth before standing up with her arms held out, holding imaginary shopping bags. "You're making a real mistake," she said in her best pouty voice. Dropping her arms, like she was carrying actual weight, she turned to me. "How was I?"

"Well, considering the line is actually 'Big mistake. Big. Huge.,' I'd say you could use some work."

She plopped down in the chair across from me. "But doesn't my version work so much better?"

"Mackenzie, babes, this is the most iconic line in the original movie. You kind of have to get it right."

"I just really want to make this role my own. My agent thinks this could get me a performer of the year nomination at the AVNs this year."

The thought of Mackenzie ruining one of the most important lines in cinematic history made my body feel like curdled milk. "You've seen the original, right?" I dared to ask.

"Parts of it," she said with a shrug. "Sunny asked me to watch it, but my acting coach, WeHo Hank, said I should avoid the source material because of bias or whatever."

"Mackenzie, with all due respect, WeHo Hank sounds like a fuckwad. How have so many people on this set not seen *Pretty Woman*?"

"I mean, if I'm being honest, I don't really think any good movies were made before *Iron Man 3*."

My brain made a record-scratching sound. "I'm going to go ahead and rewind back to thirty seconds ago when those cursed words had yet to leave your mouth." I pulled out my phone and searched on YouTube for the iconic scene. "Scoot over a little closer."

She obeyed and I hit play. We watched as the deeply early '90s saleswomen refused to tell Vivian the price of the dress she was looking at, and then told her to leave the store. I paused the video.

"Look at her," I said. "Vivian is so vulnerable at this moment. These shopkeepers have no idea how important this singular event is in the story of her life. To them, she's just another customer. To Vivian, this is a make-or-break moment."

I pressed my gauze-wrapped hand to my chest, wishing I could massage away the sudden ache there. *I* had been Vivian so many times before—not the least when I fell in love with an artsy boy who clearly saw me as someone only fit for a good time in Vermont before pursuing his computer animation dreams with his porn star ex.

Tale as old as time.

And like Vivian, I wasn't taking the world's cruel nonsense lying down. Angel could tell me all the French-flavored excuses he wanted, but that didn't mean I was ready to forgive or forget. Pas de pardon!

"We need Mackenzie in five!" someone called from the other side of the door.

I looked down at my bandaged hands. "I hope you can work a zipper on your own," I told her, doubting the possibility as the words left my mouth.

Mackenzie looked at me with doe eyes.

"Need any help?" Angel asked as he poked his head in through the door. Today he wore a sleeveless black turtleneck with jeans, boots, and a few gold rings on his fingers. The collar of the turtleneck emphasized the long arch of his throat, and the sleeveless cut revealed the tightly toned swells of his biceps and shoulders. They were lean muscles, but so lickable I could die looking at them.

No. He's the enemy.

No licking the enemy.

"How are you with zippers?" I asked.

Angel grinned and trotted into the room, unzipping the garment bag with Mackenzie's white puffy-sleeved dress with large buttons marching down the middle. I hadn't updated the look a whole lot, since it was so iconic, but I had sharpened up the tailoring to give it more structure and a slightly more contemporary vibe.

"How are your hands feeling?" Angel asked as he helped with the zip on the back of her dress.

"Traumatized. In complete agony." Although that wasn't entirely true. Other than not being able to jack off or make my own cup of coffee, I'd been fine. It was when the bandages were off that I could feel the sting of every little cut, as I had in the shower last night before clumsily rebandaging them myself.

He frowned as he continued to help Mackenzie, who truly did not seem to understand how clothing worked.

Just then, Blake walked in, already beginning to shed his clothing. "Is this my suit?" he asked as he unnecessarily slid his belt out of his loops. "Yo, Kenz, you look like a lady."

She curtsied. "Thanks, Blakey."

"Angel, hey," Blake said, with a dimpled bro smile that almost even worked on *me*. Gah! Curse his symmetrical, suntanned features!

Angel gave him a friendly smile back, and I wanted to smash up the room with my gauze paws. But no. I must have *composure*. I was above such petty emotions as jealousy.

"If you need any help with your zippers, Angel is here to assist you," I told him. I was very proud of how well I nailed my 1940s movie starlet tone. Aloof and biting. I didn't even care that Angel's ex was about to get naked and fuck in front of us all. Why would I care?

But then Angel glared at me, and I had to admit to myself that I quite enjoyed that.

Maybe I cared a little.

Blake was oblivious to the tension he'd caused by walking into the room with his horribly muscular body. "I hope these pants have more stretch than yesterday's," he complained. "I'm already rocking a semi."

Mackenzie shimmied as Angel finally worked the zipper up to her neck, and she gave a little *wee*-sounding shriek. "Isn't he such a professional?" she asked me, beaming at Blake. "Do you know how many hours of my life I've spent waiting for my costars to get hard?"

"I'm guessing more hours than you've spent watching *Pretty Woman*."

Blake, by some strange porn magic, was already mostly in his suit and buttoning up his shirt. Mackenzie slid on her gloves as Angel placed a wide-brimmed black hat on her head. With her pearl earrings and low heels, she almost sold the look. Once the curlers came out and her low ponytail was fluffed, she'd be the perfect porn facsimile of Vivian on Rodeo Drive.

"I need help with the tie," Blake announced. "I don't normally wear these things. Too stuffy."

Very believable, since I was reasonably sure Blake took his dates to baseball games, movies with explosions, or skee-ball lounges. Unfortunately, I was in no position to knot a tie with my gauze paws, and there'd be a Cheesecake Factory on the moon before Mackenzie could figure out a decent Windsor knot.

Which left Angel.

Wordlessly, Angel went to Blake and took the tie from him, looping it around his neck, and quickly adjusting the length. There wasn't anything overtly sexual about it, not objectively, but as Angel's deft artist's fingers began fixing the silk into a neat loop, tugging on it to keep it even, Blake's eyes slid to mine. I detected a hint of a smirk on his well-moisturized lips.

Jealousy burned in my gut, and I looked away. I know I wasn't supposed to care, but why did Angel's ex have to be *here*? And why did he have to be in Paris with Angel last January? If I didn't have any fuckable himbos following me around, then it wasn't fair that Angel did either!

Finally, Blake's tie was knotted, and Angel stepped back, giving it an appraising eye. "Looks good," he said. "My mom would be glad to know that dragging me to all of her boring TV network parties ended up being good for something."

Blake gave Angel's arm a familiar squeeze, and then he turned to his costar. He held an arm out for her. "Ready to bone?" he asked gallantly.

"Even more ready than I was last night," she said with a big grin. She linked her arm through his and they were on their way.

"Are those two fucking?" I asked as soon as the door shut. "Like off camera?"

Angel sat down beside me. "Probably. Blake isn't a complicated man. He likes sex and he likes it with as little inconvenience as possible." Angel said it without bitterness, just like a statement of fact. Like it was something he'd long accepted.

"So does that mean that you two aren't . . ."

"We are not."

"You certainly looked like you were with him in Paris."

Angel cut me a look that said *don't start*. "Let me see your hands," he said instead. "Show me where it hurts."

Maybe I should just rip my chest open then, I nearly said.

But instead I let him unravel my bandages in the quiet of this little break room.

"Sunny says you really saved the day out there. We only have this location for two days, so she would have been hosed without you."

"Well, I'm glad to know my vintage designer collection is good for something."

With both my hands finally free, he held them each up and began to examine them carefully.

He blew on one particularly gnarly cut on the heel of my hand, giving me instant relief from the slight sting of having the many wounds exposed.

"Death by a million paper cuts," I said. "That's what it feels like."

He blew on my other palm, his eyes locked with mine.

Without looking away or even a second of hesitation, he pressed his lips to my hand as though he could kiss away the pain.

I gasped softly, but loud enough for him to hear.

His mouth trailed down to my wrist, and oh, I liked that. I liked that far too much.

And judging by the way his long lashes fluttered and his breath hitched as he kissed along the line of my pulse, so did Angel.

Chapter Five

*A*ngel stood, pulling me with him.

I knew losing him a second time would hurt twice as much, but with his lips tracing up my arm and then to my neck, my brain shorted out every time I attempted to consider Future Luca's regrets.

Angel backpedaled to the door with his arm pulling me close to him so that our legs were no more than a tangle of limbs. With one hand, he wedged a chair under the doorknob.

"What are you doing?" I breathed, my mouth hungry for his, as he continued to place teasing kisses all over my neck, ears, cheeks, and even eyelids.

"The kind of thing that requires locked doors," he said as he pressed his hardening crotch against my hip.

He spun me around, crowding me against the wall as his hand slid down my chest and over my belt buckle until he was cupping my already stiff cock in his hand.

"Do you know how long I've been dreaming of this moment?" Angel rasped as he nipped at my neck.

"One hundred seventy-eight days, three hours, and seven minutes?"

A small laugh huffed near my ear.

"I mean, maybe it's been that long," I said with great dignity. "I don't actually know because I would never keep track of such a thing."

"No shame in that," he murmured. "I had to jack off in a bathroom stall before my flight, you know."

"Was that before or after you decided to disappear?"

He tightened his grip on my dick. "You're such a fucking brat. *You* disappeared on me."

"You love it," I said as I reached back to find his waist, hip, anything to hold on to. "God, I was so hard when I got home yesterday. But I couldn't even do anything about it."

He pulled on the waistband of my leopard print joggers—the only pants I'd been able to pull on today without pain shooting through my hands. I felt the tug and pull on the elastic like his hand was already inside my pants.

"Let me help," he said, his voice low and smooth. "That's what friends are for, right?"

My head fell forward and hit the wall as his fingers pushed past the waistband and found me completely bare.

"Luca," Angel chided, still in that low voice. "No briefs? Someone might think you were hoping for this."

I'd skipped underwear because of the hand issue, but maybe there had been a small, *infinitesimal* part of me that wanted to be ready for a sexy close-up. I mean, didn't we all do that when we knew we'd be in the same four block radius of someone who made our heart speed up? Dress to impress? Shave what needed to be shaved? Skip the meat and cheese the night before in favor of more penetration-friendly gummy bears and gin?

The minute his fingers wrapped around my shaft, I lost all sense of pride, dignity, and justice. I just rolled my forehead along the cheaply painted wall, panting as his warm grip loosely shuttled down my aching dick and then back up again. He was unfairly good at this, and you know what? I blamed art school. All those hours shaping stubborn, stiff clay and painting tiny grapes in tiny bowls to pinpoint precision. His hand was strong, certain—delicate when needed and deliciously rough every other time. He was the artist, and my body was his medium.

"Is that better?" he said, all that smoothness from earlier sounding a little rougher now, and I nodded against the wall, helpless when it came to his long, strong fingers around my aching inches. "Is that what you've been needing?"

"Oh God, so much," I grunted, my eyes fluttering closed. "Yes. Yes. Please don't stop."

Sensation skated up all my nerve endings as his fingers tightened around me, and then, with a deft flick of his wrist, he gathered the slick precum around my tip on his palm and used it to jerk me all the harder.

My thighs were tight, my pulse thrumming. Not that I would ever admit it, even if someone strapped me to a chair and made me watch a CBS sitcom with a canned laugh track, but this was the first time since January that I'd been touched by anyone other than myself. I'd like to think it was because no one in LA was meeting my quite reasonable pansexual standards of being gorgeous, interesting, empathetic, and able to sit through at least four consecutive hours of *Wife Swap* reruns. But . . . maybe that wasn't the entire truth?

Maybe the truth was that no one else was Angel Fletcher other than Angel Fletcher, and I was therefore ruined with what LA had to offer, even to such a gem as myself. Maybe the truth was that being with anyone other than Angel had felt weird and hollow and like a betrayal, and not even a betrayal to him or to the memory of what we were, but to myself, somehow. Like settling for something cheap that would only hurt me in the long run. Call it Taco Bell Syndrome.

I'd known hooking up just for the sake of hooking up when my heart was still beating for copper-brown eyes and paint-stained fingertips would only make me ache worse in the end.

"You feel so hot in my hand," Angel whispered, biting at my neck. His other hand had curled around my hip, and I realized it was so he could hold me tight against his groin, so that he could rub himself against me, stroke his erection through his jeans against my ass. With him driving his hips against my back and his fist working me at the front, I knew I was doomed. My balls were already pulling up tight to my body, my core was already tense with that gorgeous, shimmery feeling, and I was about three seconds and another earlobe-bite away from spattering this corporate-beige wall with a very organic white.

"Angel," I breathed as the pleasure sank its vicious claws deep into my belly and pulled. "I'm gonna—"

"Good," Angel said fiercely, his fist tighter and faster, his own cock fucking against me through our clothes. "You owe me this. You owe me this, and so much more."

It was too much. His hard erection wedged against my ass, his vicious fist up front.

My rough genius, my hungry artist, dry-fucking me like a comet was heading to earth and this was the last chance either of us would have to get off.

And it was so fucking hot, so wonderfully, miserably *perfect*, that I couldn't even be mad at him or myself when the orgasm ripped through my body and jerked along my dick. Thick, white pulses spilled over Angel's fist, slick and thick and wet, and they kept coming, even as Angel's hand went still and he gave me two punishing thrusts from behind. His broken exhales in my ear and the bruising hold on my hip told me all I needed to know—he just came too. From dry-humping me in the back room of a failed knickknack store.

We both slowly went still, and I opened my eyes and dropped my gaze to see a puddle of semen on the floor between my legs.

"I feel like this is usually a *front of house* problem in our line of work," I mumbled, and Angel laughed. Not his polite laugh. Not even his usual laugh. But his belly-deep giggle that only came out with the people closest to him.

My heart popped like an overinflated balloon just to hear it.

"You're right," he said, still laughing. "And oh my God, I'm going to need to borrow some pants from the costume department. Okay, you stay there, I'll get us sorted out."

After he made sure I was clean, the floor was sort of clean, and he'd changed into a pair of extra suit pants, we sat on the little loveseat in the break room with my legs stretched out over his lap. He was re-gauzing my hands, because apparently fresh bandages weren't a lie told by World War Two costume dramas.

"You should be able to lose the bandages in the next few days, I think," Angel told me.

I couldn't stop the words before they left my lips. Wit was a curse sometimes. "Oh, is that what you were doing in Paris? Your medical residency?"

"Is it always going to be like this?" he asked, glancing up at me through his heavy lashes. "You never letting me forget?"

"Considering you walked back into my life out of nowhere yesterday, yes, it is going to be like this for a little while."

Except even I wanted to let it go and just let us start all over again. Not only did I lose the romantic relationship I'd had with Angel over the last several months, but I'd lost our friendship too, which had always felt easy and casual and refreshing, if subject to ebbs and flows. But it was always there. Until it wasn't. There were no more cheeky comments on my Instagram posts or funny little random TikToks waiting for me in my DMs.

And I was all too aware of my inability to let things go. Just like a moment ago, I constantly said the kind of things I always wanted to chomp back in my mouth like a Hungry Hungry Hippo. But I'd always had a sharp tongue, and after leaving my life behind as Jeffrey in my itty-bitty small town, I swore to never again make myself smaller or more palatable for anyone else.

Angel had hurt me, and as much as I wanted to forgive him, I didn't know if I could ever let go of how insignificant he'd made me feel.

"I thought we were just a fling, and I thought we were that way because that's how *you* wanted it," Angel finally said as he finished off the last of the bandages. He straightened up and met my eyes. "Luca, you're this impossible-to-impress person. Do you know that? You can come across as cold—or indifferent even—yet somehow, you're this sort of . . . light, I guess. And you draw people in like moths to a flame."

I both hated and loved his description of me, because yes, my younger self would feel so vindicated. All I'd ever wanted was to be as coolly magnetic as Marlene Dietrich in the first forty minutes of a black-and-white movie.

And yet, I was so disappointed that Angel couldn't see through that facade to *me*.

"I thought you wouldn't even care that I left," he finished. I could hear the honesty in his voice, see it shining in his eyes. And it fucking baffled me. How, how, *how*, could he think I wouldn't care?

I pulled my hands back from him and stood. "Angel, I invited you to Vanya's birthday party! I was trying to make plans with you. How could I not care?"

"I thought you were being nice! A party invite at some artist's house—that's basically how art students say hello, you know."

"I'm never nice!" I began to shout, but then whispered that last word as I realized they were filming an epic threesome in the next room over.

"I'm sorry I can't read your mind," he said, beginning to lose his patience with me.

I could have sat down. I could have talked through this with him and truly tried to understand how he could possibly think I wouldn't care where he went and what he did after spending the best month of my life with him.

But I could feel the tears brimming already, and I hated myself for it, so instead, I threw up my arms, and said, "Big mistake, Angel. Big. Huge."

Chapter Six

I stayed on set for the rest of the day brooding until flaking out and telling Sunny I needed to go home. It didn't matter, because apparently Angel was just so damn good at my job. He was a natural! A savant! A prodigy!

Okay, no one actually said those things, but if I wasn't already pissed at him, I would have become pissed at him for being so good at my job.

So I went home. And I wallowed.

I nearly called the emergency number Vanya left behind, but sadly the only person my emotional meltdown was an emergency for was me.

I knew how people perceived me. That wasn't news. The problem with people thinking I was untouchable was that no one bothered to think twice about hurting me. It wasn't that I didn't care. It was that I cared too much.

And for Angel not to see that . . . for him not to recognize that in me made me wonder if he'd ever taken the time to understand me in the way I thought I had understood him.

That night I fell asleep with my phone in my hand, clumsily scrolling through photos of us in a bathtub back in Christmas Notch. Each photo was blurrier than the last, with suds smeared

SNOW PLACE LIKE LA

across the lens and our cute selfies turning steamy as he nibbled up my neck, his teeth nipping at my jawline.

When I woke up, I was throbbingly hard and made the immediate decision to text Sunny and let her know I wouldn't be coming in today.

She asked if I was okay, and I simply replied: I am unwell.

I felt that covered a whole host of reasons to play hooky. My unresolvable boner. My broken heart. My bruised ego.

I was unwell, indeed.

The next day I called in sick too. Sunny had texted to let me know what a great job Angel did in my place, and even though it was meant to comfort me, it made me feel even shittier.

I spent the morning curled up on my couch in my favorite caftan and rewatching my favorite episodes of *The Great British Bake Off*, flipping through old bridal magazines as I did. My hands were starting to feel usable again, so I opted to make peanut butter ramen, my favorite comfort food, rather than order out.

Just as I was settling in for an afternoon of *Love Island*, there was a knock at my door.

I lived in a Silver Lake pool house apartment behind the home of a retired voice-over actress who made a small fortune as the voice of CVS. She was rarely home and hadn't raised my rent since I'd moved in three years ago. I had access to her pool and I also had air-conditioning. It was pretty much perfect. But in order to find me, you had to know I was back here.

When I opened the door, I found Angel standing on my doormat that read, "Where the hell have you been, loca?" (My favorite quote from the *Twilight* franchise.)

"Sunny said you were sick," he blurted as I stood there with my arms crossed over my chest.

His eyes trailed over my body, hovering on my hands for a moment.

I held a fist to my mouth and let out a pathetic *cough, cough.* "So sick."

Angel studied me for a moment longer, and with each passing second, I could feel the invisible armor I always seem to have beginning to crack. If only he could see it too.

"I guess you might as well come in," I told him.

He shoved his fists into his pockets and shook his head. "Nope. If I go in there . . . I can't trust myself in there with you alone, and I'm pretty sure you can't either. Besides . . ." He peered past me to the nest of blankets and bridal magazines on my chartreuse-and-pink plaid sofa. "You could probably use some air."

I squinted at the bright blue sky behind him. He wasn't wrong. "Give me ten," I said. "Are you sure you don't want to come in?"

He shifted a moment before nodding.

After a quick-ish change into some platformed Converse, black jeans, and a white shirt that said FERAL in very small letters, I reappeared at the door, donning my sunglasses with as much dignity as I could muster. "I'm ready."

Outside, Angel led me to his old Bronco, a Teddy Ray Fletcher hand-me-down, parked out front. "Can you swim?"

"Um, I am not wearing water-appropriate attire. These are Marc Jacobs Converse."

He glanced down at my feet. "I didn't say we were actually going swimming."

WE STOOD AT the entrance of the Echo Park boathouse under a sign for swan pedal boat rentals as the employee handed us each a musty old life jacket. "And these are required?" I asked, holding mine away from my body so I didn't inhale any rare and deadly must-germs.

The teenage boy looked from me to Angel with dead eyes.

"Ignore him," Angel told him as he tightened the straps on his, somehow making the vest look hot.

He stepped onto our boat and then held a hand out for me, which I refused at first, but the moment my foot left the safety of the dock, I lost all sense of dignity and allowed him to assist me. I had a keen eye for color, but I'd never claimed to have any sense of balance.

"I'm not really a big fan of water," I admitted. "Especially being out in the middle of it with no escape."

"The no escape part is really important actually," Angel said as he began to pedal and steer our two-person boat.

The pedals spun at my feet, their plastic and metal whirring sounding very judgmental. So, begrudgingly, I began to pump my legs up and down to help Angel. "You said we would get fresh air. Not that you'd be subjecting me to manual labor. And in the middle of a body of water! Where I can't even escape!"

"Well, that's sort of the point," he said plainly as he steered us past the large fountain at the center of the lake. "My mom brought my dad out here when she told him she was pregnant with Astrid. She didn't want him to be able to run away or flip out."

"Did he?" I asked. "Flip out?"

"Legend says he stood up and dove into the water. Dad says he was so excited he fell in. According to Mom, it was more of a shock response."

"Teddy's a good dad," I told him. My parents never disowned me or anything, but they never really knew what to do with me. We did a short phone call on holidays, with very rare visits, while Teddy side hustles Christmas movies to fund Angel's and Astrid's dreams.

My dad didn't even offer to fill up my gas tank when I drove to LA after high school.

"So I guess you thought I was a flight risk?"

"Well, you did dive out a window into a bush to avoid talking to me."

I eyed the turtle swimming alongside our swan boat. He was free. Swim, little turtle! Swim! "I don't know what else there is to talk about," I said.

"How about we start with this? You broke my heart last winter."

I gasped. "That's my line and you know it! How can you even accuse me of being the heartbreaker in this situation?"

He stopped pedaling, and we came to a stop, our boat floating off on our own. "Luca, you literally deleted me from your life. You didn't even give me a chance to explain."

"You humiliated me," I told him. What I didn't say was that humiliation was right up there with a broken heart for me.

He swiveled toward me and took my hand, refusing to speak until finally I looked up at him. How was he so fucking earnest? How was he so good at tricking me into thinking I was the only person in the world?

"I'm sorry," he finally said. "You have to know that I am so deeply sorry for not telling you about Paris before I left."

"Do I have to know?" I said, looking away from him, but not pulling my hand free. "This is the first time you've given me a real apology for it."

The sun glinted off the water in bright, shimmering shards; it was the kind of hot summer mood meant for movie montages and influencer stories featuring micro bikinis and a Hadid sister in the background. We couldn't be farther away from that month in Vermont right now.

"You're right," Angel said quietly. "So here it is. I'm sorry. I found out at the last minute, and I wanted to tell you, but I went into self-preservation mode, and I'm sorry."

I inhaled and exhaled through my nostrils, a wave of emotions assaulting me. "I—I've liked you for so long, Angel. Christmas Notch felt like a miracle. I've been terrified of taking that leap with you, because I'd never get my first shot back. But now we're damaged goods, and I don't know what to do with that. I don't know how to forget how you made me feel."

"Luca," he whispered. "Nothing is ever wholly good or wholly bad. No place or person or relationship. You really want to throw all this away because we fucked it up the first time?"

My eyes began to burn with tears.

"This feels big. We feel big. I can't let you give up on us."

I finally looked back at him. "It felt like you gave up first, and that's a lot for me to forgive." I paused. It all came down to one thing. "How could you not tell me?"

Angel let out a long breath. His hand around mine was still there, though, reassuring. Like . . . like we could argue and still hold on to each other. Like we could be uncertain about everything else, but still know that we wanted to be in the same place, uncertain together.

"Do you remember who kissed whom first that night after The North Pole?" Angel asked.

The memory made my cheeks warm—well, even warmer than a swan-boat excursion in July had made them already. "You kissed me. I am *whom*."

"And who was it who said they wanted to spend more time together after? And who was it who suggested renting the house and staying in Christmas Notch a little while longer?"

"Objection! Leading the witness!"

"I always made the first move," Angel went on. "Talked first. Asked first. Was vulnerable first." He took a long breath, his eyes going down to our linked hands. "And I know part of that is me. That sometimes I can get . . . obsessive about things. Art. People. Whatever. And I was obsessed with you."

My heartbeat seized; I didn't even know what to do with myself. *I was obsessed with you.* He was? Like, really? That was better than anything, better even than love! I'd always wanted someone to be obsessed with me—and not even for *Mean Girls* quote reasons— but because there was something so bone-hummingly rich about knowing you were preoccupying someone's thoughts, starring in all of their daydreams. It was satisfying like chocolate cake or the sharp fizz of fresh champagne—a downright sensual experience.

Or so I'd always imagined. No one had ever been obsessed with me before (or admitted as much).

But I didn't miss Angel's use of the past tense there. And I also didn't miss that he still hadn't explained himself.

"Okay, so I take my time opening up," I said. "That doesn't mean I wouldn't care about someone I'd just spent a month with jetting off to Paris! With their ex! Their stupidly ripped ex!"

Angel turned as much as he could to face me. Our swan was gently rocking now, turning slowly in circles. "Firstly, I didn't go to Paris *with* Blake," said Angel. "I went and he was already there visiting his cousin and fucking his way through Montmartre. He picked me up from the airport, and then when my apartment ended up being a disaster, he took me out for the day while the place was filled with plumbers fixing the broken pipes. Nothing happened between us, and neither of us want anything to happen between us. He wants easy sex with no commitments. I want someone who understands that visual art and computer-designed art complement each other, and who will also get me a heating pad when I have a trapped fart."

I could see why that wouldn't be Blake. Even in our very open, very queer circle of art and porn, there were some men who embraced toxic masculinity to the extreme. Blake wasn't a *bad* person, but he also wasn't exactly the listening, *care about my lover's tummy ache* type of guy.

"Secondly," continued Angel, "I definitely didn't know whether you'd care if I left or not. We were getting ready to leave our little paradise, and you didn't even tell me you wanted to *date* when we got home."

"Erroneous!" I exclaimed. "As mentioned many times prior to this boat ride, I invited you to Vanya's!"

"You told me I could come to a friend's birthday party *if I wanted*. You said you'd *like to see me there*. That's not telling someone you'd like to continue things, Luca. That was you offering just enough to make me chase you again. But after so much chasing, I had to ask myself if you really wanted to be chased at all. I had to ask if maybe you were just looking for a polite way to wind things down, and if this was all some convenient fuckfest for you and nothing more."

"How dare! How very dare! I am not the convenient fuckfest type!" Which was sometimes to my great regret, but still.

I thought he was narrowing his eyes at me from behind his mirrored sunglasses right now. "How am I supposed to know that, Luca? How many serious relationships have I seen you in over the years? Scratch that, how many *relationships period* have I seen you in?"

Ooh! I wanted to jump out of this swan right now and swim dramatically to shore. "Objection! Irrelevant!"

"I don't think it is. So tell me what you would think in my shoes? That this person who never has relationships, who never opens up—"

"I do too! I have no boundaries!"

"—about anything that matters—"

"That's because of my tragic Oregonian backstory!"

"—would you think that this person might actually care for me and want to build something with me? Or that I just needed to be grateful for the time that I'd had with him, and accept that he didn't want a future?"

I sat stonily, my jaw tight, my chin threatening to tremble. "You're not being very fair right now," I managed to say without my voice wavering.

Angel didn't speak for a moment. When I looked over at him, he was staring at the skyscrapers in the distance, his throat working.

"It's hard for me to open up too, Luca," he finally said.

His voice was soft, and it *did* waver a little, and suddenly I felt like a feelings miser. Like I'd been so busy making sure he didn't know how upset I was that I hadn't made space for him to be upset too.

"It's scary for me too," he continued. "I don't have a tragic Oregonian backstory, but that doesn't mean that I'm not also scared of being rejected. Of someone not understanding me. I can get weird about art, sometimes I disappear into it, sometimes I try to disappear away from it. It makes me difficult to be around sometimes."

I couldn't stop the scoff that pushed out of my chest. "You've never been difficult to be around."

"You only have a month's worth of data to work with," he replied dryly.

"I've known you a lot longer than a month. And you might be a little sensitive, and yes, a little obsessive like you said, but you're never difficult, Angel. You are passionate and funny and you see so much about the world around you, and anyone who thinks you're difficult doesn't deserve to even look at the same sun as you do."

I stopped as I realized I was ranting now. But I couldn't help it; Angel was a hot genius who was also hilarious and who fucked like it was his profession (high praise, given the industry we were connected with). Who wouldn't adore this man???

"Sorry. I just can't even conceive of someone thinking you aren't perfect," I said.

A smile twitched around Angel's mouth. "Thanks. I feel the same about you, you know."

I was about to say that everyone thought I was perfect . . . but then I realized that might not be *strictly* true.

"Anyway," Angel said, with the voice of someone getting back to business, "the point is that I couldn't find a way through all of those feelings and fears in the minutes I had between getting my acceptance email and your flight getting called. And then I told myself that I'd straighten everything out once I landed, but by the time I had a second to breathe and connect to the internet, you'd blocked me everywhere. After *two days*. And then I thought . . . *well, Angel, you were right. Luca didn't actually want you after all.* And if you didn't want me, there didn't seem like much use in forcing the issue. In trying to talk to you through one of our friends or something."

Oh. Oh fuck.

That . . . really, really sucked to hear. That my burn notice had burned someone who'd still cared for me, still wanted to be with me.

We sat without speaking, the boat slowly spinning. The splash of the nearby fountain filled the silence, but it didn't make it any easier to bear.

I took a breath, and then another, and then it just happened on its own.

"I'm sorry too," I said. "I'm sorry I didn't give you a chance to explain what was happening. And I'm sorry I didn't give you more reason before you left to know that I . . . liked you. Wanted to be with you. I'm really sorry, Angel."

I thought it would feel horrible to say, but it didn't. The truth was that I'd spent a lot of time when I was younger thinking I needed to be sorry, because my parents were this varietal of passive-aggressive mediocrity that was impossible to entirely explain, but was still awful to live with. Because I was as pansexual as they came, and I loved fashion-fuckery, and I loved attention and the spotlight, and *yes*, okay, I loved being one of a kind. As the meme goes, I was the drama. I didn't think my parents knew what to do with that, and I spent a long time thinking that was my fault.

So the moment I'd stepped foot in LA, I decided that I wasn't going to waste a single second of my life being sorry ever again.

Except that Angel wasn't my parents, Angel wasn't the cis-heteronormative patriarchy. Angel was wonderful and lovely, and if anyone deserved the s-word from me, it would be him.

Angel squeezed my hand at the same time I turned to face him.

"We both fucked up," I said.

"I know."

"And this is still really messy," I added.

"Yeah."

"But," I continued, "I think if we don't spend the night together, I'm going to jump out of this swan just like your dad did."

Angel smiled. The diamond studs in his ears sparkled just like the water around us. "That was almost romantic until you mentioned my dad."

"Okay, how about this. If we don't spend the night together, I will pout until you kiss me."

"You'd do that anyway," Angel pointed out.

"How do you know?"

His smile deepened until subtle dimples appeared in his cheeks. "You're doing it now," he murmured, leaning forward.

"Am I?" I asked with as much innocence as I could muster, also leaning forward. I could see my reflection in his sunglasses, just like I could see the reflection of him in *mine* also in his sunglasses, and it was like a hall of mirrors, Angel, Luca, Angel, Luca, both of us into infinity.

Angel's breath was sweet and minty as his lips brushed over mine. "You are," he confirmed, and then abruptly yanked me close to give me the kind of kiss that would have made Sunny call to keep the cameras rolling.

Chapter Seven

*W*e burst into the door of my converted-garage-slash-apartment like we were trying to break it down, Angel's hands twisted in my T-shirt and our mouths sealed together so tightly that our sunglasses were going askew. Angel kicked the door shut behind him as I ripped off both of our sunglasses and tossed them in a random direction, not caring if they broke or got stepped on or landed on something embarrassing, like my giant plastic bag full of other plastic bags that I kept meaning to recycle. Angel's tongue was slick and skilled, fluttering over the tip of my tongue until I groaned, and then plunging deep, stroking my mouth like he was fucking it.

Only tripping once over a stack of bridal magazines, we stumbled back to my couch, which was covered in thrifted afghan blankets and throw pillows that Sunny had embroidered with various genitals, and Angel pushed me down, crawling over me with a knee planted on either side of my hips, his mouth giving me no reprieve, no quarter. I was dizzy, from the kissing, from the erection that was currently straining the very well-constructed zipper of my vintage black jeans. From Angel's scent and his dilated pupils when he pulled back to look at me.

"I want to spend the rest of my life with my tongue in your mouth," Angel rasped, trailing his fingers over my swollen lips. "Too bad I can think of other things I'd like to do with it."

My hands were sliding up his hard thighs to his narrow hips. I encountered the turgid ridge of his hard-on before I got to the button of his slouchy khakis, and pressed my palm against it until he hissed. The cuts on my hands were mostly healed, but there was the tiniest bit of sting as I rubbed his dick over his pants, and I almost welcomed it, savored it even. It was like confirmation that I was here, that this was really happening, that it was really him under my hand, him above my hips, and that it wasn't one of the countless, countless dreams I'd had since I got on that plane home from Vermont.

My hands shook a little as I unbuttoned Angel's khakis, the trembles in my chest and stomach too as I unzipped the pants and pulled Angel's briefs down to expose his shaft. It was thick and long and cut, so I could see the perfect flare and swell of his crown. It was art all on its own, with two veins twining up the sides, and a mathematically straight line of dark hair marching down from his belly button straight to his base. I reached into his briefs and cupped his balls, grinning wickedly when he shuddered.

"Like that?" I asked, and he mock-scowled down at me.

"I hate it. Never do it again. And you better not stroke me behind there, that would make me really miserable."

"You were the one who called me a brat," I told him, sliding my fingers behind the tightening skin of his sack and running them along the warm skin of his perineum. He grunted a delicious noise as his hips rolled forward. And then he grunted again as I parted my lips and sucked his first two fingers into my mouth, grazing his fingertips with my tongue and then pulling them as far as they would go, nearly to the back of my throat. I might have been only porn-adjacent, but I did have a nonexistent gag reflex, something I attributed to a long habit of aggressively brushing the back of my tongue twice a day. (I like having fresh breath, okay? Sue me.)

Angel's pupils were so dilated now that his irises were a thin ring of bright brown around the black, and his throat worked as I sucked on his fingers. I found his stiff cock with my hands and gripped the hot, thick length, working both hands up and down until he was rocking his hips forward, fucking my fists.

He pulled his fingers free and reached behind himself. With some tugging and scooching, we had my jeans undone and pulled to my thighs. He rewetted his fingers in my open mouth and then reached back to jerk me slowly.

The first jolt of pleasure hit me like a train. I gasped, arching underneath him, and then unable to move much because he was still straddling me, I whined for more, which he gave.

I pulled on his cock until I'd guided him forward to straddle my chest. He still had a hold of me behind him, and the angle was a little awkward, but I subscribed to the philosophy that the hand of a cute guy on your cock at an awkward angle is better than no hand at all.

"Are you sure, babe?" he murmured, looking down at where the wet head of his dick was just a few inches from my mouth. The little pet name made my heart flutter, which was saying something, because the slow, torturous handjob he was giving me was sending me into arrhythmias, fibrillations.

"Never been surer," I replied and then took his slick crown between my lips.

He tasted wonderful, salt and skin and him, and I loved feeling him jump and jerk on my tongue, like just being in my mouth was enough to make him respond.

"Fuuuuck," Angel whispered, watching his erection disappear into my mouth. "You feel so good. Fuck."

I wrapped my fist around his base and worked the bottom of his shaft while I sealed my lips around him, making as much suction as I possibly could while also caressing his sensitive frenulum with my tongue.

"I'm not going to last," he warned me, his chest heaving. His eyes were molten on mine, his hand on my cock tight enough to make an angel sing. I didn't want him to last. I wanted him to spill all over my tongue, spill right down my throat. I wanted to taste him, to feel him pulsing, and know he was as far gone as I'd been all this time.

Also I was about to jizz all over his fist.

He went first, his thighs tensing around my shoulders, his breath coming out in a punched exhale as he surrendered to the primal need to fuck and shoved his way deeper into my mouth as he swelled and swelled. The dam broke, and he poured down my throat, spurt after thick spurt, his shaft flexing with each and every hard, long jet.

He had one hand on my cock, moving in irregular strokes, and his other hand on my jaw, and it was strange to feel treasured just then, but I did, I really did. He was still getting me off, even in the throes of his own pleasure, and his expression was something between awed and greedy. He was looking at me like he was trying to memorize this moment, memorize everything about it.

The orgasm rippled through me with abrupt speed, and I came with his cock in my mouth, twisting underneath him. I could hear my Converse on the sofa, rubber against the old velour cushions, and I could hear the now-slick sound of his hand working me over and over, determined to wring every last drop of pleasure from me that he could, even as he was still using my tongue to ride out the last throes of his release.

He slid free after a minute, although he kept his fist around my now-sensitive cock. He looked back over his shoulder at my groin.

"You made a mess," he teased.

I smiled up at him, my half-dressed and all messy body more loose and relaxed than I could remember it being since our cabin in Christmas Notch. "I think I have just the thing."

Chapter Eight

An hour later, and we were in a bubble bath. A legit bubble bath in the giant clawfoot tub that I'd rescued from my landlord's curb when she'd renovated her master bathroom to have a walk-in shower with LED lights and a built-in fireplace.

And despite an Ibiza-rave level of bubbles, we weren't doing a very good job of getting clean.

It had started innocently enough, with me sitting between Angel's legs while he stroked my arms and shoulders, and then somehow I ended up in his lap, and then somehow I was straddling him, my thumbs bracing his jaw as I kissed him as deeply as I could. Our erections grazed under the bubbles, and with a long groan, Angel grabbed my hips and yanked me closer, until we could grind together properly.

"Luca," he said, breathless from kissing, "there's still some other stuff we should talk about tonight."

Ugh! We'd done so much talking already! Talking responsibly was like donating blood—yes, it was fun to feel smug about my moral fortitude . . . but I was also exhausted and wanted a cookie.

Although I wasn't *that* exhausted . . .

"Later," I said against his lips. "I need help getting clean first."

I could feel Angel's smirk curve against my mouth, and then I felt the resulting puff of breath when I found one of the hands he had curled around my hip and guided it down and over my ass to the tight ring of muscle waiting for him.

Getting clean was a lie, really, because I'd taken a pre-sexy-bath shower while Angel had taken a call from a panicked Sunny, who was now anxious about the cinematographic kinship between her porn masterpiece and *Pretty Woman*, and suddenly wanted to run the entire film through the blue *Twilight* filter instead. So by the time we'd clicked open the lid on Mr. Bubble, my body was ready and my nether entrance was clean enough to eat off of—or at least to eat, which was more important to me anyway.

But Angel accepted my pretext and rubbed his fingers over my opening, pressing and testing the firm eyelet there as he caressed me. My erection jerked, and as I lifted to give him better access, it slid against the firm muscles of his stomach, the tip breaching the bubbles to the cool air of the room. I shivered.

"Yes?" he asked in a husky voice, his finger now toying with my opening.

"Yes," I breathed. I'd die if, after everything we'd been through, we didn't have a bubble bath bonedown.

We'd earned this bubble bath bonedown!

I reached past him to the small table next to my tub, which was mostly there for tub-wine purposes, but it was also convenient for other reasons . . . like a little drawer where I stored a bottle of silicone-based lube. I took the bottle and pressed it into his bubble-dripping hands.

"The condoms are in my bedroom," I said. "But . . . I haven't been with anyone since you."

He let out a long breath, ruffling some of the curls that hung over his forehead. "I haven't been with anyone since you either," he admitted.

I knew monogamy was a construct and a prison, et cetera et cetera, but God, it felt good to know that Angel had been right there with me. Alone, pining. Hungry but hungry only for a certain person. It made me feel wanted and chosen and together with him, and okay, maybe monogamy was a construct, but sometimes it had its charms. Like right now when no one had to do the wet-foot-shuffle across the tile to go get condoms.

"Then I'm okay going without," I told him. We had gone bare in Christmas Notch, both of us recently tested, since that was basically as easy as walking into the Uncle Ray-Ray's offices on nurse day.

"Okay," whispered Angel. "Only if you feel good about it."

I brushed wet fingertips along his narrow jaw, up to his temple. Without his glasses on, he looked younger and softer. Less *genius* and more *artist*. With those dark, heavy-lidded eyes and lush mouth, he could play a tortured Victorian poet in a biopic or something.

"I feel amazing about it," I replied. And then his finger brushed against me again and I moaned. "*Please.*"

"Fuck, I want to be inside you," he mumbled, pulling his hand out of the water to open the bottle of lube.

Joke was on me, and maybe even him, because he was already inside me. In all the ways that mattered. Since Christmas Notch. Since that fateful day two years ago when I saw him painting the neon pink Uncle Ray-Ray's logo in the lobby of Teddy's tiny strip mall office.

Angel paused what he was doing, and then reached over to the table and turned the Mr. Bubble bottle around, so Mr. Bubble was facing the other way.

"He doesn't need to see this," Angel said, and then squeezed some lube onto his fingertips.

He reached under the bubbles and smeared the cool liquid against my entrance, getting some more before he started pressing against the rim, teasing me open. He slowly, slowly breached me, sliding his finger into the first knuckle, and then the second as I quivered at the intimate touch.

My breath hitched as he added another finger, and Angel's eyes searched mine.

"How does it feel?" he asked. "Good? Slower?"

I slid my hands down to press against his chest. "It feels like I want more," I told him, and he laughed in a low, rough voice.

"I can do more."

He slid his fingers free and then got more lube. There was something about feeling his hands underneath me, getting his erection nice and slick for me, that made me so hard and squirmy. And when he grabbed my hip again and urged me against the slippery head of his cock, I could barely stand it. My eyes fluttered closed as the wide tip slowly worked the pleated aperture open and gradually, *so gradually*, pushed past the rings of muscle to slide all the way inside.

I was panting on top of him, and his free hand found my chest, pressing wetly against my heart.

"Still okay?" he asked.

"I'm fine. But have you ever considered not being so big?"

He laughed, and his organ flexed inside me, making my toes curl. "My apologies."

"Sunny always said it was the lanky ones to watch out for," I mumbled as I lifted up a little and then pushed my way back down. I felt the invasion between my legs, but in my stomach and chest too, trembling, panting, shivering as I finally seated myself fully on Angel's rigid inches.

I opened my eyes to see him watching me with rapt wonder, his chest moving fast, goose bumps all over his shoulders. They matched mine.

"Now fuck me," Angel said, the words husky and bossy and sexy as sin. "I want to feel you moving on me."

I pushed my hands through the bubbles to splay against his chest as I started riding him. Slow bounces up and down, the water making everything buoyant and easy, and then I moved in deep circles that had us both gasping and groaning. My erection was sliding against his stomach, and I gripped the edges of the tub so I could lean back and take him even deeper.

His eyes were locked on mine, his hands now roaming all over my body, my thighs and my ass and my chest, like he couldn't get enough of me, like he couldn't feel enough of me. And I felt the same, all the way warmed up now, taking him to the hilt over and over, riding him right into the sunset, needing him deeper and harder and faster.

"You feel so good," I said, my words coming out fevered and broken. "Oh my God, I can't believe I went without this for so long. It feels so fucking good."

Angel responded by getting more lube and then wrapping his slick hand around my penis. I let out a ragged cry on the first hard pump of my cock, fucking myself even harder in response. He jerked me mercilessly, his cheeks flushed and his jaw tight, and his free hand possessively gripping my hip.

"That's it, babe," he rasped. "Show it to me. Show it to me."

I couldn't have stopped it if I tried. His cock was too perfect and his hand was too slippery and tight and he was too beautiful, so, so beautiful. With an almost painful contraction, my cock seized in his grip and started painting his chest with stripes of white. We both watched as Angel kept working the cum right out of me, as I pulsed heavy and hard in his hand, and it felt pulled from every corner of me, from the soles of my feet, from my chest, my throat, all of me emptying onto his chest while still spread open by his cock.

And then it receded, leaving me bereft and replete at the same time, all the gorgeous tension now replaced by something shimmery and bright. I slumped forward.

With a growl, Angel grabbed my waist and began railing into me, taking advantage of my body being open and soft, fucking me with hard, merciless thrusts that had my sensitive organ twitching, trying vainly to swell again.

I buried my mouth in Angel's neck, raking my teeth over the damp skin, and then finally sealing my mouth on the tender spot at the base of his throat and sucking as his thrusts grew erratic and shuddering. With a sudden exhale, he got bigger and harder inside of me, and then started filling me up with jerking throbs, his feet moving against the bottom of the tub as he fought to keep himself wedged as deep in my backside as possible.

He was cursing up a storm, those hands that could make such beautiful, delicate things now gripping my flesh with bruising intensity, and he kept fucking me through it all, like he couldn't stop, never wanted to stop.

I never wanted it to stop either. Who needed a job or hobbies when there was a bathtub filled with bubbles and Angel Fletcher? Who needed food or handcrafted cocktails when there was a perfect cock to sit on and the deepest, sweetest eyes to gaze into?

But finally Angel's body stilled inside me, and I stopped abusing the skin near his throat. I nestled my head against his shoulder instead as our breathing settled and he eased himself from my body.

"I think," I said, watching a clear oil slick of lube collide with an iceberg of bubbles, "we need to take a bath after our bath."

Angel laughed. "Yes, getting clean didn't work out so well for us, did it?"

Within a few minutes though, we'd drained the lingering bubbles, lube, and cum from the tub, and had a fresh bath going, with fresh bubbles too. I brought us both a glass of chilled wine and a can of fizzy water—flat water was for peasants—and then crawled back in to cuddle against Angel's chest. He had the kind of body that I sometimes felt self-conscious around, tall and trim, if not overtly muscular, and he moved with an easy, graceful strength that would make runway models topple over in their heels with envy. In contrast, I was shorter, softer, less toned. It shouldn't matter—it didn't matter—except in LA's brutal meatmarket of a dating scene, sometimes it did.

But with Angel, I never felt unsexy or unattractive. Angel grabbed and fondled and fucked me like I was the sexiest man that had ever graced this horrible city; he looked at me like he was trying to etch the memory of me into his brain so he could masturbate to it later.

Since that's how I felt about him, it was dizzying to know that it was mutual.

"I'm glad you walked onto my film set," I said softly, stroking along the inside of his wrist.

He nuzzled my hair. "Who knew my 'oh no I still don't have a real job' summer job would net me such rewards?"

I smiled, still playing my fingers along the inside of his wrist. The space between our words was filled with the cheerful fizz of bubbles and the music I'd turned on when I'd gotten our wine, music that Angel cheerfully called my *main character in an indie movie having a montage* playlist. Angel preferred really complicated and obscure electronic music, especially the kind that was supposed to sync up your brain waves or whatever. And that was *not* my idea of a post-coital vibe.

"You know," Angel said after a moment, his hand toying with the short hair at the nape of my neck, "if you ever want to talk about your tragic Oregonian backstory . . ."

"Oh, I'm sure it will come up at some point," I assured him. "But it comes up less than it used to, these days."

"Oh?"

I kissed his wet chest and then snuggled closer, savoring the feel of his chest hair against my cheek. "There was therapy, and that helped a lot, but you know what helped even more?"

"Moving away from Carharttville, Oregon?" Angel asked dryly.

"Well, that," I said with a puff of laughter, "but actually . . . I think it was the people I found after moving more than the moving itself. You, of course, and Bee, and Sunny—and honestly, your dad has been more like a dad to me than my own father. He's picked me up from being stranded on the highway and gone with me to the mechanic to make sure they don't screw me on repairs. He's helped me replace washing machine hoses and babysat my hermit crab when I've gone out of town."

"Didn't that crab die like a week later because Dad fed it tap water?"

"The point is," I said over him, "I came here and suddenly I had people I could call, people I could count on to show up, people to have Thanksgiving and Christmas with. It made me realize—like, really realize—that my family acting like they didn't know what to do with me was all about them. There was a whole world of people waiting to love me as I was."

Angel kissed my head, holding me close. "I'm honored to have been a part of that," he murmured, and I pressed my lips against his chest again.

"What about you?" I asked after a moment. "Any tragic backstory there?"

"Alas and much to the detriment of my art, no. My mom is a super fierce ally, and you know Teddy. He's a soft touch when it comes to everything. It's why he and my mom got divorced, actually. She was tired of coming home and finding random strays crashing in the guest room until they could find work. She's really generous, but she was also really protective of us. It was one thing for her husband to make porn, but to have his work leaking into the family sphere was a different story. Plus they're both workaholics. I think she woke up one day and realized she barely knew him. It broke his heart."

"Poor Teddy."

"Yeah. I guess if I have any backstory, that's it. I've spent the last ten years watching the aftermath of what being in love with someone who doesn't love you back does. It's not pretty."

His words were light, but I heard the ache laced through them. And abruptly, I wanted Angel to know. Not only because of what he'd said, and not only because the water was warm and the bubbles were fluffy and because my favorite *main character in an indie movie having a montage* song was playing. But because I didn't want to keep it to myself anymore. Because being secretive and cautious and invulnerable . . . it no longer felt safe.

It felt lonely.

"I love you, Angel," I blurted out. "I love you a lot. Too much. So much it scares me."

Angel used his fingers to tip my face up to his. I blinked up into his bottomless eyes.

"I love you too," he said simply.

"I should have told you in Vermont," I said, high on the rush of my bravery. "I loved you then. But I was terrified. I've imagined myself in love so many times, but it had never felt like this. Like I've backstitched my heart to yours, and I'll die instantly if you pull away."

Angel's hand moved, cradling the side of my face, his fingers in my hair. "Luca, I've loved you since the day you walked into my father's office with a sewing machine in one hand and a pair of old ice skates in the other. It was the best day of my life when I got up the courage to finally kiss you."

I had so much more I wanted to say—so much more I wanted to ask. What did being in love mean for us? For what came next? Could there even realistically be a *next* for us, after everything that had happened?

But I didn't want to break the spell. Of our murmured words, of the warm bath and the lingering oxytocin in our bloodstreams.

Instead, I cuddled closer and said, "It was the best day of my life too."

Chapter Nine

I woke up to my face wedged against a warm, naked hip. Crisp leg hair tickled my chin and I smelled the lingering sweetness of Mr. Bubble. Heaven.

"Good morning, starshine. What's a five letter word with A, O, and E?" Angel asked.

I rolled my head away from Angel's hip to blink up at him. The light seeping in from around my hand-sewn curtains was still gentle and soft, and I was pretty sure I hadn't played the "hit snooze fifteen times on four different alarms" game, so it must have still been early in the morning. Angel was propped against my headboard, his legs half-wreathed in a sheet, his phone in his hands.

Ah. Wordle.

I stretched and then wrapped my arms around his thigh and hugged myself to it, nuzzling my face against him. "Omega," I said sleepily. "As in omegaverse."

"Omega*verse*?" There was doubt in Angel's voice, like I'd just made this up.

"You know," I told him. "Alphas. Omegas. Knotting."

"Knotting."

"It's when a penis has this part that swells up and locks inside a partner's body until it ejaculates. Sometimes it's for male pregnancy, and it's also a wolf thing. Not that *all* the fics with knotting have wolf stuff, you know. I read a *Yellowstone* knotting fic the other day."

I looked up to see Angel looking down at me like I was speaking in tongues. "Someday I'll let you log into my AO3 account," I told him. After I'd gone through and cleaned up my bookmarked fics, of course. Some AO3 reading you just had to take to the grave.

Angel tapped on his screen. "It's *canoe*, by the way."

"Did you just spoil Wordle for me?"

"Like the same way you spoiled my innocence with all this knotting talk?"

"It's better to be corrupted," I said, pressing my face back into his thigh. "Are you sure we have to go to work today?"

"Only if you want to afford your rock and roll lifestyle of Mr. Bubble and wolf fanfics."

I pouted into Angel's leg. Why was the world so cruel?

"Also your rock and roll lifestyle of owning every bridal magazine ever printed," he said. I didn't have to look at him to know he was looking at the towers of magazines I had stacked around the apartment. "Are you making Bee some kind of epic decoupage bridal gift that I don't know about?"

"Firstly, I would never donate my decoupage talents to something as ill-advised as Bee marrying someone who unironically wears a beanie. Secondly, they're not even engaged yet! Don't hasten that curse onto us!" And then I stopped. I wasn't sure I was ready to get to *thirdly*.

Angel set down his phone and wove his fingers through my hair, gently pulling my face away from his thigh. My dick stiffened both at the pleasurable sting and the bossiness of the gesture, but if he noticed, he didn't let it distract him.

"Luca," he said. "What are the magazines for?"

I hesitated. Only Bee and Sunny knew about this, and I'd sworn them both to secrecy because . . . well, because I didn't know why. It shouldn't feel so personal, and it didn't used to feel so personal, but somehow this piece of me had become very private over the years.

But the morning sun was a lovely gold, and Angel's eyes were so deep and soft behind his glasses, and he smelled so nice, even if he did ruin Wordles for me.

"I want to design wedding dresses," I blurted out, and then buried my face in his leg again.

Once more, his fingers tightened in my hair and pulled my face away from his thigh. "Why are you acting so shy about it?" he asked. "Of all the things you're closed off about, fashion isn't one of them."

How could I explain it to him? When it didn't really even make sense to myself?

"It's kind of what I always wanted to do, ever since I saw *Enchanted* as a kid. Giselle's wedding dress was everything I thought a wedding dress should be, you know? Ridiculous and over the top, and fluffy . . . but then four years later came Bella's wedding dress in *Breaking Dawn: Part 1*, this streamlined, flawlessly tailored Carolina Herrera masterpiece, and I had to confront that everything I knew about wedding dresses was wrong and evil. But then I saw *Mamma Mia* at my aunt's house, and I saw Amanda Seyfried's perfectly bohemian wedding dress, and I just realized that wedding dresses can be anything. They can be anything and everything and they can be lacy or jewel-toned or sleek or ridiculous and every single option is something exciting and gorgeous. There's nothing else like a wedding dress. And yes, I'm including jumpsuits in my definition of *dress*."

Angel looked at me with wonder. "I've heard you talk about fashion before, and you've always sounded—I don't know—passionate about it. But I've never heard you sound like this."

"It feels a little foolish, honestly. My parents barely even kissed in front of us growing up, and here I was obsessing over the moment you sign on for happily ever after. It felt like make-believe. As fictional as magic. But even my cynicism is no match for the way wedding attire makes me feel swept away. I never thought I'd actually leave home, but when I did—when I actually did—I decided maybe make-believe could be real after all. So when I went to fashion school, I made a plan. I'd graduate, get a job as a patternmaker or sewer for someplace like Vera Wang or Monique Lhuillier until I could break out on my own." I huffed out a breath, running my fingers over the hair on Angel's thigh. "It didn't work out."

"Why not?" He sounded curious, not dismissive, which was nice. But the curiosity was uncomfortable too.

I abruptly sat up, gathering a blanket around myself like a fortification. "I don't know. It just didn't. Fashion school was too expensive and the people there were shitty about bridal wear anyway. It was too commercial, too easy, too obvious—you know, all that stuff snobby people say."

"But it got to you," said Angel softly.

I hugged a pillow. "I guess. And the loans."

"You don't need a degree to make wedding dresses, Luca. Look at the gorgeous one you made for Bee for *Duke the Halls*."

"A degree helps though," I mumbled. I was looking down at the pillow I was hugging. "Or at least being at school helps. The professors recommend you for internships, the internships get you a job, you eventually leave a fashion house to start your own. It doesn't work without school. The system. The connections."

"As an art school kid, I get it, but I hate the thought that you can't do something without going back to some expensive, pretentious hellhole."

"Angel," I said with affection, "we *live* in an expensive, pretentious hellhole."

He stroked my arm. "You know what I mean. Although—God bless my hometown—I'd say it's more parvenu than pretentious."

"I don't regret leaving school," I said and plucked at the corners of the pillow. "The only thing I wish—well, it's stupid." I'd made my choices. There was nothing left to do but live tragically with them, like a young, stubbled Miss Havisham.

Angel put his hand over mine on the pillow. "Tell me, babe."

I leaned my head back against the headboard. "It's so stupid. Too stupid to say out loud."

"Luca, remember that time we fell in love filming a movie about a time-traveling duke obsessed with chili cheese fries? Stuff other people might call stupid is fun and romantic to us."

"Well, this won't be," I said and looked away. The stack of magazines next to my bed had already been field-dressed—the promising pages torn out and stuck inside the scrapbook I used to keep track of inspiration and trends. The whole pile mocked me.

I took a breath. "Here it goes, I guess: I got offered an internship at Prada right before I left school. They wanted to expand their bridal platform and the designer leading the initiative liked my work at our school's year-end showcase, probably because I was the only one who did bridal wear. But the internship was unpaid and I couldn't afford to get to where they wanted me anyway, much less pay for rent and living expenses for six months—and they were probably only half-offering because no one else gave a shit about bridal wear at the show and they needed an easy intern pick to go back to headquarters with. Or maybe as a favor to my professor. I don't know."

"Luca," chides Angel. "You're telling me that *Prada*—the Prada that even my father, Teddy Ray Fletcher, has heard of—offered you an internship and you're acting like it was some kind of fake pity ask? I don't think Prada does that."

"I guess not," I said glumly. "They were really nice when I emailed back and told them I couldn't do it. They said I could reapply if my circumstances ever changed."

"Luca!"

I shoved the pillow to my face for a minute and let out a muffled groan. "It killed me to say no," I said as I lowered the pillow. "But what could I do? I couldn't afford to live in Milan! Hell, I couldn't even afford to *get* to Milan! Just saying the word *Milan* charges my bank account an overdraft fee."

I slumped back against the headboard. Angel was preternaturally still next to me.

"Milan?"

I managed a sad but nobly resigned nod. "That's where Prada wanted me. And even if they still wanted me, it's not like things have changed. I could maybe afford a plane ticket now, but I can't afford not to work for half a year. I can't ever afford that, not unless I become a kept man."

"Do you . . ." Angel's voice was careful. Careful enough that I turned to look at him. "Do you have a problem being a kept man?"

I was almost offended. "Me? With my bone structure and how much I love a long brunch? Obviously not!"

Angel closed his mouth. Shifted. Lifted his hands and then lowered them.

"Okay," he said. "Okay. Don't be mad."

I froze. *Don't be mad?*

My three least favorite words! After, of course, *bowl of olives* and *to be continued*!

"I promise nothing," I said regally.

Angel looked like he expected no less. "Okay, here it goes," he said and jammed his fingers into his loose, messy curls and closed his eyes. The words came out in a rush. "I just got a job offer from my dream studio last week, and it's based in Milan, and they're paying me so much money—I mean, not like 'buy a boat' money, but more money than either of us has ever made—and I'll be able to get an apartment and pay to live like an adult and I've been trying to find the right way to tell you because of how I left last time and I want this to be different but also it's exactly where I want to be and exactly what I want to be doing and they want me there in a month, the end."

He didn't move after he finished, as if braced for something bad, but I threw my arms around him, half-clambering into his lap and kissing the backs of his hands until he dropped them from his head and allowed me to kiss his mouth.

"Congratulations, congratulations, my genius Angel, I knew you'd wind up somewhere amazing," I squealed, peppering his face with kisses. "I'm so happy for you!" It was true even if the words stung just a touch.

His arms circled me and it was inside his embrace that the full weight of his revelation sunk in.

I wasn't upset that he hadn't told me until now—actually, I was glad he'd told me with still a month left to go. But that meant that in a month, I wouldn't be able to kiss him or sit in his lap. In a month, I wouldn't feel his arms around me, or smell the lingering Mr. Bubble on his skin, or get to hear the shivery way his voice got low and bossy when he was in the mood.

I wouldn't have him, and I would have wasted this entire summer being mad at him instead of pouncing on him the minute he got back from Paris, and there was nothing I could do about it.

I wouldn't ever ask him not to follow his passion, to stay in this town just because I was trapped here too—but already the feeling of missing him was unbearable. I pressed my face into the side of his so he couldn't look at me.

He seemed to feel the change in me immediately. "Luca," he said, trying to turn his head to look at me and then laughing a little when I wouldn't let him. "Luca! Listen for a minute! I want you to come *with* me."

There was a silence that spanned everything—our breaths, our heartbeats, the world outside. I pulled in a shaking inhale as I leaned back enough to look at him.

"What?"

His eyes were bright, and even through his glasses, I could see them so closely, so clearly. Copper near the pupils, with crypts and threads of dark brown, a hue and texture I'd never be able to match even with the most expensive silks or damasks or vicuña wools.

"I mean it," he said earnestly. "I want you to come with me. Live with me. You wouldn't really be a kept man, because you could do your internship at Prada, but you wouldn't have to worry about paying for anything, because I could take care of it all."

I was just staring now, no idea what to say.

"We could be together, both of us following our dreams," Angel said excitedly. "This is perfect. Say you'll come with me, babe. Please."

There was something unpleasant hooked into my guts now, behind my chest. Inside my bones, making them ache and hum. I couldn't—I wouldn't even know where to begin—

"I can't afford it," I said, and Angel laughed.

"Did you not hear what I just said? I can pay for us to live over there! And we can figure out plane tickets. My mom has so many miles, it's not even funny."

"But Uncle Ray-Ray's," I said. My voice sounded hollow and numb—I *felt* hollow and numb. "I can't leave them without a costume designer."

"They'll be just fine," said Angel. "They'll find another Luca."

"But my apartment, I can't let my lease lapse—Carol will rent this place out in a heartbeat! Do you know how hard it is to find a full kitchen *and* a place with washer and dryer hookups for this price?"

"Well, ideally," Angel said softly, "we'd still be living together, wherever we were."

The softness in his voice should have been a warning, but I was too far gone to heed it. "And I can't just leave my entire life and all my friends—"

"I don't think it's *just leaving* when you're going to follow a dream. And to be with someone you love," Angel said. "Or was that whole *my heart is backstitched to yours* thing just a slick thing to say to the naked man in your bathtub?"

That was when I realized his arms weren't around me anymore.

"Angel," I said, but I didn't know what else to say. Because obviously, I couldn't move to Milan with him! Obviously I couldn't just go scratch at Prada's door and hope they'd still take me! That wasn't how life worked! You didn't just get to have a sexy Italian sojourn with the hot guy you were in love with!

And—and—what if it wasn't really me? What if I got to Milan and I wasn't as sophisticated or worldly as I'd always thought? What if I got to Prada and I was actually terrible at designing wedding dresses or making espresso or delivering parcels?

What if Angel and I moved in together and then everything fell apart?

No. No, it was better not to push, not to seek. Better to let something—a dream, a relationship, a version of yourself—die quickly than watch it slowly fail.

"I think you should get off my lap now," said Angel after I still hadn't spoken. "I need to get ready for work."

"Angel," I said again, pointlessly, as I slid off his lap. He threw the sheet off him and then stood up, showing off his perfectly molded ass and the delicious stretch of his back. A stretch that was visibly tense. He strode to the footboard of the bed, grabbed his briefs and yanked them on with short, jerky movements.

I tried again. "I just—I need more time."

"You could follow your dream and you could do it with me," Angel said. He turned to face me, hurt written all over his face. "What else is there to think about?"

And by the time he'd finished dressing and swiped his car keys off the table, I still hadn't found an answer.

Chapter Ten

I sat in Sunny's director's chair at the rented mansion, clutching an iced latte against my chest and trying not to cry. I used to think I'd be so good at being heartbroken—a beautiful, tragic figure, dabbing repeatedly at his eyes but valiantly refusing all comfort—but this last year had proved me dead wrong. I did not wear heartbreak well. My nose got red and I couldn't focus on work and I watched the most heinously horny dating shows the internet had to offer. And this time was no different.

It had been two days since Angel had left my apartment, and he hadn't spoken to me since. Not via text, not via email, not even when we passed each other on the set of the movie.

Well, except for one message after I texted him asking if we could talk:

> I promise we'll talk, but I need a few days to think. I'm sorry.

"What does that even mean?" I lamented to Sunny. She was standing at a table next to me, eyes fixed on a laptop as she reviewed footage, not giving any indication that she was listening. Which was probably fair, since I'd rehashed The Fight and The

Text with her several times daily since everything had unraveled. "A few days to *think*? Think about what?"

"Probably about the fact that you confessed your mutual love, you opened up about your One True Luca Dream, and then when he offered you a chance at said dream, you balked?"

She still hadn't looked away from the screen, but I didn't let her inattention diminish the withering glare I gave her. "Whose side are you on?"

"I would like to remind you that I am friends with you and Angel both, and therefore your concept of *sides* is not applicable to me." She clicked the pause button, eyeing an anal scene on an opera balcony with a critical look. "Also, as your friend, I'm required to tell you when I think you're doing something I think you'll regret."

"But I'm not doing anything," I said, sniffling. I took a drink of my latte to hide the sniffle, but Sunny heard anyway.

She turned with an arched eyebrow.

"Really," I told her. "It's him who wants to go and change everything! Wants me to . . ." I cast around, trying to find the right words to make her understand. "He wants me to be someone I'm not!"

Sunny threw up her hands. "What the fuck is wrong with you?" she demanded. "You want to do porn costumes for the rest of your life? Do Hope Channel movies and pretend you don't know what anal beads are whenever you're in Christmas Notch? You've wanted to make wedding dresses for as long as I've known you, you have a chance to build a bridal presence at one of the world's most recognizable designers, and you can do it while getting boned down by the one artist in this town who isn't a pretentious dickhole. That's not Angel trying to make you someone you're not. That's Angel trying to help you be whoever you want to be."

"Non, mademoiselle, that is Angel springing something absolutely fucknuts on me with no warning. Live together? In *another country*! We've only just gotten back together! And my life here—"

I paused, unable to properly defend my life here, because . . . well, Sunny was kind of right. I loved my Uncle Ray-Ray's family, and I had a weird amount of fun making *Duke the Halls* and would go back to Christmas Notch to dress people in bland sweaters in a heartbeat, but did I really want to be here in five years? Ten years? Did I want to be living in someone's backyard with stacks of sun-faded bridal magazines?

I shook it off. "Look, even if my life here isn't everything, and even if Prada would still take me—a huge flipping *if*, by the way—Angel still shouldn't have just sprung this on me! Living together is a huge step!"

Sunny shrugged and turned her attention back to the opera anal. "Luca, you left everything to come to LA. You dropped out of fashion school when it didn't feel right anymore. You're a person of huge steps. Or at least you used to be."

I frowned. It wasn't mean—or untrue—but I didn't like how it felt to hear. Was that really how people saw me now? Someone scared of making big steps?

"Maybe I've gotten older and wiser," I said, taking a wise sip of my latte, which I'd wisely ordered with a nut milk that wouldn't make me gassy later.

"You're twenty-four, broski. If there was ever a time for moving to Italy for an impossible dream on a hot artist's dime, this is it. And if everything falls apart, then you can come back and crash on my couch here in sunny California. Ooh, do you think Sunny's California would be a good LLC name? I think I need to be an LLC."

"Why not? I saw Blake's paycheck stub and his LLC name is Your Mom LLC."

"What does Vanya think about all this, by the way?"

I watched as Sunny bookmarked a spot in the anal opera scene and then clicked over to Mackenzie getting railed at a horse race. "We talked yesterday while she was on a break at her breathwork retreat. I think the alternate nostril breathing is turning her into a real snotwaffle right now, because she had some . . . unwelcome words."

I took a long pull of my latte so that I would stop talking. But Sunny wasn't about to let me get away with that.

"And what unwelcome words would those be?" she asked as she swiveled her head to look at me. Sunny revered Vanya, as did most people who met her. One time Sunny overheard Vanya say that she liked to wear an amethyst around her neck to support her third eye, and the next day, Sunny showed up to work with an amethyst tattoo on her left palm, which has since faded almost completely away.

"Shesaidicanthaveitbothways," I grumbled, not making eye contact with the traitor named Sunny.

"What was that now?"

I mumbled it again, just a bit louder.

"Still can't hear you!" Sunny said in a singsong voice.

"She said I can't have it both ways!" I said fussily. "There. Happy?"

Sunny smiled beatifically before turning back to the horse track fucking and bookmarking something. "You know what, I am happy."

I groaned and slumped in the chair. "Vanya said I couldn't spend months wishing that Angel would have asked me for more, then get cranky and defensive when he does ask for more. She also said that she's un-burn-noticed Angel and that I should eat at her favorite trattoria in Milan when I get there."

Sunny clicked a few more times and then pulled up a fresh scene. Blake and Mackenzie in a bubble bath.

And instead of tea-bagging or salad-tossing or wheel-barrowing, Mackenzie was sitting in Blake's lap, her arms looped around his neck, bubbles up to their chests. Their foreheads were pressed together as they slowly, lingeringly kissed, and Sunny had managed to capture every pause, every hitched breath. The wet curl of Mackenzie's hair on her neck, the way Blake's eyelashes fluttered between kisses. It was shockingly romantic.

And abruptly, all I could think of was my own bathtub, of Angel's thighs under mine, of his gorgeous throat, his dark, pupil-blown eyes.

Of how safe I felt curled in his arms as the bubbles fizzed around us.

And that was it, wasn't it? I felt safe with him. Alive, yes, horny, yes—but safe too. If I got to Milan and had to leave, or if we ever decided to break up . . . it would be okay. It would suck and I'd cry and I'd have to watch so much bad reality TV, but it would be okay.

I would be okay, because I was strong and he was safe.

It came in bits and pieces, the epiphany, and then like a fashion sketch, it all came together in one singular idea.

Yes, it was okay that I needed time to think about such a big change. But it was also okay for Angel to ask. And it was definitely time that I stopped living like heartbreak was just around the corner.

Sunny was right—I had stopped taking big steps, had decided at some point that every leap of faith was actually a plummet right into a terrifying abyss, and what had all that wariness gotten me? Was I happier for playing it safe? For thinking bravery and vulnerability were the emotional equivalents of feeding yourself to carnivorous mushrooms?

No. I wasn't. And I was about to lose the one person who was worth being slowly digested by every man-eating mushroom in the world if I didn't do something.

I jumped to my feet. "Oh my God," I breathed, staggered by the enormity of what I could lose. Ecstatic that I might still have a chance to keep it.

Sunny hummed at the laptop. "I know, it's great, right? I had no idea Blake could smolder like that—"

"Where's Angel?" I demanded. "Is he here at the mansion?"

Sunny looked at me with an expression of dawning glee. "He's at my apartment getting it ready for the fire escape scene. Are you going to do a grand gesture at him?"

"The grandest gesture," I said, and Sunny clapped her hands and squealed.

"We are most amused!" She clapped and skipped her way over to a nearby tote and then presented me with a bundle of fake red roses she'd dug from it. It was cinched shut with a thin bondage cuff. "Here, you need this more than Blake will. And take the Uncle Ray-Ray's Jeep!" She fished a key with a miniature dildo on the ring from her pocket and pressed it into my palm. "Go make Julia Roberts proud, Luca."

"It's all I've ever wanted," I told her sincerely and then practically ran toward the door.

I DIDN'T HAVE time to touch up my makeup or change into not-heartbreak clothes, and the roof to the Jeep was off, meaning that by the time I rounded the corner to Sunny's apartment complex, my luscious hair was more wind-ravaged than wind-tousled. Plus, I had no opera music anywhere on my Spotify playlists, and so I had to improvise as I started rolling up the block. "Grace Kelly" by Mika it was. That could be a grand gesture song, right?

I honked as I got close, knowing Sunny's unit was on the side closest to the road and hoping against hope Angel would hear me, because Sunny's building manager had finally fixed the broken front door and I had no way of getting up there on my own. I parked, honked some more. Mika was singing about being purple and hurtful, and cars behind me were honking now too, because strictly speaking I was parking on a six-lane street where it was— strictly speaking—illegal to park.

Just as I was about to pull around and try again, the sash to Sunny's window flew up, and there was Angel wearing a white T-shirt dotted with paint stains, a black blazer, and jeans. He squinted down at me, his face creased in the most adorable confusion.

"Luca?" he shouted down. "What the actual hell are you doing?"

"Don't go anywhere!" I yelled and frantically turned off the Jeep, accidentally dropped the keys under the seat, and fumbled with the roses desperately enough that fabric petals were dropping everywhere as I scrambled out of the vehicle. "Wait! Wait!"

"I'm not going anywhere," he called down. "But you can't park there."

"Watch me!" I said, with the courage of someone driving his boyfriend's dad's porn car, and then jogged over to the fire escape. When I dressed in my long-sleeved T-shirt and my kilt today, I had not expected physical exertion. I was already glistening like a Christina Aguilera music video extra by the time I reached the bottom.

"Luca," Angel said, and when I looked up, I saw something almost like a smile playing on his mouth. "That metal ladder is going to be scorching hot. Please go move the Jeep and then I'll let you in the front."

I wasn't going to give him a chance to chicken out when it came to talking to me. I pulled down the metal ladder, squeaked when it indeed cooked the insides of my palms, and then stuck the fake roses in my teeth, determined to see this through.

"Luca!" Angel exclaimed, and then I heard the window opening above me, followed by the clatter of his shoes on the metal landing.

I whimpered as I climbed the rest of the way up. The theme for the summer definitely seemed to be *fuck Luca's hands*. And also the plastic stems of the roses did *not* taste good.

But somehow I made it to the top of the ladder, only having to climb up one flight of steps to meet Angel, who was clambering down, concern all over his face.

"Oh my God, are you okay?" he asked, grabbing my hands and raising my palms to his lips.

The soft kiss felt so good on the stinging skin that I sighed—which meant the bouquet fell right out of my mouth and then tumbled onto the metal railing of the fire escape. It bounced on a nearby tree branch and then exploded into a shower of green plastic sticks and fake rose petals, raining down onto the half-dead bushes below.

"Well," I said. "Shit."

Angel laughed, sending warm air dancing across my palms. "It's okay," he said. "I'm more of a hyacinth guy anyway. What are you doing here?"

Luca, do not fuck this up! This is your freeskate quadruple axel with gold on the line!

I took a breath. "I'm sorry. I'm sorry I panicked when you asked about Milan and said no as a reflex. And I'm sorry that every time you've been ready to be brave and open with me, you've been met with a brick wall. I think I could probably name seventeen different reasons why intimacy and love and commitment scare me, but I also know that I don't want a single one of those reasons to be the thing that keeps me away from you. You're the one person in the world that I am happy to be scared with, Angel Fletcher. I love you. And I don't know if I'll be ready to move with you when you go . . . but I want to be."

Angel's face softened even more. "Luca . . ."

"I love you," I said again, moving my scalded hands so I could lace my fingers through his. He took a step backward, pulling me with him, so that the steep metal stairs going up to Sunny's apartment were at his back. He pulled me into a tight embrace, burying his face in my neck.

"I love you too," he mumbled into my skin. "And I'm sorry I needed time to think. I wasn't trying to ghost you or break up with you; I was just so hurt that I wanted to make sure I was still making all the right choices. I'm happy to try long distance if that's what you want. I'm happy to try anything. I don't even have to take the job at all. Let's just stay together. Please."

I could feel his glasses dig in just below my jaw, and I almost wanted to cry. How was it possible to miss something as inconvenient as giant glasses always getting in the way? And yet I had. I'd missed everything about him, even after only two days. There was not a snowflake's chance in LA that I'd make it for however long his new job would have him there. And he had to go to his new job. I wasn't about to let him make his own dreams smaller just because chasing my own had become strangely terrifying over the last two years.

"You're going," I told him, pulling back so I could see his face. "And I'm going to do my damndest to go too. After all, if Prada won't have me, then I'll make sure Moschino or Versace will. And if not, then I'll brood mysteriously at coffee bars until someone notices my genius and funds my own brand."

"That's the spirit," Angel murmured, his eyes dropping to my mouth. "I'll do whatever makes you happy, babe."

"Whatever?"

"Whatever."

"Then," I said, leaning forward, "kiss me."

His mouth crashed forward against mine, hot and hard, his tongue finding mine in a slick demand and stroking until my knees were weak. His hands dug into my hair and our legs tangled as I twisted my fingers into his blazer and held him close. He tasted like cinnamon gum and coffee and sunny mornings halfway around the world.

"I missed you, and I missed *this mouth*," he growled.

I gasped as he bent his head to nip at my neck. "I don't think Sunny and the actors will be here for a while—"

Just then my phone rang. I nearly ignored it, except it was Sunny's ringtone: The Fairy Godmother from *Shrek 2* singing "I Need a Hero."

With a huff, I pulled my phone from my kilt pocket. Angel's head fell back against a metal stair; an eager erection was currently pressed into my hip.

"I hate her," Angel groaned. "I hate her, I hate her."

I accepted the call and held the phone to my ear. "Yes?"

"Firstly, does this mean your grand gesture wasn't grand enough? Because I thought you'd be skewered like a 1970s party appetizer by now, if you get my drift—"

"Ahem," I said.

"Secondly," she went on, undeterred, "I forgot to tell you the secret Bee and I have been keeping!"

"What secret?" And then I remembered the barbeque, and Bee's promise to tell me a secret if I went. I made a wounded gasp. "This secret is *so overdue*, Sunny."

"Life got busy," she sniffed. "Anyway, Bee overheard a telephone call between everyone's favorite hot mommy manager lady Steph D'Arezzo and the Hope Channel. To help launch *Duke the Halls* on Hopeflix, the Hope people want to do a series of featurettes on the making of the movie. And they want to do one about the wedding dress you made for Bee. Ten minutes of just you and your bridal fashion genius, right at the click of a button."

A dizzy sort of shock stole over me. "Really?"

"Yes, really. So make sure you tell those people at Prada that you're Hopeflix-famous, okay? Okay. I'm rounding up Blake, Mackenzie, and the crew to head your way. Be done fucking in my apartment before then, maybe?"

She hung up before I could answer.

"Well?" Angel asked, his eyelids half-lowered, his cock still stiff against me.

"Sunny said Hopeflix is going to do a featurette about the wedding dress I made," I said, dazed.

Angel gave me a warm look. "Of course they are, because that dress was perfect and you're brilliant."

My cheeks burned. I didn't even have a smart, self-confident remark. I was too shocked. Could this really be happening in my life all at once?

Recognition? Opportunity?

Love?

But then my eyes caught Angel's again, and I remembered the actual most important part of the call. "Sunny said that we have until she and the performers get here to finish fucking in her apartment."

"Well, then," Angel said, grabbing my hand and tugging me up the fire escape steps. "I think we'd better get started. Don't you?"

Epilogue

Five Months Later

*Y*ou're being ridiculous," Angel said, watching with an amused expression as I gingerly stepped to the edge of the heated pool, my teeth chattering. My balls had already retreated into my abdominal cavity by this point.

I glared at him with as much dignity as I could muster while also wearing neon yellow swim briefs. "It's Christmas Eve in the Alps, you dick. My nipples hurt!"

"Oh, poor baby," Angel said with an expression of immediate concern. "Come here and I'll help you with that."

When I stepped into the very warm water, splashing my way down the pool steps, he was there to greet me, immediately folding me into his arms with my back to his chest and his hands finding my nipples under the water.

"Oh, they are so hard," Angel crooned. He rubbed at them with his thumbs, sending pleasure zinging through my body, which was very confused by now. It had just been freezing cold, now it was deliciously warm, and also his fingers were sending wicked thrills right down to my briefs.

"Is that any better?" he murmured into my neck.

"No," I said with a mournful sigh. "You might have to keep doing it."

The huff of his laugh tickled the damp skin of my throat. "I'll have to think of something more comforting then." He wrapped his arms around my waist and lifted me so that my feet were on top of his, and then he walked us through the water to the edge of the infinity pool.

The hot water lapped just below our shoulders, and steam drifted around us as we looked out onto the wind-roughed surface of Lake Como. Green and white mountains cradled the lake, and all the ochre and terra-cotta houses perched around it. The forecast had promised a light dusting of snow later, but for now, the sky was a high, pale blue.

Behind us was a three story confection of a villa—bright pink, with balconies and shutters galore, and the tackiest possible decorations inside. I was in love with it, and had been since the moment Angel's new boss had asked if we wanted to house sit over Christmas so he could go to the Seychelles for the holidays with his new wife.

"We're basically the Clooneys now," I told Angel, leaning back against him.

"Mm," he agreed, but his interest was still obviously elsewhere, as one hand continued to caress a nipple and his other hand slipped down my stomach to my briefs.

"Do you think your boss knows Amal—*oh*."

Angel had slipped his fingers into the waistband of my briefs, grazing my swelling penis and stroking the sensitive tip until I shuddered against him.

"Feeling warmer now?" he asked softly as he worked my briefs down over my hips to my ankles and then off my legs altogether.

"A little," I mumbled as he wrapped his long fingers around my erection. "Still a little cold."

"Well, that just won't do." He moved us both a single step to the side, and then my eyes rolled back into my head. I stood in front of one of the gentle pool jets, and the jet was right at cock level, and oh my God . . .

My head fell back on his shoulder as he toyed with my dick in front of the jet, making sure the stream stroked and tickled me everywhere, moving me even closer so that the water was just forceful enough . . .

"Fuck," I panted.

"Warmer now?" he asked in tones of grave worry, but I could feel the outline of his own erection pressed against me, feel the rapid rise and fall of his chest.

"Yeah." I was beyond warm; I was simmering, boiling, made of sweet fire as my hips rocked forward and my hands came up to grip the edge of the pool. Now my balls were tight for an entirely different reason, and the pressure building in my core was almost unbearable.

Angel kissed my neck as he forced me to endure the torturously wonderful caress of the jet, his firm body holding me in place as I squirmed and moaned and twisted.

"How does it feel?" he asked in a low voice.

"It feels good. I'm—I'm about to—"

The climax came with a shuddering surge, and I curled forward, my hips bucking of their own accord as the pleasure pushed through my groin and up the length of my organ. With pulsing quivers, I came into the pool, my cock still being stimulated by the jet, which in turn made the orgasm last forever and ever and on and on—

I slumped back against Angel, who was practically shaking behind me. When I managed to tilt my head enough to look at his face, I was met with a hard mouth and burning eyes.

"Are you done?" he rasped.

I twisted in his embrace and pressed my face against his shoulder. My body was still trembling from the aftershocks. "Yes," I said faintly.

He didn't speak. Instead, he took my hand and tugged me back to the pool steps, onto the freezing balcony overlooking the lake, and then back inside the warm villa. We didn't even make it past the kitchen before he had me slammed against the wall, his tongue in my mouth and his hands roaming all over my body.

I was still naked, and he was trying to tear off his trunks without his hands leaving my body for longer than a second at a time, and we ended up dripping a trail of water as we kissed our way to the bedroom, where Angel spun me around and bent me over a desk. When I looked up, I could see Lake Como stretched out like a sapphire field before me, the snow-capped Alps, the fresh clouds beginning to wreathe the mountains with something like fog.

"Fuck, you're beautiful," murmured Angel as I heard the plastic click of a bottle cap.

I wanted to give him a seductive smile, but I was still tingling and limp from my orgasm in the pool, and so all I could muster was a quivering moan as a slick finger found my entrance and caressed the muscle there. His mouth came down on my neck, biting, kissing, as he pushed inside me and began stroking.

I, of course, was always very aloof and cool about everything, but it was hard to be aloof when someone as sexy and naked as Angel was behind you, and even harder when I looked back to see him slowly working lube up and down his shaft with his free hand. My own dick was stirring to life, and I squirmed on the desk, watching him over my shoulder with my mouth open and my ribs jerking with short, heavy breaths.

"Ready?" he asked, a slippery hand curling around my hip as his other hand guided his erection to where I wanted it.

"Always for you," I whispered and he gave me a wicked smile. Without his glasses, I could see with absolute clarity the sinful gleam in his eyes. The gleam that reminded me that however terrifying it was to make a huge step, sometimes the payoff was so incredibly and deliciously worth it.

"Good," he said and began working his way into me.

The hot slide of him stole my breath away, and by the time his hips were flush to me, I had my face against the cool plastic of the vintage-but-still-hideous desk and was panting hard enough that my breath fogged the surface over and over again. When his hand found me, I was fully erect, and it didn't take long before another climax was tearing its way up my thighs.

We came together, heavy and hard, him deep inside me, and me all over the ugliest desk in Italy. Outside, the first snowflakes were beginning to fall, dissolving over the heated pool and disappearing into the steam.

"This definitely beats Christmas in LA," Angel said with a laugh that I could feel in my ass.

"Just you wait," I told him, too come-drunk to sound smug. "I have plans for you tonight."

"Sexy plans?"

"The next best thing."

His voice brightened. "Food?"

"Sì, certo."

AFTER WE CLEANED up and then bundled ourselves in coats and scarves, we took the bus from the little village closest to us to Como proper, where the Christmas market was in full swing. Wooden stalls lined the vias and piazzas, Christmas lights sparkled everywhere, and the stone-paved streets were filled with people laughing and shopping and sipping mulled wine. Angel had roasted nuts in one hand and a paper cup of fried olives in the other, and I was on my second mulled wine, trying to calm my nerves. I was a survivor of eastern Oregon, Taylor Swift presale tickets, and rush hour on the 105. I could do this!

For the millionth time since getting off the bus, I patted the pocket of my ankle-length wool coat, making sure the ring was still there.

I had taken a huge step in coming here with Angel last August, and it had been the best decision of my life. Prada had indeed welcomed me into their intern fold, and had even offered me a small stipend while I was there. They'd also hinted more than once that after the six-month internship, I should apply for a real position as a patternmaker, and I was considering it. There were a couple movies I wanted to come back to Christmas Notch for—the second *Duke the Halls*, and also an absolutely unhinged Santa Claus movie starring none other than former INK member Kallum Lieberman— but for the most part, my life was here in Italy. Because that's where Angel was.

And Angel loved working for this studio. They were growing fast, and there was some talk of opening up an LA location, but neither of us were too anxious for that to happen. We loved our friends and family, but we didn't miss the constant, desperate grind of LA, and also . . . well. There was something kind of honeymoon-ish about being on our own over here. Just the two of us exploring and fucking and hanging out with fashion and art people who hadn't also known us as awkward undergrads.

Plus just when I thought we were in an inviolable bubble of sex and gelato, Sunny or Vanya or Angel's sister Astrid would find some flight deal and wind up crashing on our secondhand couch for days at a time and never seeming to leave. So there was that too.

Angel stopped in front of a stand selling a million different kinds of torrone. His eyes were wide behind his glasses. "Must have torrone," he told me in tones of great urgency, and because I am a hunter-gatherer, I bought him some torrone and had it bundled up for us to take back to the villa. Then we finished our snacks and wine, and wandered over to the massive Christmas tree in the corner of the square and stopped to admire it.

The blue-white lights of the tree added a silver sheen to Angel's eyes as he took in the scene, and there was a soft smile on his lips as snowflakes drifted gently down from the sky to catch in his hair and on his shoulders. And of all the Christmas shit I'd seen over the last year, this was the most magical. This quiet moment after fried olives and wine, just a free tree and fickle snowflakes and Angel's soft, content expression.

Without thinking about it, I got down to one knee.

Angel didn't notice at first, didn't notice until he turned to murmur something about how designing light in animation could be tricky without the right depth buffers, and saw I wasn't standing next to him. And when his eyes finally dropped and he saw me kneeling with the ring box open, his lips parted.

"Luca," he said, and the breathlessness in his voice made my chest ache.

"I love you," I said. "I love you so much that I'll kiss you even after you eat fried olives. I love you so much that I'll listen even when you talk about render layers. I love you so much that when I think of a future without you, it feels like a future without happiness or joy or hope. I want to keep taking huge steps with you, Angel, and I want to take our next one tonight. Please marry me. Please marry me and let's be the most talented, tragically handsome couple that everyone knows for the rest of our lives."

Angel's lips were still parted and a tear trembled on the edge of his eyelid as he looked down at the ring in my hand. I hadn't had the biggest budget, and so I'd been scouring every secondhand shop, flea market, and creepy estate sale in Milan, until I'd found this in a tucked-away shop in a case next to several old pocket watches. It was a thin gold band, twisted with Art Deco designs, and dotted with tiny ruby and sapphire and emerald chips. It reminded me of colors on a palette, of Angel when he paints. And it would always remind me of Milan, the new home we'd made together.

"Oh, Luca," Angel said, the tear spilling over and racing down his cheek. "Yes. Yes. Of course."

"Really?" I asked, looking up at him, barely able to hope I heard right. "Yes?"

He laughed. "Sì, certo, Luca. I mean it. Yes."

My own eyes were burning as I tugged off his vegan leather glove and slid the ring onto his finger. It was a perfect fit, since I'd already measured his finger with a length of string while he was sleeping. Very normal stuff!

For a minute, I just admired how it looked on his hand, winking in all the Christmas lights, and then he grabbed me by the lapels of my coat and hauled me to my feet, crushing me into a bruising, scorching kiss. I could taste the spiced wine, feel the snowflakes on our cheeks, hear the cheers and applause of the other Christmas revelers in the square, and I could hardly stand it. After an entire lifetime making fun of Christmas magic—including the time I was on the set of a movie designed to *promote* Christmas magic—there was a little Christmas magic in the air, just for me. Perfect night, perfect man. The rest of forever just waiting for us to take it.

As our mouths slipped apart, Angel pressed his forehead to mine, his hands cradling my face. It took a light breeze off the lake to make me realize I was crying.

"I hope you know I'm getting an engagement ring too," I sniffled. "A giant, ridiculous one. So people think I'm a trophy fiancé."

Angel laughed and kissed me again. "We'll figure it out."

"And I call Bee and Sunny for my bridesmaids."

"I figured."

"And I think Vanya should marry us, but isn't your dad a licensed officiant?"

"It's a long story, but yes." Angel rubbed his nose against mine. "And we'll have food and music and dancing . . ."

We were kissing again, snow falling all around us, and slowly our hands met and laced together. His tongue was soft and perfect, his lips warm, the sounds of Como at Christmas cheerful and bright as they echoed through the square.

They say there's no place like home—and it's true that there's no place like LA.

But there's really no place like being right in front of the person you love, knowing there's nothing but kisses and the rest of your lives ahead of you.

That—*that* is home.

And worth every huge step it takes to get there.

Can't get enough of Julie Murphy
and Sierra Simone? Don't miss the
first installment in their brand-new, college-set,
extra-spicy Academic Affairs series

Fundamentals of Being a Good Girl

Available January 2026!

From #1 *New York Times* bestselling author Julie Murphy
and *USA Today* bestselling author Sierra Simone comes a
brand-new college town raunch-com about a sexy single dad
professor and a feisty law school grad turned nanny in this
steamy tale of Academic Affairs . . .

Class is in session.

Turn over to read

Seas and Greetings

the steamy enemies-to-lovers
Christmas in July rom-com set on a
cruise ship where a *Twilight*-inspired
musical is being produced . . .

Turn over to read

Snow Place Like LA

the spicy second-chance romance set during
one steamy Los Angeles summer . . .